PRAISE FOR
A STEADFAST HEART

"This book has a great storyline, compelling and believable characters and both action and heartfelt moments. I found myself drawn into the story, and wondering how things would work out. I highly recommend this book, and based on the first two Wind River Mail-Order Brides stories, I am looking forward to the rest of the series."

—LEIS, GOODREADS

"Beautiful, comfortable prose, faith-filled story of love, and kind, thoughtful characters are a boon to this second book in the series. It is very engaging, full of action, with emotions to commiserate with and a happy ending to cheer for."

—NATASHA, GOODREADS

"Emotional! I loved all these characters, even the secondary ones that added so much to the story. So much heartbreak and pain but the healing that takes place will have you crying too! Read about the power of family and love and never giving up. This story is amazing!"

—VALRI, GOODREADS

"The first chapter snagged my attention and I didn't want to stop reading. I was drawn to Drew and Kaitlyn as they faced the same problem—rejection. The threats to

Kaitlyn, the needs of the children and Drew's fears of failure really pulled me in. It's a great story."

—DESIREE, GOODREADS

"Mesmerising! I kept wanting to read the next chapter, and before I knew it I had devoured the entire book at one sitting."

—JEANNETTE, GOODREADS

A STEADFAST Heart

WIND RIVER MAIL-ORDER BRIDES

A Steadfast Heart

Lacy Williams

Martha Hutchens

sunrise PUBLISHING

A Steadfast Heart
Wind River Mail-Order Brides, Book 2

Published by Sunrise Media Group LLC
Copyright © 2025 Sunrise Media Group LLC

ISBN: 978-1-963372-27-4

For more information about Lacy Williams or Martha Hutchens, visit their websites at lacywilliams.net and marthahutchens.com.

Cover Design: Sunrise Media Group LLC

This book is dedicated to my husband. Honey, I noticed
every chore you picked up, every time you said,
"Let's eat out," because you knew I was too tired to cook,
and every time you told me you believed in me.
Thank you. You are my Prince Charming.

"For I know the plans I have for you," declares the Lord, "plans to prosper you and not to harm you, plans to give you hope and a future. Then you will call on me and come and pray to me, and I will listen to you. You will seek me and find me when you seek me with all your heart. I will be found by you," declares the Lord, "and will bring you back from captivity."

Jeremiah 29: 11-14a

One

March, 1893

HOW ON EARTH DID I END UP AT AN-*other socialite's mansion?*

Drew McGraw shifted, the cobblestones foreign beneath his cowboy boots that were far more accustomed to the long prairie grasses back home.

Dread pooled in his stomach as he looked at the three-story building, then compared the address to the letter he held. Maybe Leona Fitzsimmons was a servant here? He checked the mailbox. No name that he could see. His cousin had a better angle, since she stood on the side. "Merritt, do you see a name on the mailbox?"

"It says Fitzsimmons."

Drew rubbed the back of his neck. What was he even doing here?

His suit coat pinched his shoulders. A decade of ranch

work would do that. He resisted the urge to adjust his tie. It felt like it was choking him. He lowered his hand.

Merritt stepped up beside him, her head tilted to the side as she studied the house. "You don't have to go through with this."

This being a mail-order marriage he'd arranged over the past months of corresponding with one Miss Leona Fitzsimmons.

"The kids could go to school regularly if they spent weeknights with me," Merritt went on.

Sure they could. His eyes slid closed briefly. He hadn't realized how bad things were until he'd seen David struggling with a math problem out of a fifth-grade math book. If he went to school in town, he'd be placed with children three years younger than he was—just because his father had needed every available hand on the ranch and hadn't noticed the problem developing right before his eyes.

His girls were struggling too. Tillie burst into tears at random moments, and he never knew what would set her off. Or how to comfort her when she cried. And Josephine? Drew rubbed the ache in his chest. Her long, angry silences proved something was wrong in his second child's life. Bad wrong. What child didn't want to go to church when church meant seeing the neighboring families?

He loved the ranch his father had started and his brothers shared, but it was too far out of town for the family to attend church every Sunday, much less for the children to go to school regularly. That probably contributed to Jo's problems. He'd noticed the town girls hanging together and giggling behind their hands when Jo got close, had tried to discuss it with her—if "How was Sunday school?" counted as trying. If her mother were alive, she'd know what to say, might even help Drew know what to do. Then again, if Amanda were alive and things had gone according to her plan, Drew wouldn't know Jo at all.

He needed help. Had no money to hire a tutor, nanny, or cook. And when Merritt's mail-order ad had brought her husband Jack into her life, he'd thought for once he had the answer he needed.

He laid a hand on his cousin's shoulder. "I appreciate the offer, Merritt. I really do. But if I send them to you, I'd only see them a couple of days a week." Not to mention his cousin was a newlywed. She and Jack didn't need three kids underfoot. He shook his head. "No, the children need a mother, one who can give them the fundamentals of an education. A few manners wouldn't hurt either." If Leona Fitzsimmons lived here, she ought to be qualified.

A sense of misgiving settled over him. He and Leona had exchanged several letters after he'd posted his mail-order bride ad. Why hadn't she told him she was from a wealthy family? Why did she want to trade *this* for his Wyoming ranch?

Amanda had certainly thought it a bad bargain. Had told him in plain English she'd made a mistake in marrying him.

He inhaled deeply, but the smoke-laden air of St. Louis did little to brace him. He could still remember the first time he'd stepped onto the front stoop of his former father-in-law's estate. He'd been naive then, shoulders straight with pride and heart full of determination. The world had been his to conquer.

It had conquered him instead.

He was doing this for the kids. David, Josephine, and Tillie were all that mattered. He crossed the porch and knocked on the door.

The door opened to reveal a man dressed in a black suit. "May I help you?"

Drew didn't miss the man's brief perusal nor his quick frown. Too bad. Drew had spent two years dressing to society's exacting standards. No more. "Mr. McGraw and Mrs. Easton to see Miss Leona Fitzsimmons."

From somewhere deeper in the house, a few giggles, quickly shushed, reached his ears.

"Won't you come in, sir? I will see if Miss Fitzsimmons is available."

If she's available? They'd settled their plans weeks ago. Wouldn't she have told her family, the staff, that he was coming? The unsettled feeling in his stomach grew bigger, knotted tighter.

The man led them to a formal room furnished with matching armchairs and sofas. Floral prints abounded, from the upholstery to the wallpaper. A piano stood against the wall, the tiger oak veneer competing for attention with some fancy carved overlay.

"It's not too late. We can still leave." Merritt's gaze widened as she glanced around the room. Drew had once been impressed with displays of wealth like this, back in the early days of his marriage. It'd taken years for him to realize the simpler life on the ranch was better.

"I told her I'd see her today." He led Merritt toward the

sofa and took the seat closest to the main door. He wanted to see his intended as soon as she entered.

A second door in the back of the room opened a crack. Shuffling sounds drifted across the room, but the door opened no farther. Merritt gestured in that direction, and he nodded slightly. With their hearing deadened by life in the city, the spy most likely thought he was being quiet. Probably a servant. No society miss would meet with a man alone, even to accept a proposal.

When the main door opened again, a young lady sailed in, her dress dripping with lace and her sleeves puffed all the way to the elbow. A river of blonde curls flowed from under her ribbon- and feather-decked bonnet that wouldn't last ten seconds in the Wyoming wind. She was young. The youthful look of her face hit him hard in the solar plexus and made him feel older than his thirty-three years.

This was Leona?

Drew rose to his feet. "Leona." He moved toward her, but she held up a hand to stop him.

His pulse pounded in his temples at the gesture. They'd never met before, but he'd expected a warmer welcome than this.

She stood there, and he did too. He could feel a muscle ticking in his cheek. "Is there a problem?"

"I didn't think you would actually show up, thought surely when you saw my house you'd turn around and leave."

"What's that supposed to mean?" He could feel his temper sparking like flint against tinder. They had an agreement. Surely she wasn't backing out now. He'd come hundreds of miles. He'd spent time writing her those letters. Told the kids he was bringing home a wife.

The society miss looked past him to that cracked back door. "You can come out now." Several young ladies dressed just as lavishly entered the room, smothering their giggles behind pristine white gloves. Their stares and obvious amusement pricked his skin with heat.

Miss Fitzsimmons turned back to him. "Your letters have provided the best entertainment of the year for myself and my friends."

His temper flashed so hot it robbed him of words. Maybe Merritt sensed it. She sidled close, hovering behind his elbow. "That's a very cruel trick to play on another." She sounded like the schoolmarm she was, her voice snappy and commanding.

"You didn't really think that someone in my position would accept a proposal from some two-bit rancher, did you?"

The longer he looked at her, the more she came to resemble his late wife. The disdain in the curl of her lip. The glittering ugliness in her eyes, judging him.

He felt sick. "I didn't think much on it, as you didn't tell me of your position."

Her blue eyes widened in exaggerated shock. "Didn't I? How careless of me. Here, take your letter with you. And a word of advice, if you should try this again. Next time, put a little romance in your proposal. Not that it would have mattered in this case, of course, but no woman wants to be married just to look after a bunch of brats."

He opened his mouth to respond, to blast her with words

she surely deserved. Miss Fitzsimmons had played a vicious joke. He should speak to her father, should—

He forced his whirling thoughts to steady. He didn't want one more thing to do with this young woman who played with the emotions of others. Jagged breaths cut like glass inside him. There was nothing left for him here. He left the house to echoes of laughter, Merritt beside him.

It was cooler outside, but the fresh air did nothing to dampen his anger.

They crossed the park before they sank onto a bench out of sight from the house. Merritt reached for his hand. "If you ask me, this was a lucky escape. Imagine. Some poor man is going to end up married to her."

Drew laughed bitterly. "I pity him."

"You have other replies to your ad."

"I do." And he'd burn them just as soon as he got home. There had to be some other way to get his kids some schooling. He'd rather they grow up ignorant than be exposed to what that "lady" would teach them. Or any city woman like her. He should've known better. Hadn't his doomed marriage to Amanda taught him anything?

The brightness of Merritt's joy with her new husband had blinded him. Convinced him that a mail-order relationship might work. That and the feeling he was failing his children.

"It would take a while to choose another candidate though." Merritt bit her lip. "Meanwhile, Nick can help with the kids' schooling. It's worked okay so far."

Sure it had. If you defined *okay* as Nick spending an hour or so each evening tutoring his nephew and nieces after putting in a full day on his own homestead. An hour divided between three kids, no less. Drew's youngest brother looked more tired every day.

Ed tried to pick up some of Nick's work, but the land agent would be inspecting his property at the end of May to make sure he had complied with the Homestead Act. If he didn't meet the requirements to prove up his land—namely, build a structure to live in—he would lose it.

And Isaac. Drew's chest tightened. Isaac had returned to the ranch months ago without his badge and without the confidence that had been such a part of him since they were kids. If it hadn't been for the McGraw jawline, Drew almost wouldn't have recognized him.

And their neighbor, Heath Quade, was waiting in the wings, ready to snatch their land out from under them.

Drew swallowed the bitter taste of failure. Some job he was doing of keeping the family ranch going. If they didn't prove up the homesteads, he might even lose the land that Pa left him.

And now he'd failed in finding his kids a new ma.

They made their way back to the cable car, then to the train station. He left Merritt in the waiting area, then approached the ticket counter. Changing his tickets to an earlier departure date only required a minor fee, but the station agent refused to refund his money for the ticket that his bride would have used. He crumpled the useless piece of paper in with his final letter and his ad, then left the wadded-up mass on the counter. A gust of wind picked it up and carried it away.

Pointless. This entire trip had been pointless. He and

his brothers had three homesteads to prove up, and he had wasted a full week.

If only he hadn't told the kids the purpose of this trip. Tillie was going to be heartbroken when he returned without the new ma he'd promised her.

Michael picked up my mail.

Kaitlyn Montgomery exited the St. Louis post office, her quick steps sending her skirt swirling around her ankles. Her pulse was buzzing in her ears, blocking out the sounds of carriage wheels clattering on cobblestones. Even though it was only March, the midafternoon sun hitting her tweed walking suit felt stifling. She wove between the people clogging the sidewalk, moving faster than might be considered socially acceptable.

She had to get home.

Her offer letter from the Piedmont School District, with its accompanying train ticket, was supposed to have arrived today. Accepting the role as teacher was supposed to be her way of escape.

How had Michael even known about the secret PO box?

No point in asking why the clerk had handed over her letters. Her brother could charm honey from bees without getting stung.

She was the only one who knew his true nature.

Her mind raced. What could she do now? If he'd read the letter, he would know she'd made plans to leave St. Louis. He would be angry.

Thoughts swirled as she dodged a mother pushing a baby

carriage. Was there anyone she could ask for help? A newsboy's shout of "Read all about it!" reminded her that her own name had figured prominently in the society pages of late, and the papers hadn't gotten much correct. Why bother with truth when her brother's lies sold more papers?

Even worse, her supposed friends now believed those lies. Had conveniently been "not at home" when she'd called on them. Pretended not to see her when they met in public. Who would believe her if she told them Michael had stolen her mail? Who would care?

No one.

She caught the cable car and stared out the window. The houses got larger as she reached the outskirts of the city. She exited at Dolman Street, then hurried past the three-story homes that faced Lafayette Park. Past the Holdens' place, the Whitlaws', the Fitzsimmonses'.

She stopped just outside the wrought-iron fence that surrounded the house. She could hardly call it home anymore. It loomed above her, three stories high with large windows leering at her from every level. She'd once loved the warm wood floors, the long, elegant hallways inside. Chasing dust motes, curling up in her window seat to read . . . Those memories were tainted now.

She inhaled deeply. No help for it. Her only hope for escape lay behind those doors.

The gate screeched as she opened it, announcing her return to anyone listening. She climbed the steps and opened the door. "Michael?" Her brother didn't answer, but the door to the office was open, so she moved in that direction.

Michael was waiting for her when she entered, seated

behind what had once been Father's desk. He didn't bother to stand. He might be dressed as a gentleman in his dark suit, silk tie, and black shoes, but he never bothered with the manners that went with the title unless it suited him.

He'd inherited their father's honey-blond hair, just as she had, but the similarities ended there. He had brown eyes just like his mother and had their father's height, while she had her mother's green eyes and short stature.

She hesitated only slightly before moving closer. There was no use avoiding this confrontation.

"Where have you been?" His voice was cool, his question flat.

"Where's my mail?" She crossed her arms over her chest.

"This mail?" He smiled while holding up a letter. As she watched, he slowly tore it in half.

She lunged to reach the ripped letter, but he stood and held it over her head, lighting one corner with a match. Then he tossed it into the fireplace grate to watch it burn.

Kaitlyn rubbed a hand against her chest, but it didn't ease the tightness. The ashes of her letter fell through the grate, disintegrating like her hopes. She blinked rapidly. What now?

Maybe she could send the school a telegram. They wouldn't be happy about the wasted expense of that train ticket . . .

"I don't know why you would want to leave St. Louis," Michael said. He gestured to the room around them. "Father left us this beautiful home. All our friends are here."

All of *his* friends were here. He'd slowly isolated her from each of her closest allies. Spread gossip. Told lies.

And now this.

He sauntered across the room to the sideboard and poured a drink. "I'm having some guests for supper tonight. We'll want your company."

She had no intention of joining him. But maybe . . . "The pantry is much depleted. Is there anything left of our allowance for the month? I can go shopping."

Her allowance. It was her allowance, but Father's will had made Michael the legal custodian until her twenty-fifth birthday or until she married.

"Don't worry about that. You'll want to spend some time making yourself presentable for our company."

Her stomach lurched. "Why?"

She saw the way his eyes glittered as he faced her again. "Brian will be here. He wants to see you."

Her skin crawled, tiny pinpricks of disgust marching up and down her arms and neck like ants. "I don't want to see Brian."

Her brother's so-called friend was known to run several of the gaming halls in town and was believed to run many less-reputable businesses. He was powerful and vicious. She hated the way he watched her whenever they were in the same room together. His eyes followed her with an intensity that made her deeply uncomfortable, especially after what had happened years ago.

"You'll be the consummate hostess tonight." Michael moved toward her.

Kaitlyn pressed her lips together. She would do anything in her power not to attend her brother's gathering tonight. There was something he wasn't telling her.

"Don't test me, Kaitlyn. I'm your protector."

She wanted to laugh. Michael was not a protector. He was a predator and she was the prey. She eyed the door. The room was small, and Michael had positioned himself to block her retreat.

"Brian Matthews wants to marry you," Michael said.

Her stomach churned.

"He'll come courting first, of course."

She shook her head, backed another step, then held her ground. Any farther and she would be against the wall.

Michael adjusted the sleeves of his suit coat so that his shirt cuffs peeked out by the perfect half of an inch. "You will dote on him tonight."

"No. I won't."

She spun and ran for the door, but Michael grabbed her arm before she could pass him.

"Let me go."

"You will attend my gathering tonight." Michael gave the order through gritted teeth. "You will hang on Brian's every word."

A part of her was terrified. She knew exactly what Michael was capable of. But she still shook her head. No.

He gave a wordless growl and pulled her bodily down the hall. She struggled against him, but he was bigger and stronger. His grip bruised her forearm.

He thrust her into a storage closet. "You'll hostess, or you'll stay here all night." He slammed the door and banged the bolt into its holder, trapping her inside.

"Michael, don't! Michael!"

He didn't answer her. His footsteps faded away even as she pounded on the door.

The walls closed in. It felt as if the air grew warmer and warmer.

She pounded louder. Screamed.

No one came.

Breathe, Kaitlyn. There's plenty of air. It only feels like you're suffocating.

It didn't help. Her breaths were jagged, cutting through her chest.

Michael was a monster. Brian was worse.

She couldn't stay here. She'd hoped for escape with her train ticket to Piedmont—that wasn't an option now. Even if she used her own meager funds to get there, it would be the first place Michael would look.

She knew him. She knew what he could do. He would turn the school against her, and she'd be right back under his protection. If she went farther afield, he'd track her down.

Michael was determined she marry Brian.

She couldn't. She wouldn't.

What was she going to do?

A sob burst from her. Then another. Fear rolled over her in waves. There was no one to help her. No place she could go to find safety.

She heard a whisper of her mother's voice through the clamor in her head. *You're the smartest of all, Kaitlyn.*

It wasn't real. She knew it was only a figment of her memory.

But it was enough to cut through her terror. Unlock

her chest just enough that she could draw a breath. Then another.

Michael had locked her in.

Was there a way out?

"Think, Kaitlyn." She closed her eyes and pictured the latch on the other side of that door. A simple piece of hardware—just a bolt that turned and slid back and forth in its barrel. There had to be a way to defeat it from the inside.

As her eyes adjusted to the darkness, the light from around the door allowed her to see what remained in the storeroom. He'd cleaned all the tools out of it. She ran her shaking hand along the floor. Nothing. She stood, and the room swirled around her. A deep inhale and slow exhale steadied the floor. What had she brought into the room with her? She had money in her handbag, but little else. Hairpins? No, too short to be of much use.

There had to be something. Maybe on the shelf? She couldn't see that high, but she could reach it, run her hand along it. Something poked her fingers. She grabbed it, pulled it down.

Wire. It could form a loop, hold its shape. She wiped her damp palms on her skirt, then held her hands in front of herself, frowning. They were still shaking slightly, but she'd have to manage it. No time to wait for them to stop.

She quickly bent the wire, then slid the curve through the crack in the door, running it down to the place where she could see the bolt. It took several tries before she could capture the knob holding it in place, but once she did, it was only a matter of moments before she was out of the closet.

She slipped across the hallway to her own room. No time

to regret hiding most of her emergency funds in her desk. Michael had surely found that when he'd picked the lock to find the rest of her correspondence with the Piedmont School District. But she removed two ten-dollar gold coins from the pocket attached to the outgrown corset she'd left in her closet.

She glanced around her room, daring only a minute's delay. She had planned her exit carefully, but now she had no time to follow her packing list. Michael might be back at any time. Still, the shopping basket she'd put in her closet might make her look like a servant out on errands. The perfect fit of her suit with its simple velvet trim would only stand out to someone with an eye for fashion. Most wouldn't see past the basket, which made it worth the seconds it would take to pack it.

What to take? Her silver brush, comb, and mirror set had belonged to her mother and could be sold if necessary. Her mother's Bible went in next, and then all of her own jewelry. She hadn't been able to afford nice pieces on the allowance her brother gave her from her inheritance, but they might bring in a little cash. Some clean underthings to muffle any rattle. That would have to do. She didn't have time to consider more carefully.

She opened her window and lowered the basket to the ground outside. She had to raise her skirts to a scandalous level to follow her belongings out the window, but then, scandal already clung to her like a heavy cloak. She cut across the back of the Fitzsimmonses' place to the sidewalk, then across the park, careful to copy the scurrying walk of the maids sent out on errands.

She didn't know what to do now. Piedmont wasn't an option. There was no friend to call on, no one to help.

She wouldn't go back to Michael, who wanted to marry her off to Brian.

The only way out of town was the train, so she hurried north. Her heart thudded in her chest. She didn't dare look over her shoulder, couldn't break her pretense. When she arrived at the train station, she examined the schedule. Her heart sank. Only one train scheduled, and the only place available was a sleeping car. Her remaining funds wouldn't take her far enough. Michael had far-reaching connections. She backed away from the counter, her knees shaking.

Lord, please help me. What do I do now?

She retreated toward the ladies' waiting area, staying close to the wall in case her legs needed extra support. A less expensive train left early tomorrow morning, but that would be too late. Michael would find her.

Her foot brushed something that crinkled. Why someone had thrown it to the ground instead of into a wastebasket, she couldn't guess. A flash of green banding caught her eye. That looked like . . . She knelt to pick up the wadded bunch of papers and pulled out the one with the green band. It said *Cheyenne, Wyoming.* She checked the date and time on the ticket.

The train was scheduled to leave in ten minutes.

And thanks to this ticket, she'd be on board.

Two

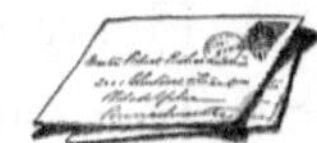

WHAT IF HE DOESN'T WANT ME?
Kaitlyn hurried along the walkway, the boards uneven beneath her feet. Habit had her glancing over her shoulder. After three days of broken sleep on a rocking train, her nerves jangled at every sound. Michael might be a thousand miles away, but who knew what threats lurked here?

Behind her, the train whistle screeched and the porter shouted, "All aboard!"

She could turn around. Buy a ticket for farther west. Find a school that needed a teacher.

She shook her head. And Michael would find her as soon as that school contacted her alma mater to check her references.

She forced her feet to continue moving forward. She had practically memorized the letter Drew had left at the train station. A man willing to go so far as to find a mail-order bride because he was concerned for his children was a man worth knowing.

And Michael couldn't force her to marry Brian if she was already married to Drew.

Her heels clicked on the boardwalk. It didn't matter if Drew didn't want her. She ignored the ache of loneliness the thought brought. Better to be needed than wanted any day. But she couldn't convince him he needed her until she got to his ranch. A town like this must have a livery. She just had to find it.

A door opened a couple of buildings down, and two people strode out onto the boardwalk. Here was someone who could help her. One of them was a bear of a man, unsmiling, his hands on his hips. He towered over the . . . woman? Kaitlyn's jaw dropped. A woman in pants?

The woman stood tall, her shoulders straight. Then she turned, and Kaitlyn saw the metal star on her vest. A woman as sheriff? Or deputy? Were things that different in the West?

She hoped so. She really did.

Kaitlyn moved closer. "Ma'am? Deputy?"

The woman pivoted, her boots squeaking against the wooden boardwalk. "Marshal, actually." Her coffee-colored gaze was coolly assessing.

Kaitlyn straightened her shoulders a fraction and pushed away the worry that told her not to talk about her destination in public. What did it matter if she left traces for Michael to follow? By the time he picked up her trail, she'd be safely married.

If Drew McGraw would agree.

Please let him agree.

"Could you give me directions to the livery?"

"It's at the end of this street." The marshal cocked her head questioningly. "Where are you headed?"

"To the McGraw ranch. Do you know them?"

The big man shouldered his way next to the marshal. "What business do you have with the likes of them?"

"The McGraws are good folks." The marshal sliced a look at the man, as if daring him to say different.

"Of course, Marshal." His gaze swept Kaitlyn from head to toe. "My spread is out that direction. It'd be the neighborly thing to do to offer a ride. Traveling alone in these parts can be dangerous."

Kaitlyn eyed the man in front of her. Neat suit and tie. Dark hair and eyes. Mustache. Traveling alone was dangerous anywhere, but could she trust this man she'd barely met? She shook her head. No, the livery was her best plan. "Thank you, Mr. . . ."

"Quade. Heath Quade. Glad to be of service."

"I appreciate the offer, but I think I'd better stick to my original plan."

Kaitlyn stepped past the two on her way to the livery. The spot between her shoulder blades itched, as if the man's gaze bored into her back. She resisted the urge to glance over her shoulder. Instead, she slipped into a business two doors farther down and made her way to the window. The marshal and Mr. Quade had disappeared. She let out a pent-up breath. Her imagination was working overtime.

She left the store and continued toward the livery. A block farther down, a crowd spilled onto the boardwalk from the saloon. Loud laughter. Shoving. A man at the back of the crowd noticed her and nudged his neighbor, who also looked her way.

She crossed the street. Rowdy groups of men could be trouble. No point in getting any closer than she had to. She kept an eye on the two men. They crossed the road toward her. Heading to the business she'd just passed, no doubt. Most men weren't like her brother.

Except their angle would take them right in front of her. She sped up.

They altered their path. Her stomach turned over. They intended to block her way. If she could only get to the livery. Surely someone there would help her.

The men's voices reached her.

"Hullo, sweetheart."

She ignored the man who'd called out so familiarly. Her face burned and her pulse pounded.

"I saw her first." The other man spoke even as they closed in on both sides.

Kaitlyn spun around. The jail was only a few doors down. Her heels clattered on the boards but couldn't drown out the sound of her heartbeat in her ears, nor the sound of the men's boots as they passed her.

"Where ya goin' in such a hurry, missy?" The first man hulked in front of her, blocking her path.

His friend stopped beside him. "Why doncha stop and chat with us?"

Please let the marshal be there.

Horse hooves thudded in the packed dirt of the road, then clattered onto the boardwalk behind her. She whirled around to see a huge brown horse standing between her and the men, Mr. Quade in the saddle. "What do you boys think you're doing? Harassing a young lady like that."

The other men backed into the street, muttering apologies.

Her knees threatened to melt in relief. "Thank you, Mr. Quade."

He swung down from his horse. "Why don't I escort you to the livery? I'd hate for more trouble to find you."

He hadn't had reason to, but he'd come to her rescue. One of the rough men glanced over his shoulder, eyes narrowed and angry.

With her heart still pounding in her ears, it was an easy decision. "I'd appreciate that."

The livery wasn't far, even with shaky knees. When they reached its stable yard, Kaitlyn glanced back to see the men still watching her. Not good. Not good at all. They likely had horses nearby, and who knew how far it was to the McGraws' ranch?

"Mr. Quade? Are you still willing to show me the way to the McGraws'?"

Quade looked back toward the saloon. "It's either that or follow you. Couldn't risk that bunch finding you. Can you ride?" He wrapped his reins around the post outside the livery.

"Yes."

It only took a few minutes to speak to the hostler, then Kaitlyn found herself in the saddle of a mare that seemed sturdy and gentle.

Mr. Quade kept his horse at a walk. Kaitlyn eased up beside him.

He smiled at her. "You never told me your name."

"Kaitlyn Montgomery."

"I hope you won't judge our entire town by a few bad actors."

Bad actors. As if they hadn't accosted her on a public street. Still, he had stopped to help. "I'd say you and the marshal even things up. I'll keep an open mind."

His smile widened. "A diplomat's answer. You sound like my middle daughter. She's always trying to smooth ruffled feathers."

At the edge of town, the road narrowed into a dirt path barely wide enough for the two of them to ride side by side. Kaitlyn took a deep breath, the air scented with grass instead of coal smoke like the past days on the train. The prairie stretched as far as she could see to the east, and to the foot of the mountains that stood a few days' ride to the west. No buildings hemming her in. Judging by the marshal's attire, there might be fewer expectations as well.

Unless Drew felt differently.

She shook her head. No point in worrying about it. She'd face Drew's expectations when she got to the ranch.

Quade guided his horse closer to her, away from the tall grass beside the path. "Why are you headed to the Mc-Graws'?"

And wasn't that the question. Not like she could tell him what she was running from, and she wasn't sure what she was running to. She forced a light laugh. "That would be telling. It wouldn't be fair to give you the gossip before anyone else, now, would it?"

His hands tightened on the reins. "I'm not the kind to indulge in gossip, Miss Montgomery, but I do like to look out for my neighbors."

"Have you been neighbors long?"

"Years." He glanced her way. "Long enough to know them well. Their spread is small and like to get smaller."

"I see." Not that she really did. If they were to lose land, wouldn't they lose it all?

"Not like my place. I've got the biggest spread in the area. Largest herd too."

There we go. His weak spot. If she could get him talking about his ranch, he'd quit pushing her for information. At least for now.

"How'd you get started out here?"

"Got lucky in the mines west of here. Earned enough to buy my first spread. Added to it as opportunities came."

He told her the story of his spread. She only understood about half of it, but she nodded in what she hoped were appropriate places. When he wound down, he asked, "What about your family?"

A topic she'd like to forget. "My parents died when I was young. I have one brother named Anthony." Not that he used that name, since he liked his middle name better. "He runs the family business." *Runs it into the ground, that is.* "Do you have a family?"

Was that a flash of disappointment? It passed too quickly for her to be sure.

"Three daughters." He glanced down at his hands on the reins. "My wife passed several years ago."

Disappointment over daughters, or grief over his wife? It could have been either. "I'm sorry to hear that."

"Still, three girls that are worth their weight in gold. Nothing like that crew of McGraw's. I figure he's wised up and hired a tutor for those hooligans of his. You'll have your hands full. Those kids have run wild since their mama left on a train." There was something calculating in his gaze, waiting for her response.

Her hands jerked. Drew's letter had said he was a widower. How could he be asking for a bride if he still had a wife? *Think, Kaitlyn. Don't reveal what you know. Or think you know.* "Left?"

"She ran off. Got tired of fighting against the land, and even more, fighting with her husband."

Kaitlyn bit her lip. She'd built up Drew McGraw in her head since reading and re-reading the letter she'd found at the station. The man who'd written it was thoughtful, intentional. Not eloquent or long-winded. She'd pictured him as kind. Like her father on most days.

But if what Mr. Quade had said was true, Kaitlyn had been completely wrong.

What had she gotten herself into?

No luck. Wasn't that the story of his life?

Drew backed away from the brambles he'd been searching. Where had Curly gone to give birth? He'd have thought a cow that had been bottle-raised would find safety nearer the house when her time came, but he'd spent the last several hours searching and found no sign of her. That wasn't unusual. Cows liked to pick remote places to give birth.

He strode back to his roan's side and swung into the saddle. Solomon had seen him through many an adventure, but the stallion was surely feeling the cold just as much as Drew. In the wooded areas, the trees blocked what little warmth the sun provided. Late March, and they still had snow on the ground.

Didn't matter. He had to find that cow. Curly Jo was the first calf David had bottle-raised. She'd been missing since yesterday, and Drew was determined to find her.

Drew had returned to the ranch a week ago without the new ma he'd promised the children. Their responses had demonstrated all the problems he'd hoped his wife would find a way to solve. If anything, their disappointment had made the issues worse.

David had said little, as if having a ma made no difference one way or the other.

Or maybe the girls' extreme responses had hidden David's. Jo had muttered "Good riddance" and been almost pleasant for the next couple of hours. Tillie's crying had ended the happy interlude. Jo had snapped at her sister and stormed out of the house, slamming the door behind her.

Tillie. Well, Tillie was the reason Drew found the cold outdoors more comfortable than the warm living room. Her expression had crumpled as she'd asked, "Don't she want us no more, Pa?"

Her questions hadn't gotten easier as the days passed. "Will she change her mind, Pa?"

"Maybe she came on today's train, ya think, Pa?"

"Did she decide three kids was too many, Pa?"

He'd had a few words with Jo after that last question. She was the most likely to have planted the poisonous idea that it was Tillie's fault Leona had backed out. Jo had denied it, complete with another slammed door.

Drew sighed. How did he tell his children that they'd been the subject of a rich girl's joke?

He didn't have an answer.

He guided Solomon out of the stand of aspens he'd searched and back into the sunlight. Where to next? He glanced at the sky to judge the time and stopped short.

Buzzards. His eyes squeezed closed.

Lord, please, don't let it be Curly.

But he had a bad feeling.

He struggled to pull in his next breath. What was he going to tell David? At thirteen, David already knew about loss. But Curly was special.

Drew had been nine when he'd learned not to name all the creatures on the ranch. He shook his hand, trying to forget the feel of Calico's fur beneath his fingers. That cat had followed him through his chores for the year, always glad when he sent a stream of milk her way.

Coyotes had gotten her.

You gave her a good life, his father had said. *That's all you can do, son.*

Drew hadn't liked the words then, and he didn't like them now.

He just didn't have any better.

Hoofbeats sounded from his right. That would be his

brother, Ed. He didn't even need to look. The second youngest McGraw had the knack for always being where he was needed most. He'd never left the ranch, unlike Nick, who'd had a brief stint in teaching school, and Isaac, who'd been with the U.S. Marshals for several years before returning home last year.

No doubt he'd seen the buzzards too.

Drew nudged Solomon to a ground-eating canter. Maybe, just maybe, it wasn't too late.

Ed guided his bay gelding, Lightning, beside them, matching the pace. He looked up at the birds circling their intended prey, then at his brother, his eyes somber.

A few moments passed before the terrain forced them to slow down.

Ed pushed his hat back on his head. "Mr. Cummins stopped by. Had some news from town. He said that Robbins sold out."

Drew hadn't heard. "When are they leaving? We'll have to get over and get the logs they promised we could cut."

"Cummins said they're already gone. Pulled out last Monday."

"What?" He guided Solomon around a bush. How were they supposed to prove up homesteads with no logs? Their pa had left the original family claim to Drew in his will, but Drew's brothers needed to prove up their new claims, and he'd promised he'd help. But when? Bills had to be paid and supplies purchased, leaving precious little money for lumber. Aspens might be pretty, but they'd never make a cabin. "Did you hear who bought it?"

Ed shook his head.

It didn't make sense for the Robbins family to pull out.

Quade. It had to be. Thousands of acres, yet the man still craved more. He'd been buying up so much land that surely his ranch took up a quarter of the county by now.

He wanted the McGraw spread and its water access and had made no secret of it.

Drew loosened his too-tight grip on the reins. Quade had made another offer on their property just last month. He'd said they'd be wise to take it, as everyone knew they'd never manage to prove up by the deadline. Had he known about their deal with Robbins?

No doubt he had. Had probably pushed the other family into leaving.

Ed pulled Lightning closer. "If we have to, we can tear down the bunkhouse and salvage the wood to build our cabins."

Drew shook his head. Where would his brothers sleep?

Ed seemed to follow his train of thought. "Nick and I can bed down on the living room floor for as long as it takes, and Isaac . . . doesn't seem to want a roof over his head these days."

Another problem. Jocular, outgoing Isaac had come back from his last marshal job silent and solitary, and without his badge.

Lord, if it's true You won't give us more than we can handle, I sure wish You didn't trust me so much.

Drew glanced over his shoulder to meet Ed's gaze. "We'll find a way. We have to."

Someday he'd like to do better than just *find a way*. Pa had made it look easy, but in the decade since Drew had taken over, he'd learned it was anything but. He'd made a promise to his ma, that he'd take care of his brothers. If they didn't get those homesteads proved up, he'd fail at that as well. No way could a single homestead support four men and three kids.

And Quade now owned the best stand of lumber trees.

Solomon sidestepped. Drew dragged himself out of his thoughts to see dots of red splashed across the patches of snow. He followed the trail to a patch of brush, then looked away.

Too late.

Curly wasn't moving.

Ed reined in beside him. "David is going to take this hard."

"He'll survive it. We all did." But the words felt hollow somehow. Like Drew inside.

This was Drew's fault. It was that bull he'd bought. He had taken one look at that Angus bull in the sale ring and just known it would improve their stock. Now he had five dead cows and a soon-to-be-distraught son.

Curly's calf stood on wobbly legs next to her dead mother, then folded onto the ground. The cold, wet ground that would suck the life from her as well if they didn't hurry.

Drew swung down from his horse. That calf had to live. It was the best possible salve for David's heart.

He grabbed the blanket from behind his saddle and wiped down the calf.

Ed went behind him, rubbing where Drew had dried, trying to improve the calf's circulation. "We've lost a lot of cows in calving this year, more than normal."

The words were salt in the wound. Drew knew. "Has to be the bull." Guilt coiled low in his stomach. He should have been able to predict the problem. Should have realized that the bull was too big for his otherwise healthy herd. "I'll be selling him the first opportunity we get." They might take a loss on him, but less than they were losing now.

Ed stood back as the calf struggled to her feet. "Why don't you take this little one to the barn? Lightning wouldn't like the smell of blood on her."

Solomon wouldn't like it either, but he'd do it because Drew asked it. "Someone will have to butcher Curly." Drew's stomach turned at the thought, but there was no help for it. Painful or not, they couldn't afford to waste the meat.

Hooves sounded in the distance. That'd be Isaac, drawn by the sight of the buzzards. Nick was on kitchen duty today.

Ed tipped his head. "Isaac and I can handle it."

Drew nodded. "Appreciate it." He swung into the saddle. "Hand me the calf?"

Ed wrangled him across Drew's lap. They had missed some patches of blood, and it smeared across his pants and shirt. Oh well. His clothes would wash.

Ed gave Solomon's neck a quick rub, which the horse tolerated. "You'd better get this baby to the barn. The sooner she's warm and fed, the better. Isaac won't be much longer."

Drew turned Solomon toward home. His horse shook his head at the slow pace Drew set but didn't argue otherwise. Not that Drew blamed him. Solomon knew there was grain waiting in the warm barn, just like Drew knew there'd be a pot of hot coffee on the stove in the kitchen. "Not much longer, boy. Just over that rise." As if the horse didn't know his way home blindfolded.

They topped the hill that gave the best view of the homestead. The setting sun cast shadows across the clearing where they planned to raise Ed's cabin. It was empty except for the haying equipment waiting for repairs. The barn door still didn't shut completely, since no one had fixed its broken track.

Drew's dream of handing this land on to a new generation of McGraws was slipping from his grasp. The legacy his father had begun was crashing down around him.

He rode on, listing the things he would need to do tomorrow.

Starting with finding a new source of lumber.

Then he noticed the strange horse tied to the corral fence. Company? When all he wanted was clean clothes and a hot cup of coffee?

And they wouldn't be bringing good news. Not unless his luck had changed drastically in the last thirty minutes.

Three

N O ONE WAS HOME.

Kaitlyn eyed the scratched-up door she'd hoped someone would open. One of its hinges must need tightening since the door drooped to one side. Hollyhocks straggled here and there at the front of the house. Someone had cared enough to plant them at one point in time. They just needed a little coddling.

"Who are you?" a young voice demanded from behind her.

Kaitlyn spun, the porch boards shifting beneath her feet.

Two girls and a boy watched her from the bottom of the steps. The suspicious question must have come from the middle child. She stood in front, her hair in a single braid that hung over her shoulder, her grimy hands on her denim-clad hips. Did all females wear pants in the West? No, she'd seen plenty of women in dresses on the train and at depots.

"Jo, where are your manners?" The older boy nudged his sister. His mud-spattered pants ended two inches above his ankles, and the muck on his boots had a suspicious odor. The youngest child stood next to him, wearing a too-short dress that was stained and in need of a wash.

Misgivings swamped her. Were these ragamuffins her soon-to-be charges? The lace at the neckline of the blouse she wore under her tweed jacket seemed to mock her desire to fit in.

The middle girl shoved her brother. "Don't you talk to me about manners, David McGraw. Anyone can see she don't belong here." Jo strode toward the steps and Kaitlyn.

Her brother, a head taller, rushed forward and wrapped his arms around her from behind, hoisting her off her feet while staying away from her flailing legs. "Don't matter who she is, Jo, exceptin' she's our guest."

His sister's elbow found his stomach. He flinched but kept her feet off the ground.

Uncertainty plagued Kaitlyn. These brawling children belonged to Drew McGraw?

She swallowed hard as she turned to track their tussle. She had survived Michael. She could survive three pint-sized hooligans.

She took a step forward, and her skirt rose nearly to her ankles, as if snagged. Cheeks heating, she snatched the fabric of her skirt and gave it a good tug.

She met the guileless brown eyes of the youngest, who must have slipped up beside her while the other two wrestled. "I's just checking your shoes."

Kaitlyn could barely hear the girl's voice over a dog who

had joined the two older kids and added loud barks to the melee. "My shoes?"

"You must be a princess, so I wants to see if your shoes are glass."

Kaitlyn smiled at the little girl, then glanced around to make sure she was alone with the kids. She raised her skirt just enough that her shoes showed.

The little one touched the toe of Kaitlyn's shoe. "It's leather, just like mine. Why isn't it glass?"

"Don't be dopey, Tillie. She's not a princess." Jo had escaped from her brother and marched up the stairs. David followed close behind.

"She is too."

"Is not!"

"Is too."

Tillie parked her hands on her hips and stuck her tongue out at her older sister. Jo lunged for Tillie, who backed into Kaitlyn's legs.

Kaitlyn couldn't control a flinch at the noise and turmoil surrounding her, but she forced a steadying breath, then lowered her skirt back to its full length. Mr. Quade had underestimated this crew. *Wild* didn't begin to cover it. She placed the ad and letter on top of the saddlebags by her feet. The letter that hadn't said anything about his children being this boisterous.

Then again, he'd probably exchanged more than one letter with Leona. Maybe he'd been open with her in previous exchanges. At least he'd had the good sense to leave once he'd met his supposed bride in person. *Mean-spirited* was the kindest description she'd ever heard applied to Leona.

Crowded, Kaitlyn took a step back, but the kids followed her, pushing in too close.

"Have you gots a magic wand in there?" the littlest asked, her fingers fiddling with the buckle on Kaitlyn's bag.

David grabbed his little sister, his arms brushing Kaitlyn's skirt as he pulled her back. "Sorry, Miss. You know better than to go through other people's things, Tillie."

Enough.

Kaitlyn put two fingers between her lips and whistled long and loud.

The children gaped at her, and Kaitlyn took advantage of the silence. "I'm here to speak with your father. Where is he?"

Ignoring her question, Jo crossed her arms over her chest. "How'd you do that? Can you teach me?"

"Kids, quiet."

The deep voice behind Kaitlyn had her spinning in place. Her cheeks burned. Even her ears felt hot. Was this Drew? He seemed young to have three children, and his hair was lighter than theirs, but his stance made it clear he expected them to listen. Had he seen her raise her skirt? She straightened her shoulders.

The man smiled at her, the expression reflected in his dark-brown eyes. "Drew is out on the range, but he should be back soon. David, Jo, Tillie, why don't you ask our guest inside?"

"Unca Nick!" Tillie ran to the man, then pointed toward Kaitlyn. "She's a princess, but she's disguise-ed, 'cause her shoes aren't glass."

Uncle Nick. This must be Drew's brother. Younger brother, by the looks of him.

Nick scooped Tillie up and grinned at her. "If she's in disguise, we can't call her Princess. Wouldn't want the evil stepmother to find her." Nick glanced her direction, the humor in his eyes contagious.

Tillie raised her hand to her mouth. "I sorry, Princess—I mean, Miss. She won't find you here. Pa won't let her."

Kaitlyn felt a pang of wistfulness at the certainty in the statement.

Nick put the little girl down and gave her back a gentle push to get her moving. "Okay, crew, inside—no, not you, David, not until you take those boots off. Get cleaned up. Supper'll be ready soon."

The girls bolted inside, leaving two sets of muddy tracks behind them. David followed once he had removed his foul-smelling boots. Footsteps thudded as they scampered upstairs. If Kaitlyn stayed, those imps would be her responsibility. Could she handle it?

She took a deep breath. Her only other choice was Brian. That was no choice at all.

Nick nodded toward the door. "Nick McGraw. You look like you've been traveling awhile."

"I have." Kaitlyn shored up her slumping shoulders. "All the way from St. Louis."

Whatever warmth she'd seen in his welcome, it disappeared instantly.

"You head on in. I'll find Drew."

Nick leaned over to grab her things. He crossed the parlor and dropped her bag just inside the dining room. At least it was away from the mud the children had tracked in. He said nothing more but kept walking through the house, his boots echoing against the wooden floor. A door opened and closed in the back of the house.

Kaitlyn's heart sank into her not-glass shoes. She didn't understand why Nick's welcome had changed. She hesitated at the threshold before stepping into the parlor. At least, she thought it was a parlor. Mud-smeared coats sprawled over the chair closest to the door. Pieces of tack better suited to the barn were piled beside the fireplace. Dirty footprints marked paths on the floor. A sofa faced the front door and divided the parlor from the dining area, which had a large table with chairs on one side and a bench on the other. It didn't have any dirty dishes on it but desperately needed a wipe.

A door opened and closed upstairs, reminding her that the children were still inside.

Kaitlyn hovered near the dingy window, watching as a tall man in a dark hat rode into the yard. Was this her intended groom?

There was some kind of bundle across his lap. Nick approached him, his arm gesturing toward the house. Drew shook his head. Nick gestured some more. What was he saying?

The man dismounted and handed his reins to his brother, who placed a hand on a bundle still slung across the saddle. Nick headed to the barn, and the rider—Drew?—approached the house.

Kaitlyn scurried away from the window. Wouldn't do to have his first impression of her be as a nosy Nellie. Should she sit? Stand? Her etiquette lessons hadn't come close to covering this. Her hands ached. She unknotted her fingers and forced her shaking hands to her sides.

The man flung open the front door while she was still deciding, and she turned to face him, standing halfway between the sofa and window.

"Miss Fitzsimmons, we have nothing more to say. I can't imagine what you're doing here—" His thundering voice stopped abruptly as he reached the doorway. "Who are you?"

Oh, he was handsome. Or would be if he were smiling. Dark hair peeked out from under his almost-black cowboy hat. He was taller than Michael, his shoulders wider. His eyes were the color of pewter and equally cold. A shiver passed through her. He was inspecting her with the same expression she might use when looking at a bug that had crawled onto her dinner.

She bit her lip. "Are you Drew McGraw?"

He nodded, remaining framed in the doorway.

He's only a man. One who needs my help. Kaitlyn pushed away the trickle of unease that wanted to become a flood. No matter how strong he appeared, his letter had made it clear his children needed a mother.

She swept a look up—way up—to his face, then back to his feet. His shirt and pants were wet in places and stained red in others. Was that blood? And why didn't he move?

"Who are you?" His deep voice had softened, but retained an edge of annoyance.

"Um, you see . . ." Kaitlyn clutched the back of the chair by the fireplace. Her pulse raced. Where were all her fine arguments? She'd practiced this moment for three days on the train, but none of the polished phrases returned to her mind. "This isn't going how I planned."

"Plan? What plan?"

Finally, he strode across the room and stopped by the fireplace. His presence seemed to shrink the room.

"What are you doing here?" He crossed his arms in front of his chest.

"My name is Kaitlyn Montgomery." Footsteps sounded overhead. The children. She lowered her voice. "I'm here to answer your ad. For a mail-order bride."

For a moment, his only movement was a muscle twitching along his jaw. Then his eyes narrowed. He opened his mouth, but before he could speak, the children pounded down the stairs. Tillie ran to Drew and threw her arms around his legs. "There's a princess here, Pa, 'cept, we're not s'posed to say that, cause she's running from the evil stepmother. But you'll protect her, won't you, Pa?"

Kaitlyn's gut plunged. The girl had said the words with pure innocence. She couldn't have guessed how close her assessment was to the truth.

David and Jo lagged on the last stair, watching.

Drew gave Kaitlyn a dark look before he reached down and disentangled his daughter. "Why don't you take our visitor into the kitchen for a cup of water."

The smile he gave Tillie gentled his expression, but Kaitlyn's jitters didn't ease. After all, he hadn't smiled at her. Hadn't responded to her statement. And now he was sending her out of the room.

Tillie took Kaitlyn's hand. "Come on, Princess. The kitchen's this way."

Kaitlyn followed the little girl past the dining table and chairs and into the kitchen.

She could hear Drew's voice behind her. "I brought a new calf down. Nick is in the barn and will need your help with it. Her mama didn't make it."

Kaitlyn felt a burst of compassion as she followed Tillie to the counter where a bucket and dipper rested. There was a murmur of voices from the parlor and then an exclamation from David.

"No! Curly's not dead!"

"I'm sorry, son. We gave her a good—"

"She can't be dead. Why didn't you do something to help her?"

Tillie tugged at Kaitlyn's skirt. She had a dipper of water in her hand, her lip caught between her teeth.

Kaitlyn took the dipper from her, took a sip, and replaced it in the barrel. "Who was Curly?"

In the other room, a door opened and slammed shut.

Tillie's lip trembled. "She was David's special cow. Do cows go to heaven like my mama did?"

So Drew *was* a widower.

Kaitlyn knelt down to face the girl. What should she say? What had her mother told her, back when her pony died?

"I don't think anyone knows for sure, but we know God loves all His creation, and we can trust Him to do what's right."

The words hit with a force they hadn't had when Kaitlyn was nine. She'd trusted God and He'd taken Mama.

Kaitlyn had been left with Michael trying to control her every move, plotting against her. She'd had no choice but to take care of herself.

Tillie stepped back with a sniffle. "I better go check on the calf." Before Kaitlyn could protest, she skipped out the back door, her skirts flying behind her.

Kaitlyn hesitated. Nothing about her arrival had gone as planned. She hesitantly moved into the doorway to the front room. There was no sign of David or Jo. Drew sat at the dining room table, his head in his hands, his shoulders slumped.

As if he sensed her presence, he straightened and then stood up. His expression was stony. No hint of the smile he'd given Tillie.

Drew just wanted this day to end. He wanted his pillow and the relief of the oblivion of sleep. For a few hours.

I'm here to answer your ad.

Drew reached for his hat brim to pull it lower, but of course he'd left it on its peg by the door. Without it, he'd have to work harder to hide his expression. He ran his hand through his hair, eyeing the woman standing in the kitchen doorway.

A princess. Tillie's words whispered in his head. The woman across from him really did look like she'd wear shoes made of glass.

She was pretty, with her blonde hair and green eyes, but it only took a glance to know she lacked staying power. It was there in the fine cloth of her dress that wouldn't stand up against ranch work. The fair skin that would burn under the sun.

And he hadn't missed her inventory of his clothing when she'd first seen him. Just what he needed. Another finicky city girl. Within four years of their returning to the ranch, Amanda had left him for a man who'd promised a life together in Boston. This Kaitlyn didn't look like she would last four days.

He was too tired to be polite. "There's nothing for you here."

She blinked and glanced to the side. He waited for the waterworks or some other kind of manipulation. Something Amanda would've done.

He just wanted this woman out of his house. He'd given up on the idea of a wife.

After a long moment, she met his gaze again. This time she didn't look away. "Your children are wild." She winced, like maybe she hadn't meant to blurt it out like that, but then hiked her chin up stubbornly.

"This is the West. Things are different than you're used to." He didn't try to hide the bitterness in his voice.

Kaitlyn met his gaze steadily. "Not that different. Another year or two and your older daughter will be ostracized for wearing pants."

Was that the problem with the girls at church? Jo's pants? Then why didn't she wear the dresses she had?

"If your son needs tutoring in math and reading, I can do that too. As well as teach the girls."

"What are you talking about? How'd you get here, anyway?"

She bit her bottom lip, then pulled some papers from her saddlebags and handed them to him. "I think these are yours."

His face flushed as he thumbed through them, an echo of the humiliation he'd felt back in St. Louis growing. "Where did you find these?"

"Where you left them. At the train station, with a ticket attached."

"You read my mail?" He walked to the window, breathing deep, trying to quell the anger he felt. So what if she knew what'd happened in St. Louis? It was Leona's shame, or should be.

Her cheeks had pinked, but she still didn't drop her gaze. *Stubborn*, he thought again.

"I did."

"Well, I'm sorry to say you came a long way for nothing. I don't aim to get married."

She bit her lip. "I can't change your mind? What about—I can pay you." She took a deep breath. "When I marry, I'll have access to some money."

Irritation poured through him. Another heiress thinking she could buy her way out of whatever had brought her here. Like Leona. Like Amanda. Well, not this time. Thoughts of his family's legacy had him considering it for a broken moment. But he didn't need money badly enough to shackle himself to another helpless city girl. To be labeled a mistake in another rich woman's life.

Through the window, he saw two horses coming off the foothill. Isaac and Ed. They'd need help when they tackled the butchering.

This was the real life he lived here. Amanda had refused to help with terrible jobs like this. Surely this young woman would too.

He pivoted and caught her gaze. "You want to prove you belong here? Come help with the butchering."

Kaitlyn's eyes narrowed. "Fine."

She followed him out to the barn. Brief introductions to his brothers followed, and Nick mentioned she'd ruin her clothes. David was sent to the house to fetch one of Drew's shirts. Kaitlyn put it on over her suit.

Drew thought it made her look like a child playing dress-up. In fact, it reminded him of the time Tillie had put on one of David's shirts. It had dragged the floor, and she'd pretended it was a gown, twirling and spinning as if she were at a ball.

The last thing he needed was a supposed princess reminding Tillie of unrealistic fantasies.

Kaitlyn stared at the carcass his brothers had hung from the ceiling. Her throat worked as she swallowed. Her face had gone pale, but she asked, "What do I do first?"

She didn't back down, not even when she turned green in the lantern light. She stayed with the men through the entire process, from removing the hide to splitting the carcass, even helping split it into smaller sections. When Tillie came to tell them that the stew Nick had assembled and left Jo to watch was ready, Drew insisted Kaitlyn accompany Nick and the kids back to the house to eat. He didn't miss the brief flash of relief that crossed her expression. Or how quickly she vacated the shed.

She was more stubborn than he'd expected.

But she still couldn't stay.

Darkness had fallen before he and Ed finished the butchering. By the time he'd eaten the plate of food warming on the back of the stove and been upstairs to help settle the girls in bed, the rest of the house had emptied. David had been sent to join his uncles in the bunkhouse. His son hadn't spoken to him since he'd broken the news about Curly.

Where had their unannounced guest gone?

She wasn't in the parlor. He moved through the kitchen, idly noticing his bloodied clothes were gone from where he'd left them by the back door.

There was a rustling noise coming from the lean-to. He headed that way but stopped short in the doorway.

Kaitlyn knelt over a washboard, rubbing his shirt across it.

"I didn't ask you to do that." His words emerged sharp, an uncomfortable feeling twisting in his belly.

She didn't look up. "You didn't. But the stain will set if it's not taken care of. I'm sure you've had a long day."

Taken care of.

Slow warmth spread through him. It'd been a long time since someone had thought about whether he was tired and needed his bed. Amanda had often left the kitchen a mess and been fast asleep when he'd come in after a long day of work. She'd claimed the work too much for her.

He blinked those memories away. "I'm not looking for a wife. I don't need anyone to take care of me."

She scrubbed his shirt up and down the washboard once, twice, before she let it drop into the water and looked over her shoulder to meet his eyes. "Do you need someone to take care of the kids? Your ad said you did."

No. He didn't. Not anymore. But the words stuck in his throat.

When he didn't answer, she tipped her face down to the washtub. "My brother is an unkind man. He tried to force me to marry someone . . . unsuitable."

There was something more behind the words. Earlier, she'd tried to out-stubborn him, staring with her chin tilted just so. But now, in the quiet and shadowed room, she didn't look at him. Trying to hide the vulnerability? Was this the real Kaitlyn?

"So you ran away?" he asked.

"I didn't have a choice." She found another item of clothing and squeezed water from it.

There was a resignation in her voice that he understood all too well. He leaned against the doorframe. "Clearly, I need help with the house and kids."

He'd taken a look around earlier, seen the house with fresh eyes, as Kaitlyn must have seen it. When had things gotten so bad? It needed a deep cleaning and someone to stay on top of the clutter and accumulating dirt, but when would he or his brothers find time for that?

And the kids.

Tonight, when he'd tucked Tillie into bed, her hair had been tangled beyond his ability to tame it. Kind of like his life.

Kaitlyn looked up now, a hint of her earlier stubbornness in the way her lips pressed together. "What if we can help each other?"

She was a complete surprise. Showing up like she had. Pitching in to help. With the butchering and with dinner—Nick had told him in a low voice that she'd charmed Tillie into eating her supper and taken it upon herself to clean up after.

There was too much work to go around. Too little of him. She'd been right about the children's education, about Jo growing up before his eyes. It was why he'd tried to make a match with Leona.

"So you'd be willing to marry a stranger to avoid your brother's choice?"

Silence stretched for a long moment before she gave one brief nod. What kind of choice had her brother made for her?

"And you're not looking for love? Because I can tell you, you won't find it here."

Amanda had taught him that lesson. He had nothing to give a woman, especially not a woman like Kaitlyn.

Her fingers paused on the washboard. "I don't need love. A little kindness might not hurt."

He smothered a smile. She didn't mind calling him out, but that was a good thing. His kids would run right over someone who didn't have a backbone. "It's a deal, then. Escape and kindness for you. Help with the kids for me."

She looked at him, her cheeks growing red. "I can't stay here unless—I mean, there's, um, no other women."

He felt his own cheeks warm. "There'll be a wedding, but no marriage. This is a business deal we'll both profit from. Nothing more."

Four

WHAT HAVE I DONE?

Early the next morning, Kaitlyn looked around the bare room where she'd passed the night. No pictures on the rough wooden walls. A single window that needed a good scrubbing. If she went through with this marriage, she would be trapped out here in the Wyoming wilderness.

But Michael would hold no power over her once she said *I do*.

Drew would.

She got out of bed, trying not to trip over the hem of her borrowed nightgown. She picked up a handful of extra fabric, but the hem still brushed against her ankles.

Last night, Drew had escorted her to his room and told her it was hers now. He'd sleep downstairs with David. Some of his first wife's things were in the bottom drawer of the bureau, he'd said. Kaitlyn could use what she needed.

There'd been several awkward moments with him standing out on the landing and her inside the room. This morning, she had to wonder whether he was still in love with the woman who'd worn this very nightgown. He'd certainly made it clear he had no interest in Kaitlyn.

And you're not looking for love? Because I can tell you, you won't find it here.

His words from last night had given her pause. She'd been so concerned about escaping Michael's grasp that she hadn't fully considered what it meant to marry a near-stranger. Drew seemed determined that this would be a business deal, no emotions involved.

She hadn't thought about it in a long time—not since girlhood dreams had faded—but she'd always imagined having a family of her own. A husband who loved her.

Was this business deal worth what she would give up?

What choice did she have?

Kaitlyn hiked her chin.

She wasn't looking for love, was she? Being needed was better. People didn't throw away what they needed.

Bickering voices filtered through from the kitchen, interrupting her thoughts.

Kaitlyn threw on her traveling dress and shoes, then quickly put up her hair. She'd never thought she'd be grateful for Michael's spendthrift ways, but at least his inability to pay staff meant she knew how to help with the work around here.

Two girls' voices rose higher as Kaitlyn descended the stairs. Knots curled in her belly. She knew how to manage the cleaning and cooking, but her main job was caring for the children. She'd been shocked yesterday at how wild they'd seemed. Surely the memories that had plagued her as she'd tossed and turned in the unfamiliar bed had exaggerated just how rowdy and improper the children had acted.

She pushed away the uncertainty. She had planned to teach in a classroom. This couldn't be that different.

And she had no other choice. Michael had stripped them all away.

The clatter of a log shifting in the wood-burning stove drew Kaitlyn to the kitchen doorway. Tillie stood on a chair, cracking eggs into a bowl, and Jo rolled out biscuit dough while one of the brothers—was it Nick or Ed?—sliced ham. The worktable in the center of the room easily accommodated all three of them, the girls on one side and their uncle on the other.

"Jo, I dropp-ed more shell in."

Jo grabbed a fork and moved to lean over the bowl, sighing as if this wasn't the first time. "You're such a baby, Tillie. If you could do anything without help, I'd be able to go work in the barn." Jo scowled as she flicked the piece of shell onto the counter and then returned to the biscuits.

"Jo," the man warned, though he didn't even look up at the squabble.

Tillie's lower lip stuck out. "I'm not a baby."

"Yes, you are." Jo ran the rolling pin across the biscuit dough. "You still need someone to look after you all the time." Jo's complaint in the last words probably meant she was usually assigned the task. "And I can't even take you to the barn, 'cause you're too loud."

Ed-or-Nick looked over at Jo sharply, and at the same

moment, Tillie looked over her shoulder and caught sight of Kaitlyn. The girl jumped off the chair and ran to Kaitlyn. Kaitlyn dropped a hand on her shoulder as the girl hugged her waist.

Jo dropped the rolling pin on the counter with a clatter. "Finally. You slept late. Uncle Nick, can I go to the barn now?"

Kaitlyn might've hoped for a warmer greeting. She shored up her smile. Jo must still be getting used to the idea of Kaitlyn staying here. It was an adjustment for all of them.

At least Nick was glad to see her, if his smile was any indication. "There's coffee on the stove. Finish the biscuits, Josephine," he said firmly.

Jo scowled again. "I don't want to. I want to help Pa and David in the barn."

Nick's chin dipped and for a moment, the only noise was the *snick-thump* of his knife before he answered Jo. "You are a lot of help in the barn, short stuff. But your pa tasked you with making those biscuits for the family."

"But I don't want to. David never has to help in the kitchen."

Tillie moved back slightly and tugged on Kaitlyn's hand. "Will ya help me crack the eggs?"

Kaitlyn followed her to the worktable, nose wrinkling slightly at the scattered flour and bits of eggshell on the dirty surface.

Jo glared at her sister. "You're useless. If you could do the eggs by yourself, I wouldn't be stuck in here."

Tillie's shoulders shook as she swallowed a sob. "I'm not useless, am I, Miss Kaitlyn?"

"Of course not." Kaitlyn pulled the child into her arms. "You're just little."

"That means the same thing." Jo smirked.

Tillie wailed.

Kaitlyn ran her hand along Tillie's back. Was it too late to go back to bed and start over? The wool fabric of the girl's dress was rough beneath her fingers, and her cries didn't abate.

Of course they didn't. Kaitlyn's head spun. What did she know about comforting a distraught child?

Jo pushed hard on the rolling pin, working the dough to nearly pie-crust thickness. Intentionally sabotaging the biscuits, no doubt. Kaitlyn bit her lip. Step into the girl's trap, or eat burnt crackers for breakfast? Neither choice appealed.

Jo dug one end of the rolling pin into the dough and dragged it, ripping the mixture down the middle. Her smirk grew wider.

Kaitlyn's stomach tensed. She knew a challenge when she saw one. Unfortunately, the odds weren't in her favor, no matter how she chose to respond. Still, how much madder could the girl get? Kaitlyn released a still-sobbing Tillie and moved next to Jo. "I think you got the dough a little too thin."

"We like it that way. What do you know about living on a ranch anyway?"

"Not much, but I can learn."

Jo scoffed. "You ain't gonna be here long enough for that. You'll leave, just like Ma did."

"Josephine McGraw!" Nick's cheeks flushed, and his lips folded into a flat line.

Kaitlyn's stomach tightened. Could there be truth to Mr. Quade's story? Was Drew divorced, not widowed? She leaned against the sharp edge of the worktable to steady her weakened knees.

Nick sighed and put his knife down. "Tell you what, Tillie. Why don't I teach you how to cut out biscuits. Jo can check on the chores in the barn."

And wasn't that just how her parents had treated Michael? Whatever it took to get him to quiet his current tantrum. Still, Kaitlyn needed answers, and she wasn't likely to get them with the girls in the room. As soon as she found her footing, she'd be prepared for Jo's stubbornness.

Jo threw the rolling pin into the mess of torn dough and ran out the back door.

Kaitlyn tweaked one of Tillie's crooked pigtails. "Why don't you go with her?"

Nick's eyes squeezed shut, but he didn't argue.

Tillie, her tears miraculously calmed, ran after her sister.

Nick picked up his knife and cut another slice of ham. "I wish I could tell you that was unusual, but so far, this has been a fairly typical morning. Still, if you can handle the butchering, I don't guess a few dramatics will chase you away."

"What chased the children's mother away?"

"Amanda. Her name was Amanda."

"And?"

He sighed. "Drew wouldn't be happy to hear us discussing this." Even his ears were red.

"I have a right to know if the man I'm about to marry is a widower, divorced, or even . . ." Her cheeks heated and her eyes dropped to the worktable. She gathered the biscuit dough into a ball and rolled it out.

Nick paused in his chopping and turned to face her. "No, Kaitlyn. He wouldn't . . . I mean, it never crossed my mind that you'd think—" His Adam's apple bobbed. "Let me start over, okay?"

Kaitlyn nodded.

"Amanda came from money. She couldn't adjust to life here, or maybe she didn't want to." He chuckled. "I know she would never have pitched in like you did last night."

Kaitlyn's shoulders relaxed just a bit. She'd done something right, anyway.

Nick returned to slicing meat. "I guess I should be kinder. She stuck it out for almost four years. Then she ran off with one of the hands. Said it was a mistake for her to come west with Drew and she was going back to Boston. She took both girls, but David was out working with Drew. The train derailed. Amanda died."

Kaitlyn shuddered. No wonder Drew didn't want to talk about it. She swallowed hard. "The girls?"

"Cuts and bruises. Jo had a broken arm."

"How old was she?"

"Five."

Kaitlyn's eyes squeezed shut. So young to have her world turned upside down.

Nick sighed. "Nothing's been the same since." He shook his head. "No, nothing's been right since."

Kaitlyn wandered to the window and pushed aside the curtain. The dirty glass felt cool beneath her fingers. Drew was hunched over a piece of farm equipment. Tillie stood next to him, watching. Jo had vanished, probably into the barn.

Amanda had told Drew he was a mistake. Had left with another man, fracturing this family. Kaitlyn's heart ached. David had held back from her. Jo had pushed her away. Tillie had latched on to her, holding tight. All responses to the trauma of their mother dying.

Was she supposed to fix this? And if so, how?

Ouch!

Drew pocketed his file and examined his fingers. No blood, thankfully. He should know better than to get distracted while sharpening a plowshare.

Laughter drifted across the barnyard from where David and Ed stood outside the weathered barn, chatting. Drew's stomach tightened. David had been avoiding him all morning. He leaned back toward the equipment, the cold from the frozen ground seeping through the knees of his pants. His file screeched against another burr. Whoever had put up the plow last fall had forgotten to coat it with oil. Now it would take nearly a day to get it ready. One more chore in an endless list.

Hoofbeats stopped nearby. Drew glanced up, swallowed another sigh. Isaac waited, all kitted out and obviously not planning on staying at the homestead today. Drew put down the file and walked over.

"You headed out?" Drew ran his hands over his pants legs, wiping off the dust from the plow.

Isaac nodded. "Thought I'd check on the new calves and the last few pregnant cows."

"I'll see you tonight, then."

Isaac shook his head. "I heard some wolves pretty close. Thought I'd make sure they weren't building a den somewhere nearby."

Isaac's voice sounded steady but lacked the note of humor that used to be a near constant. What had killed Isaac's laughter?

Drew rubbed the back of his neck. "Last night you said you wanted to talk to me."

Isaac looked toward the path he'd be riding, his face expressionless. "It can wait. You've got a lot on your hands."

The conversation had already waited too long, to Drew's way of thinking. He glanced down at his brother's waist. No pistols. Isaac hadn't worn them since he'd returned home without his badge. "Isaac—"

"I said it could wait." He guided his horse toward the pastures.

Drew turned back to the plow, his heart heavy. When had Isaac lost his smile, his joshing good humor? Growing up, he'd been behind most of the mischief the brothers had made, and most of the fun as well. Now he seldom smiled. Never laughed. Looked like he never slept.

The file jerked in Drew's hand, caught on another burr. He wiggled it, but it wouldn't move forward or back. Drew sighed and left the file where it lay. He had bigger fish to fry. What could he do to help his brother? Isaac needed more than Drew could give him. For now, only the vast empty land seemed to give Isaac peace. If the cost of that peace was more work for Drew, so be it.

He stood and jostled the plow handles. The rungs had worked loose again. They'd have to be tightened before he plowed more land for the hay his larger herd needed. Maybe he'd expanded too fast. Drew pushed the thought away. His brothers deserved their own land, their own places. They'd just have to make it work. With the old plow.

But for now, he needed to get the team. A few minutes later, he led the dappled grays out of the barn to the wagon. Ed ambled up and took one horse, quickly moving to the front of the wagon.

Drew's shoulders relaxed. He could always count on Ed to jump in with whatever needed doing. They busied themselves with straps made stubborn by the cold.

Ed adjusted a buckle for a better fit. "We could start tearing down the bunkhouse while you're gone, to recycle the lumber."

"No need. I'm headed to town. I'll see what I can get for that bull and price lumber while I'm there."

Ed nodded. "The bull needs selling, but where will we get money for a new one if we use the money from his sale on lumber?"

"I'll handle it." And without touching his bride's money. That wasn't part of their deal. If Kaitlyn could just help Jo, she'd more than pull her weight.

Except he couldn't let his brothers pay the price for his

own pride. The ball of guilt that had taken up permanent residence in his gut grew. The original homestead couldn't support four families. It made sense that he'd inherited it, as he was both the oldest and the only brother with a family.

But if it made sense, why did he feel like a thief?

The front door slammed, and Jo stomped down the porch steps. "I don't wanna wear this dress," she hollered. David followed her, stopping to kick at something.

Ed cleared his throat. "Are you sure about this marriage?"

Drew adjusted a strap that already lay perfectly smooth. Fact was, he wasn't sure about anything. "It isn't real, you know. The marriage, that is."

"Once you're in front of that preacher, it's as real as it gets. No going back."

David moved closer to Jo, his expression scornful. He said something Drew couldn't hear, and Jo took a swing at him. David danced back out of reach.

Was this marriage the right thing for the kids? He shook his head. He couldn't predict the future. He only knew they couldn't continue as they were now. David longed for more education than Drew could provide, and Jo? Well, he didn't even know what Jo needed.

The front door opened, and Tillie stepped onto the porch. Kaitlyn followed. Tillie's hair was pulled back into a bow. A bow, of all things. He didn't even know they had ribbon. Tillie took Kaitlyn's hand and pulled her toward the wagon, her smile wider than he could remember seeing. Drew's heart lightened.

Ed stopped beside him and placed a hand on his shoulder. "Are you sure, Drew?"

"I'm sure. I'm getting married."

Five

Y OU GOT A BROTHER?" TILLIE ASKED
from the wagon bed, where she rode with her siblings.
"What's his name? When do we get to meet him?"

Kaitlyn's head spun. Who knew such a little girl could have so many questions? She looked around for a distraction for the girl. The side street off Calvin's main thoroughfare was lined with small bungalows and empty of town folk.

The wagon jolted as the wheel hit a low spot, sending her sliding across the seat before she could brace herself, and landing her against Drew's strong shoulder. Again.

"Sorry," she muttered as she moved back to a proper distance. Unlike her, he seemed to shift with the jolts of the wagon, never losing his balance.

At least, not physically.

She'd seen his shoulders droop a bit more every time David snubbed him on the trip to town.

Tillie grabbed Kaitlyn's arm. "When we gonna get there?"

Kaitlyn gritted her teeth. It had to be the hundredth time the girl had asked during the long drive. She forced a smile. "Soon, Tillie. Soon." It had to be soon, didn't it? They'd reached the town, after all.

Drew pulled the team to a stop in front of a small house near the church and secured the reins. "Now, Tillie. We're here now."

"Yay!" Tillie stood in the wagon bed. "I want to go with you, Pa."

"Nope. You stay with Kaitlyn." Drew rubbed a hand across Tillie's head, then climbed down from the wagon.

A man of few words, her soon-to-be husband.

Husband.

Her nerves hummed, and an itching sensation skittered across her skin. She didn't know this man. He'd barely spoken on the trip to town, and yet his steadfast presence had been impossible to ignore.

She forced a deep breath, her mind racing back through the past twenty-four hours and stopping on the image of Drew at the table, his face buried in his work-roughened hands. Her next breath came easier. He worked hard and cared about his children. Both good recommendations.

She turned to David and Jo, who had ridden quietly in the back of the wagon. Too quietly. David looked somber, his arms draped to his sides and his attention focused on his father. Jo's arms were crossed over her narrow chest, and she glared at Kaitlyn.

"What do you want to do while we're in town, David?"

He shrugged, and Kaitlyn's heart sank. The boy was hurting, and she didn't know how to help.

"I want a candy stick." Tillie danced in place, excited over the outing.

"Candy's for babies. I want a new headband for Sunny's bridle." Jo stood in the wagon bed and leaned on the back of the seat, then backed away. Probably realized her enthusiasm had put her too close to enemy camp—Kaitlyn.

Tillie ignored Jo's verbal jab, so Kaitlyn did too. All siblings snipped at each other. It was normal. Wasn't it? But then, what did she know about normal sibling relationships?

The door to the house creaked open, and an older man stepped outside. Drew gestured toward the wagon, but Kaitlyn couldn't hear what he was saying. The man's eyebrows rose. He studied the wagon for a moment, then spoke earnestly to Drew. Drew nodded, then returned to the wagon. He extended a hand to Kaitlyn. "Pastor Carson said he'll wed us now."

Kaitlyn placed her hand in his. She had never thought her hands particularly delicate, but against his calloused palm, her hand appeared no larger than Tillie's. Heat soaked through her glove and traveled straight to her heart. Doubtless, Drew only aided her descent out of good manners. He'd do the same for any woman. She pulled her hand from his and took a wobbly step. Her feet tingled and burned.

Drew's eyes narrowed, and he retrieved her hand to carefully tuck it into the crook of his arm. When her next step faltered, his arm tightened, lending her his strength until she found her footing.

Her face heated. "I'm sorry. My legs seem to have deserted me."

He smiled at her. Not a full smile, just a quirk of his lips, but it warmed his eyes from pewter to something closer to the dapple gray of the draft team pulling their wagon. "It was a long ride."

He guided her to the boardwalk, then released her, but watched for a moment to make sure she was stable. Her heart lost its rhythm for just a moment. When was the last time someone had cared enough to help her find her footing?

Kindness is a part of our agreement. It's a business arrangement, and I'd do well to remember that.

"Thank you. I've got my balance."

He nodded once, then moved to the wagon bed to lift the kids out. Kaitlyn examined the boardwalk from one end to the other. No crowd walked her direction. No unease prickled the back of her neck. Any apprehension she felt arose solely from doubts about fulfilling her job, not from what her brother might do to her. For the first time since her father died, she felt free. In just a few minutes, Michael wouldn't be able to touch her ever again.

She followed the short path that led to the pastor's house, then entered. The inside felt dim until her eyes adjusted from the bright sunlight outside.

In moments, Mrs. Carson showed her to the parlor. Drew, the kids, and Pastor Carson entered soon after. The kids shed their coats and hung them on hooks by the door. Drew followed suit, leaving his hat as well.

Drew shifted to face her, and Kaitlyn had to swallow hard. He'd dressed up. Her gaze traveled from his white shirt and black vest that emphasized his broad shoulders to his well-shined boots and back to his dark hair that curled a bit at the back of his neck. But when her eyes caught his, he looked away, flushing. A muscle ticked in one cheek. What had she done wrong? Shouldn't he want his bride to appreciate his efforts to dress up?

A rock formed in her stomach. What was she doing? He'd probably loved his first wife, and she'd left him. Maybe she'd had good reason. Kaitlyn should have kept running, found a job—anything other than marrying a stranger.

Drew tapped David's hat, and the boy hurriedly placed it next to his father's. He looked around to see if anyone had noticed his lapse, and Drew ran a comforting hand along his son's back. David shrugged away. Tillie reached her hands up, and Drew stared at his son's back for a long moment before looking to his youngest and slowly lifting her, pretending she had grown too heavy for him since yesterday.

His love for his children couldn't be clearer.

The tightness in Kaitlyn's chest eased. Drew needed her. The children needed her. Partnerships had thrived on less.

Drew had said little on the trip into town, but he showed no hesitancy as he crossed the room to stand next to her in front of the pastor. He took her hand, tucked it once again into the crook of his arm, and a sense of safety flooded her. He'd steadied her steps when her legs had protested the long wagon ride. Somehow, she knew he'd stand beside her come what may.

The pastor cleared his throat. "Dearly beloved, we are gathered here in the sight of God . . ."

Kaitlyn's stomach squirmed. In the sight of God? How was it she had never listened to the words of a wedding ceremony? What would God think of the promises she was about to make?

Drew's arm shifted, and she looked up to see a question in his eyes. *Are you sure?* they seemed to say, and the tightness in her chest relaxed just a bit. Besides, God was the one who had left her with Michael in the first place.

"Will you, Drew, take this woman, Kaitlyn, to be your wedded wife? Will you love her, comfort her, honor and keep her in sickness and in health; and forsaking all others, keep only unto her, so long as you both shall live?"

"I will."

The certainty in his deep voice seeped into her soul. He was making those promises to her, no one else. Kaitlyn released the breath that had been stuck in her chest. So what if he'd told her he'd never love her, if he only wanted her to take care of his children? He still wanted her, Kaitlyn Montgomery.

"Will you, Kaitlyn, take this man, Drew, as your wedded husband? Will you love him, comfort him, honor and keep him in sickness and in health; and forsaking all others, keep only unto him, so long as you both shall live?"

As long as you both shall live.

The pastor's words settled in her chest like a heavy weight. This was a life sentence. Her mind winced, then settled on the image of facing the same sentence with Brian in place of Drew. Michael would find her eventually. A marriage certificate was her only protection.

She forced a breath past the weight in her chest. "I will."

"I now pronounce you man and wife. You may kiss your bride."

Kaitlyn swallowed hard, then looked up to meet her new husband's eyes. They hadn't talked about this. What would he do?

"Kiss her, Pa." Tillie clasped her hands in front of her, her eyes shining. David and Jo watched from nearby.

Kaitlyn's heart thundered in her chest as Drew lowered his head. His hand still clasped hers. Kaitlyn twisted her free hand into her skirt. Drew's lips barely grazed her cheek. As Drew let her go and turned away, expression inscrutable, Kaitlyn lifted one hand to the spot his lips had brushed. She felt as if his touch had been a red-hot branding iron.

She was still trying to catch her breath when Tillie wrapped her arms around Kaitlyn's legs. "You're my mama now."

Drew led Jo and Tillie toward the lumberyard while David showed Kaitlyn to the telegraph office. His bride wanted to notify her lawyer of their wedding as soon as possible.

His bride.

He'd felt nauseated when her gaze had raked him head to foot, but then he'd caught uncertainty, not scorn in her eyes. Her hand had trembled when he'd tucked it into the crook of his arm, but she'd moved closer. Closer to the man she'd first seen covered in mud and muck. The man who couldn't manage his kids.

The man Amanda had spurned.

The hitch in his chest had made it difficult to keep his voice steady as he spoke his vows.

Had he felt the same when he'd spoken vows to Amanda? He mostly remembered the overpowering scent of flowers and his own joy when she'd promised she'd never leave him.

Turned out she'd only meant for as long as circumstances went her way instead of for as long as they both should live.

His marriage to Kaitlyn was supposed to be a business arrangement, but when she'd looked at him with guileless eyes and promised to stay, he'd almost believed she'd meant the vows she'd spoken.

Luckily, he'd regained his senses before he'd actually kissed her.

"We don't need a new ma."

Drew started, then spun to face his middle child. She'd stepped off the boardwalk into the lumberyard while he wasn't watching.

Jo glared at him, her arms crossed over her chest. "Well, we don't!"

Her glare faltered for a moment, and something else flickered through her expression. Fear? Hurt? If he knew the answer to that, maybe he wouldn't need Kaitlyn. But would she be able to interpret Jo's expressions any better?

He gently took Jo's shoulder. "Follow right behind me. A lumberyard can be a dangerous place."

Tillie slipped her hand from his and raced toward a butterfly. He caught her within a couple of steps and swept her up against his shoulder. Best not to trust her to her own feet.

He crossed the yard, moving through stacks of green-cut wood, checking behind him to make sure Jo was following.

She glared at him. "I'm not a baby. I know how to follow you."

He entered the office. Mark Haskin sat at his desk, eyeing the mounds of paper that covered the surface. It looked a lot like Drew's desk at home.

"Got a minute, Mark?" Drew set Tillie on her feet.

"Glad to take one." The man ran a hand through his salt-and-pepper hair. "I didn't start this business so I could spend my days moving papers from one pile to another."

"I hear you." Drew eyed Tillie, then Jo. "Stay inside the building, girls."

"What can I do for you, Drew?" Mark waved to a chair across from his desk, and Drew sat down.

"I need to put up a small cabin on my brother's homestead. I'm looking to trade for the lumber—a butchered cow." Drew forced his hands to still. Bartering was a perfectly acceptable alternative to cash. "What do you think?"

Mark sighed. "Wish I could do that, but . . ."

Drew tried to ignore the heat that swept the back of his neck. "I could work a couple days a week. Or sign a note. I'm good for it."

"I know you are." Mark's gaze held compassion. Or was it pity? "I just can't do any credit right now, and I barely have enough work to keep my current men busy."

Drew shoved his fisted hands into his pockets. It had

been a long shot, but he had hoped. He'd just have to sell the bull quickly. The best place to get leads on a buyer was the general store. "I appreciate your time. Let me know if you need more workers."

He stepped from the office and replaced his hat. If he was lucky, it would hide the heat in his cheeks. He took Tillie's hand and signaled Jo to follow, then he crossed to the boardwalk, where David and Kaitlyn waited for him. "Get your telegram sent?"

She nodded but didn't quite meet his eyes. Her hands twisted in her skirt, and roses bloomed in her cheeks.

The memory of their wedding kiss roared back through his mind. Except it hadn't been a kiss. Would never be a kiss.

"I need to pick up some supplies." His voice sounded gruff, even to his own ears. He cleared his throat and eyed the tweed traveling dress she still wore instead of Amanda's old things. If those wouldn't work, they'd have to find substitutes. "We'll try to find you a couple of dresses and some shoes as well."

"My shoes are still in good shape."

"Shoes that work on eastern sidewalks can cause problems here."

She took a deep breath, her hands fingering the hem of her jacket and her eyes still refusing to meet his own. "I looked through the dresses in the bureau. They're too big, but I could alter them, if you don't mind, um, seeing them."

Relief flooded him. She needed both clothes and shoes, and he needed to save every penny he could for his brothers' homes. Amanda had never worn a hand-me-down in her life. When Kaitlyn had appeared in her own dress, he'd assumed she felt the same. She kept surprising him.

"That would help out." Was that gravelly voice his? He took her arm and guided her into the shoe section of the general store. "Kids, you can look around, but don't touch anything."

Jo and Tillie shot to the exact places he would have expected. Jo to the horse tack and Tillie to the candy. Neither was touching anything, so he'd count that as a victory.

David surprised him. He moved to the boys' clothing. Drew's heart squeezed. The boy needed new pants so badly. Since Kaitlyn was remaking Amanda's dresses, maybe they could afford a single pair.

Mr. Thomas was tied up at the counter, filling orders for a customer, and three more waited in line. Plus, several people searched the store for items on their own lists. He'd better help Kaitlyn, or no telling how long it would take to get out of here. Or how much trouble his kids would find in the meantime.

He took Kaitlyn's arm. "Let me see your shoes."

She glanced around the store, her cheeks rosy red. "I couldn't."

"No one will see but me, and I am your husband, after all."

Her eyes flew to his. "But we're . . ."

Sleeping in different rooms. He could easily finish her thought. His own cheeks warmed, but her embarrassment had to be more intense. Best he play things down. "Yep, we are. And will. Still means I'm allowed to see your ankles."

She looked around again, then lifted her skirt high enough for him to see the tops of her shoes.

Tillie joined them and tugged at the bottom of his coat. "I told you, Pa. Her shoes aren't glass."

Nope. Definitely not glass. But they might as well be, so far as practicality went. Okay, the heels were only a couple of inches high, but they were so narrow. And how on earth did she fasten them without a buttonhook?

Kaitlyn dropped her skirt back to the floor, looking around to see if anyone had heard Tillie's comment. She sank into the chair set out for people trying on boots.

"Tillie, go find your brother."

Tillie trudged off. Drew glanced over the women's boots. "What size?"

"Five." Kaitlyn's voice was low.

He found a size five in a simple lace-up leather boot. "Here, try these."

She didn't move to take them. He smothered a groan. She probably thought they were beneath her, but she had to have them. Or something like them. Too bad Merritt was busy teaching. She could probably explain it better.

He held them closer to her. "I know they aren't fashionable, but you need them."

"You don't understand." Her voice was pitched so low he barely heard her.

He squatted beside her. "Explain it to me."

Her voice lowered further. "I, um, can't get to my shoes easily." She looked everywhere but at him. She hugged herself, trying to disappear. "And I didn't bring my buttonhook."

His mind flashed back to watching Amanda with her shoes. Long skirts and corsets made it difficult to reach them. She had usually removed her shoes after her dress. Certainly not an option here.

His collar felt as if it had shrunk two sizes in the last thirty seconds, but he ignored it. The more matter-of-fact he appeared, the easier this would be for Kaitlyn. Right now, she looked like she'd spent hours over a hot stove. In July. With the windows closed.

He cleared his throat. "Since you appear to have misplaced your lady's maid, I'll be your buttonhook."

"I didn't have a lady's maid."

Kaitlyn's family had enough money for a lawyer but not a lady's maid? What kind of family did she come from?

He shook his head. He'd probably never know. "We can't exchange sizes easily. You have to try them on."

She hesitated, then nodded.

He knelt in front of her and brought her foot toward him, a cloud of ruffles following his movement. The hem of her petticoat brushed his hand. He quickly undid the shoe fastenings, then slid it from her foot. His fingers brushed against her lace stockings, warm from contact with her skin. Her foot jerked in his hand. He released it.

Jo marched up to them. "Pa! Tillie's touching all the candy."

That was all he needed. Being forced to pay for damaged merchandise. "Tell her to keep her hands to herself. And go help David watch her."

Drew reached for Kaitlyn's other shoe and undid the buttons. This time he carefully kept his hands on leather as he slid it off. It didn't keep his fingers from remembering the texture of lace.

"Mrs. Tyler's cat had kittens." Jo couldn't have gone to the front of the store and returned so quickly. "Can we take one home?"

"We have kittens at home." He glanced up in time to catch his daughter's quick smirk. "Go help your brother. I mean it, Jo."

His daughter muttered as she walked away.

He helped Kaitlyn into the new pair of boots. After he tied them, he backed away. "You can wear them in the store to check the fit."

She nodded, then walked quickly toward the back of the store. He moved to the front, resisting the urge to rub his fingers against his pants. It probably wouldn't wipe away the airy texture of lace anyway.

He needed a distraction.

He handed Mr. Thomas his list of supplies, then glanced around to locate his kids. Tillie and David still stood by the candy shelves. Could he afford three candy sticks? He shook his head. No, not unless the bull brought a great price.

Where was Jo? He finally spotted Kaitlyn and his older daughter looking at the horse tack. What had she said? That her horse's bridle needed a repair? He scrubbed a hand across his face. No money for leather. And Kaitlyn's boots weren't cheap. He'd better skip the new pants for David.

But at least the kids weren't making a mess.

Drew joined the men gathered around the wood stove.

One of them looked up at him. "Heard you got news, Mc-Graw."

Drew forced a smile. Much as he needed to discuss his bull, he'd have to give the gossip mill a misdirection first. "It took a long time, but Kaitlyn finally got here. We got married this morning."

"Congratulations."

"Glad to hear it."

"Great news!"

After a flurry of back slaps and handshakes, Drew held his hands toward the warmth from the stove. "Hear about anyone looking for a bull this year?"

The men looked at each other, shaking their heads. Bob Phillips looked back to Drew. "You might talk to Quade. He's about the only man buying right now."

Quade was buying all right, but not from the McGraws. Unless it was their entire ranch for sale. Drew forced his hands to relax. Why could nothing be easy?

Kaitlyn came back to stand beside him, but with a good foot or more between them. One of the men's eyes narrowed. Drew's stomach dropped. He was going to have to do something if he didn't want questions circulating about them. He offered her his arm, and she moved closer to rest her hand at his elbow. Her tiny hand. He shook his head. *Focus, McGraw.*

"Gentlemen, I'd like to introduce my wife, Kaitlyn Mc-Graw." He placed his other hand over hers. "Kaitlyn, these are some of your new neighbors: Tom Fisher, Bob Phillips, and Charles Hastings."

Kaitlyn smiled at the men. "It's so nice to meet you."

The silence stretched for a beat too long before Bob managed a simple "Likewise, I'm sure." The other two looked thunderstruck. Drew scowled at them. They acted as if they'd never seen a pretty woman.

Kaitlyn's grip on his arm tightened. "I think the wagon is loaded," she said softly.

He squeezed her hand gently. "Good to hear. It's a long ride home."

Home. He was taking his wife home.

He shook his head, trying to clear his mind.

No. It was a business arrangement. She got a safe place to stay, and he got a tutor for his kids. That was all.

He insisted that Tillie ride in the back of the wagon on the way home. All three kids fell asleep before they reached the halfway point. No surprise, really. Chores started early on a ranch, and the sun was setting.

Kaitlyn laid her hand on his arm, its heat soaking through her gloves and his coat. She bit her lip, then released it. "I heard you trying to sell your bull."

If she'd heard him mention it, she'd heard that no one had accepted his offer. How could he have been so mistaken about that bull? He'd been sure it would improve his herd.

She bit her lip. "Word will get around. I'm sure someone needs a new bull."

She was probably worried. Best not to feed her fear. He forced his tense muscles to relax. "Time will tell."

"You're doing a good job, you know."

He jerked his arm from under her hand. He didn't need false praise. "Glad you can tell, seeing as how you've been here all of two days."

"It doesn't take long to see how much the kids love you."

Yeah, well, love was the easy part. Food and clothes and holding on to the family land was much harder, and he was failing a little more every day.

Six

WOULD THIS DAY EVER END?

Drew banged the gate to the pen shut, then yanked his hands back as the cow inside slammed against the fence. She needed time for her injuries to heal, but if she didn't settle down, she'd only make them worse.

He turned and led Solomon to the back of the barn, where his stall hid around the corner from the main doors.

He removed the horse's saddle and rested it on the wall of the stall, ignoring the pull of muscles against the bruise he'd received from a calf's hooves. It had taken hours to round up the cattle from the ravines. Hours that'd made him more behind on the spring planting.

The older orphan calves stirred in the big birthing pen, but they wouldn't start bawling until they heard the kids headed this way. The animals knew who fed them.

David had put Curly's heifer off by herself. It would take a while for her to learn to drink from a bucket.

Drew slipped off Solomon's bridle. "Let me knock off the first layer of dirt, then I'll get your dinner." The stallion lipped Drew's collar. Drew grinned. Rescuing the big lug had been one of the best decisions of his life. Once Drew had finally gained his trust, Solomon had been a faithful friend for years.

Longer than Amanda had stayed with him.

Would Kaitlyn have staying power?

Drew grabbed a currycomb and started running it over Solomon's flanks. Kaitlyn. She had definitely surprised him so far. It had only been a few days, but already the house was cleaner. While her meals had mostly been simple stews, they had been more flavorful than anything he'd tasted since Ma got sick.

Ma should have recovered from the fever and cough. The rest of the family had. But somehow the sickness that had been a minor inconvenience to everyone else had settled into her lungs. She hadn't been able to fight it off. Or perhaps hadn't wanted to. He swallowed the bitterness that rose with the thought. With her husband gone, perhaps her children and grandchildren hadn't been enough motivation for her to fight.

Or maybe it was simpler. Drew hadn't been enough.

Solomon stamped a foot, and Drew's thoughts slipped to Kaitlyn.

Tillie loved her. David didn't like trading off kitchen work with Jo, but Kaitlyn was right. Cooking was a useful skill. The first few meals he and his brothers had attempted had proved that. But if she had implemented the change to win Jo over, it hadn't worked. Jo remained suspicious and standoffish.

Drew finished Solomon's hooves and crossed to the storeroom to measure his oats. One calf snorted, then gave a loud bellow. When the other four joined in, the cacophony was loud enough that Drew wanted to cover his ears.

Outside the open barn door, Tillie giggled. "It's okay, babies, we's bringing your dinner."

"Don't see you carrying no bucket, Tillie," Jo grumbled.

Drew glanced out the storeroom door and watched as David slipped inside the barn, carrying a bucket in each hand. Kaitlyn had two as well, while Jo carried one. Tillie skipped alongside them. None of them noticed him in the shadowed back corner of the barn. They were too focused on the calves. He'd join them when he was done with Solomon, who still shied around Tillie's energetic movements. Drew took his horse's dinner back to the stall.

The children's footsteps stopped outside the large calf pen, and the buckets thumped to the floor.

"Oh, they're so cute." Kaitlyn's voice was warm and happy.

There was a soft slurping sound, and Drew glanced through the stall door in time to see Kaitlyn pull her fingers away from the calf and wipe them on her dress.

She laughed. "I guess she's hungry. Do we pour the milk into bottles?"

David shook his head. "Pa says the buckets are easier to use 'cause you can clean 'em easier. Sure wish we didn't have to use the separator to get the cream though. My arm hurts."

Drew grinned, then moved to the front of the stall to pour Solomon's oats.

"Could another cow nurse the calf?" Kaitlyn asked.

Jo snorted. "It don't work that way. You can't just give a beast a new mama."

"That's not true, Jo. At least, not always." David's voice was easy, calm. "Most of our breed don't make milk enough for two, so we'd have to find a cow that's lost her calf."

Drew rubbed a hand along Solomon's neck, swallowing a sigh. David would make a fine rancher someday, if only Drew could keep the land for him.

"Some mama cows won't even feed their own calves." Tillie's voice held more sadness than a six-year-old should know about.

"I'm gonna feed the older calves," David said. "Jo, you take that last bucket to the newest baby."

Drew listened to his older children make their way to the different pens, but no gates opened.

"Let's go see the baby, Kaitlyn," Tillie said. Her footsteps pattered across the barn to the side that held the smaller calf pen. Kaitlyn's followed.

"Do you want to feed the baby, Kaitlyn?" Jo asked. The calf bawled, knowing a meal was on the way.

Drew didn't even need to see Jo's expression to know the mischief that sparked there. He hurried from the stall toward the calf pen. Jo's eyes widened when she spotted him, but it was too late.

He lifted a hand, trying to get Kaitlyn's attention. "Kaitlyn, don't—"

But Kaitlyn had already stepped into the pen with the calf that weighed over half as much as she did. Crash! The calf butted the bucket, and at the unexpected force, Kaitlyn stumbled and fell backward.

Drew winced even as he strode toward the tableau. No telling what she'd landed in.

Jo doubled over laughing. She pointed at Kaitlyn. "You landed in manure."

Tillie started crying. "Your dress. It's all messy."

Jo scoffed. "Stop being a baby."

Kaitlyn scrambled to her feet, suspicious green smears on the yellow dress she'd finished hemming last night. Drew stepped into the enclosure and maneuvered the calf into a corner to prevent it from following Kaitlyn out of the pen. She still had the bucket, and the calf would follow the bucket. Once she was out, he followed her and closed the pen gate behind him.

From outside the stall, David's eyes widened at the smears on Kaitlyn's dress.

Kaitlyn stood stiffly, holding her messy hands away from her skirt.

Drew snagged a grooming towel and handed it to her.

She wiped her hands, her nose wrinkled in distaste. "Well, I suppose I'll know better next time."

The calf bawled her displeasure over her spilled dinner. Drew turned to Jo, but Kaitlyn tugged his sleeve to draw his attention back to her.

She shook her head slightly. Her voice was drowned out

by the racket the calves were making, but he read the word *no* on her lips.

What did she mean *no*? No child of his was going to get away with a trick this cruel. He tried to ask the question with his eyes, but Kaitlyn either didn't or couldn't reply.

Tillie was still crying, and Kaitlyn laid a hand on her shoulder. "It's all right. The dress will wash."

Next, Kaitlyn eyed Jo, and Drew's throat tightened. His daughter deserved the tongue-lashing Kaitlyn probably had planned, but he was the parent.

But Kaitlyn didn't waver. "That wasn't very kind to the little calf. I'm afraid I spilled the poor baby's dinner."

Jo's eyes widened, and her laughter disappeared.

Drew knew his expression must be showing the surprise he felt. How had Kaitlyn known Jo's soft spot for animals would mean more than any anger she could show about her soiled dress?

Still, it wasn't enough. Especially with David and Tillie watching. The last thing he needed was all three of them thinking it was okay to treat Kaitlyn this way. He glared at his daughter. "Josephine McGraw, I'm disappointed in you. You apologize to Kaitlyn."

Jo's shoulders slumped. "Sorry," she mumbled.

"Get the dirty bucket." Drew pointed into the pen. "You'll have to scour it before we can feed the calf. And you will scrub every stain out of Kaitlyn's dress before you go to bed tonight. Plus take extra chores tomorrow."

Jo's shoulders slumped farther at the thought of more work. Her mouth pressed into a thin line. "They won't go to bed hungry, will they?" She gestured to the calves.

He made a show of examining the amount of milk in the remaining buckets, buying time to consider what the best answer would be. Jo had reacted to the idea of extra chores, but Kaitlyn's comment about the calves had driven the point home. He didn't want to waste this moment. "I think we'll have enough if we don't spill any more. But the longer it takes you to scrub that bucket, the longer the baby will wait for her dinner. And don't cut through the pen. The cow I put in there is crazy."

Jo grabbed the bucket and ran for the house.

"David, go get the rest of the milk and bring it here. Take Tillie with you." Best if the kids weren't here when Kaitlyn put away that fake smile. The kids trooped outside.

He turned to his wife. "I'm sorry."

Kaitlyn shook her skirt. Bits of straw and manure fell off. Her smile disappeared. She blinked a few times, but no tears fell. At least, not yet. Would she save them for him tonight?

David came back carrying two buckets. Tillie trailed behind him. Jo trudged in with the bucket she had scrubbed. Drew divided the milk between the buckets, and David carried one bucket into the stall with Curly's baby. The calf butted him, but he stood his ground.

"He's better at it than I am." Kaitlyn gave her skirt another shake, her knuckles white from her grip.

"He's had practice." Drew tried to keep his voice steady. Wasn't sure he succeeded. He wished he was surprised that Jo could do something so mean, but he wasn't.

Kaitlyn bit her lip, then released a long breath. She leaned against the pen. "What are their names?"

"Tillie named the first four. Freckles, Boo, Buddy, and Chip." Drew pointed to the calves one after the other.

Tillie looked up to Kaitlyn. "I pick-ed good names for them."

Kaitlyn nodded. "That you did." Then she looked to David. "But the baby doesn't have a name yet?"

David shook his head, eyes tight. The calf bumped the bucket again, and David pulled it back. "Don't do that, little one, or you won't have enough supper."

Kaitlyn's hand flexed. "Names take a while. You'll have to tell me what you choose."

Drew stepped into the pen beside David and laid a hand on his shoulder. Drew hadn't named an animal for a long time after he'd lost Calico. David pulled away.

Kaitlyn leaned against the wall and watched as David patiently convinced the calf to drink when she wanted to suck. "How long will it take her to learn?"

David kept his head down. "Some take longer than others. You just keep working at it."

"Who taught you how to feed them?"

Tillie looked up from the pebbles she was playing with, her tears gone but a streak of dirt across her cheek. "Pa did. He's the smartest man in the world."

Drew winced. The words hit hard. If he was so smart, why was the ranch failing? They'd go under if he didn't hold on to the grazing from the other three homesteads. And Kaitlyn knew at least some of the problems he faced. She knew he needed to sell the bull. He stiffened. What would she answer?

Kaitlyn met his gaze for a long moment, then knelt down to face Tillie. "I think you're right, Tillie."

Drew shook his head. She couldn't really think that.

Jo muttered, "You barely know us."

"I know enough."

Tillie tipped her head questioningly. "How do you know?"

"Well, your papa has a big ranch to run, right?"

Tillie nodded.

"But he still managed to teach you so much. David's doing great with his math, you already know your alphabet . . ."

Drew glanced at his middle daughter. She had gone very still, was pretending not to listen. Would Kaitlyn even be able to find a genuine compliment for Jo? His middle daughter certainly didn't deserve one today. He faced the other direction, not wanting to watch when Jo was hurt.

"And Jo doubled that biscuit recipe without even having to use paper to figure out the numbers." Kaitlyn said the matter-of-fact words, and surprise turned his head.

Kaitlyn hadn't even paused. When she had every reason to say something mean, she'd complimented instead. David stood a little straighter, and Tillie bounced on her toes.

Jo kicked at the dirt a couple of times, then left with the empty bucket. Kaitlyn bit her lip as she watched Jo leave, then focused on the other kids. Her smile was a bit tight, but David and Tillie didn't seem to notice. They jabbered on about what they'd conquer next in schoolwork, as if the whole idea had been theirs all along.

Drew's eyes caught on the huge stain on Kaitlyn's skirt

as she bent close to listen to something Tillie leaned up to whisper.

I know he is.

His stomach did a funny flip when he thought about the way Kaitlyn's eyes had shifted to meet his for a millisecond as she'd uttered those words of agreement.

She'd complimented him . . . like a real wife might've. That wasn't a part of their agreement.

As the kids cleared out and Drew went to wash up, the swirling thoughts itched like a burr under the collar of his shirt.

Did she expect him to compliment her? Amanda would've. And would've pouted if she hadn't gotten what she wanted.

Determination stole through him. He'd told Kaitlyn that theirs would be a loveless marriage. It didn't matter if she said nice things or treated his kids like they mattered.

A deal was a deal.

Fork, spoon, bowl.

Kaitlyn whirled from the table she was setting, wiping her forehead with the back of one arm. Her yellow dress was finally clean, though it had taken Jo three days of soaking and scrubbing to accomplish the feat.

Everyone would be in for dinner soon, and it wasn't even close to ready. She stirred the stew simmering on the back of the stove. A large bubble popped, spitting hot broth on her arm. She jerked back, then wiped her arm with a damp rag she'd used to wipe down the preparation table. It was time to add the potatoes, and they weren't even peeled yet.

She sank into a chair next to the worktable. It had been such a long day already. She should have asked one of the kids to peel the vegetables before they'd left the house, but she wasn't up to one more power struggle.

David had grudgingly turned his attention to working with fractions but had eventually thrown his pencil down in frustration. Tillie had caught on to the idea that letters made sounds and spent the entire day pointing to things in the house and naming the letter they started with. At least one of the children was excited to be learning, but the constant chatter made Kaitlyn's ears ring.

And Jo. Kaitlyn buried her face in her hands. Jo. The child who needed her the most seemed to hate her.

Today, Jo had split her lesson time between staring at the first arithmetic problem and glaring at Kaitlyn. She could have solved the simple word problem about how much feed a herd of cattle needed in minutes. Jo knew it. Kaitlyn knew it. Jo knew Kaitlyn knew it.

It was a power play, one that Kaitlyn would have to counter before they could move forward. She'd sent the girl outside a half hour ago just for some peace.

She pulled the bowl of potatoes next to her and picked up the knife. At least she knew what to do with these. She cut the potatoes smaller than usual so they'd cook faster. Then she picked up David's math. She had to figure out where he had gotten stuck.

Thirty minutes later, a sharp whistle from the corral shattered the silence. Kaitlyn moved to the window in time to see David pointing to the front of the house. She caught the sound of hoofbeats approaching.

Company. Drew had told her there were a few women living on nearby ranches. She whipped off her apron and draped it over the chair, then ran her hands over her hair, finding a few tendrils that had escaped her hairpins. She quickly secured them by feel. She rushed through the front door and onto the porch.

Seconds later, a cowboy pulled his horse to a stop near the stoop, looking around carefully before tipping his hat to Kaitlyn. He must want to talk to one of the men.

Kaitlyn pushed aside her disappointment. A visit with a local woman would have been a blessing. "Are you here to see Drew? I can send David to find him."

He studied the house with calculating eyes for a moment, then leaned down to hand her a sealed envelope. "I brought this for you. Mr. Quade was in town and thought you'd want it as soon as possible."

She moved to the second step and took the packet. A telegram? Was it from Michael? Her heartbeat raced, and she took a deep breath to try to settle it. The telegram was probably from her lawyer.

She pressed trembling lips into a smile. "Can I offer you some tea?"

"Can't stay." He juggled his horse's reins to adjust his leather gloves. "But if you want to send a reply, I can take it to Mr. Quade. He'll be heading back to town tomorrow. You'll have to give it to me quick though."

The bushes beside the porch rustled. Probably Patch.

That dog loved the kids, but he tended to hide when Tillie wanted to tie sunbonnets on him.

Sizzling came from the kitchen. "Oh no! My stew!" She waved at the cowboy. "I'll have to reply later. I have to go!" She tucked her telegram into her skirt pocket and hurried through the parlor and into the kitchen.

Kaitlyn grabbed a rag to move the stew pot to a cooler part of the stove. Smoke tickled her nose from the places where the stew had cooked over. She tested the potatoes with a fork. Ready to serve. A glimpse into the oven confirmed that the cornbread was nicely golden on top. She pulled out the pan and placed it on the stovetop.

Someone was already ringing the bell hung on the back porch. Nick had told her they could hear it over the front half of the ranch, but everyone was working close to the house today. She'd only have a moment to read her unexpected telegram. From her lawyer. It had to be from her lawyer.

She stepped onto the porch in time to see Jo slip into the trees around the edge of the yard. She'd probably rung the bell. Probably moved the stew to the hottest part of the stovetop to make it overheat as well. Kaitlyn shook her head. Jo was an issue for another day. The telegram was all she could handle right now.

She moved to lean against the porch railing, the cool air a relief after cooking over the wood stove. Everything smelled so much fresher in the West. She enjoyed a couple of bracing lungfuls of mountain air before finally tearing open the envelope.

Her knees almost gave way at the signature. Her lawyer, not her brother. She scanned the note.

Received letter STOP Need further documentation to honor request STOP Send proof of marriage STOP Best wishes STOP

Proof of marriage? Her word wasn't good enough?

Footsteps pounded from the corral to the front of the house.

"Wash up," she called as the noise moved inside, and she pushed the telegram into her pocket.

In a matter of minutes, everyone had taken their seats and passed their bowls for Kaitlyn to fill. Drew said grace, and everyone dug into their dinner. The tightness in her chest relaxed. The silence said more than a thousand compliments could.

Jo's spoon clanked against her bowl. "Our new ma got herself a visitor today."

Nick's eyebrows rose, but Kaitlyn thought it was more over the *new ma* comment than the visitor.

Drew spoke around a mouthful. "Mrs. Boutwell?"

Jo smirked. "Sure looked like one'a Quade's hands."

Drew's gaze sharpened as he finished chewing. "Is that true?"

"Um, yes." She paused, took in the sea of angry expressions that surrounded her. "He brought me a telegram from town."

Drew's features tightened. "How long was he here? What'd he ask about?"

"I don't understand. Why does it matter?" Didn't neighbors do favors for each other out here?

Drew took a drink, then set his glass down a little too hard. "I don't want any of Quade's men on the ranch."

"Mr. Quade himself saved me from some ruffians on the boardwalk when I first arrived. He rode with me out here, delivered me to your doorstep." Kaitlyn swallowed hard, memories clashing inside her heart. Memories of the men in town following her before Mr. Quade had taken over. Memories of her brother forbidding visitors.

Drew caught his youngest brother's eye. "You didn't tell me Quade brought her here."

Nick added butter to a third piece of cornbread. "I didn't know." He scoffed, then turned toward Kaitlyn. "He probably sicced those cowboys on you in the first place."

"Quade is a snake." Drew's voice was sharp. "Most of his hands are even worse."

Kaitlyn searched his face for a long moment. He believed what he was saying.

That didn't mean he was right. "Surely one visit can't hurt."

"Probably only took one visit for them to burn down the Robbinses' barn." Ed reached across the table to refill his bowl.

Tillie tugged on Kaitlyn's sleeve. "Is theys gonna burn our barn?"

Kaitlyn looked around the table. All the expressions were stern. Except Jo's. Her smirk had widened and her eyes gleamed. She had brought up this subject. How had she even known one of Quade's hands had been here?

The rustle in the bushes. Jo must have been spying, gathering information to create this hornet's nest for Kaitlyn to stumble into.

"Don't worry, Tillie. Our barn will be fine," Nick told the little girl.

Kaitlyn couldn't force herself to meet any of their gazes. "He can't be that bad."

Drew snorted. "Yes, he can. He held a gun on our pa. Tried to bully us into selling after—" Drew glanced around the table, his gaze resting on Tillie's pale face the longest. "Never mind."

The rest of the meal was quiet. Kaitlyn thought through every moment of her time with Quade. The man Drew and his brothers had described sounded a lot like Michael. Was she really that bad a judge of character?

Or could Quade hide his motives as well as her brother?

Kaitlyn pushed the food around on her plate. Her face burned all the way to her ears. Would Drew raise his hand to her after everyone left them alone?

She didn't know him well enough. Maybe she never should've entered this marriage. When everyone had finished eating, they left the table. Except Drew. Kaitlyn got up to clear the dishes.

Drew stacked some of the dishes and followed her to the kitchen. "The kids can handle the rest."

She nodded and crossed the room to stand in front of him. Her throat seized and knotted. She pulled the telegram from her pocket and handed it to him. "Here. You can read it. I wasn't keeping anything from you."

She moved to the front porch. Here was another hurdle

to receiving her money. Things weren't going well with the kids. What she knew about cattle could be written on a postage stamp.

Did Drew regret the marriage? If things didn't get better, would he make her leave? Her brother had never troubled himself for her, but she'd always had a roof over her head. Then again, he had needed her allowance. If she didn't hold up her side of the deal, help with the children, Drew would have every reason to kick her out.

Where would she go? She'd be on her own in Wyoming, not knowing a soul or having a friend.

Easy pickings for her brother.

Seven

HE HAD A SHORT-TERM SOLUTION FOR his money woes.

Drew clicked his tongue, and Phantom increased his pace to a lope on the lunging line, following the oval corral fence. Instant response, flowing movements, complete trust in his handler, all the result of a week of intense training. Drew had hoped to keep this blue roan stallion, dreamed of one day starting a side business selling his colts and fillies.

But if he sold the horse, he could afford the lumber they needed.

Urgency spurred him on with breaking the three-year-old. They couldn't delay building the cabins. Not with the news Ed had brought from town yesterday.

Ernie Duff was the new land office manager. He never should have gotten the promotion. Not when he'd been behind the town almost losing the lot the school stood on.

Now he was in charge of inspecting the improvements on homesteads. The Fogelsons had wintered in town after their cabin had burned, or been burned, and Duff had denied an extension for rebuilding. He'd taken back the claim when it was only one week past the deadline. No grace for extenuating circumstances, and only two days for packing.

The lunge line bit into his hand, and he relaxed his too-tight grip. They only had a little over a month to finish Ed's claim. Six weeks to put up his cabin, and they didn't even have the lumber. Isaac's and Nick's claims wouldn't be due for six months after that, which would give them a little breathing space, but they had to get that land. The one claim they owned outright couldn't support all his brothers. Plus, he'd expanded, counting on the new claims for grazing land. If they lost those homesteads, they might even lose Pa's land.

Phantom's body stiffened and his ears flicked back. Drew yanked his mind back to its proper place, slowly exhaling the fear that had built in his stomach. He had to sell this horse. The McGraw legacy would not end with him.

The colt rounded the western edge of the oval, and Drew pivoted in concert just as Kaitlyn came into view in the distance. She and Tillie paced out the area that he would need to plow for the family garden, Kaitlyn's movements graceful despite the uneven ground she covered. She seemed excited at the idea of tackling a new project. Tillie giggled, and Kaitlyn tweaked the little girl's braid, her smile bright. His gaze lingered.

He'd found himself watching her more than he should. *Pay attention to the horse, McGraw.*

He signaled Phantom to slow, then stop. Drew approached the blue roan's head and pulled one rein, then the other. Phantom easily followed the directions to curve his nose to his shoulder, a necessary skill before he'd be safe to ride.

"Pa, can I help?"

Phantom flinched and sidestepped.

Drew ran a hand along the horse's neck, then flicked a quick look to his son, who had his boots on the bottom railing with his arms crossed over the top.

"Not today."

He needed to get in the saddle if he was going to sell the horse this weekend.

"How come?"

Drew breathed through a pulse of annoyance. *Because I don't have time. Because you're supposed to be caring for the calves. Because I said so.*

"Not today," he repeated, avoiding the question.

David shuffled off and Drew moved the stirrups around the horse's sides, letting them brush his flanks. Finally, he gave them a firm yank. Phantom flinched at that, so Drew repeated it a few more times till the colt no longer responded.

When he looked up next, Kaitlyn had taken David's spot, her arms folded over the top railing and her chin resting on them. Tillie was playing with the dog out in the field past the house.

He attempted to focus on the horse, but prickles of awareness skittered up his spine.

He tipped his chin toward her. "You need something?"

"Just watching."

Huh.

It shouldn't bother him. The kids liked to watch him break horses, especially David. This wasn't any different.

Only it was.

He felt self-conscious knowing she was staring at him as he fed out the lunge line and started Phantom circling. Walk, then trot.

"You're patient," Kaitlyn said.

He felt her words like a physical jab against his skin. He hadn't been patient with David. Hadn't even taken the time for an explanation.

He chewed on that thought for a few moments, watching the horse go through its paces.

"I was a little short with David. Would you apologize to him for me?" he finally asked.

"I could." She tilted her head, considering.

He paused the horse, watching Kaitlyn—her wrinkled forehead and downcast eyes.

Finally, she met his gaze. "But I think it would mean more if it came from you."

He felt the frown as it formed on his mouth. He was the one who'd asked her to meddle in his business. She'd been careful to work on tutoring with the kids, but she left the discipline to him. As she should. She wasn't their ma.

"He looks up to you. Values your opinion," she said after a prolonged moment of quiet.

He didn't know about that. He started Phantom lunging again and then began reeling the colt in slowly.

"And anyone with eyes can see how much you love your children. All three of them."

This time, he couldn't help the snort that escaped. He sounded more horse than man. Apt.

"It's true." She sounded slightly affronted, and he took his eyes off the horse long enough for a quick glance. She had a determined pinch to her lips. Something was chasing around in the depths of her eyes and then it seemed like she came to a decision.

"My father wasn't like you." She said the words quietly, firmly. Like a fact you'd find in a schoolbook.

He shouldn't pry. Shouldn't ask. But that didn't stop the words from tumbling out as he jostled the stirrups again. "What d'you mean?"

"I can give you an example. Once, when I was nine years old, Michael interrupted me while I was having a snack that our housekeeper had left out for me. He and I were alone in the dining room."

Her body tensed.

She looked in Drew's direction but not at him. "He demanded I give him my food. I refused."

Drew held Phantom's bridle, focused on her. Her voice had gone soft and far off, like she was lost in the memory.

"He could've gone into the kitchen to make something for himself, but instead, he pitched a fit. Things escalated, and he picked up my teacup and threw it—at me or at the table, I don't know. It shattered and tea splattered—everywhere."

He heard the catch in her voice, saw the quickly hidden tremble of her lip. It couldn't be more obvious that her brother had frightened her, and a protective urge rose up inside him.

"My father must've been nearby in the house, because he appeared in the doorway. Michael lied and said I'd broken the cup, but I protested."

He wanted to hear her say that her father had done what he should have and taken a switch to Michael's behind. But he guessed that she wouldn't.

Her lips thinned into a line, and she spoke the last quickly and matter-of-factly. "Father sent me to my room. That was the last I heard of it. Michael rarely got punished."

She seemed to shake herself out of the memory. "For a long time, I wished I had a father like you."

He almost recoiled at her words. She had to be joking. He didn't know what he was doing raising three kids. Couldn't seem to get through to Jo no matter what he tried.

Kaitlyn was gazing at him with a small sincere smile on her lips.

And his gut was twisting with remembering David's slumped shoulders as he'd shuffled toward the barn.

He passed a hand over his face. "Would you excuse me?"

He needed to talk to his son.

Kaitlyn stood beside the corral railing, watching the saddled colt where he stood. She rubbed her chest, trying to erase the ache that remained after sharing that memory with Drew.

She refused to let Michael or the past have any hold over her new life here.

She wouldn't have told him the story if it hadn't been for David's dejectedness and the concern she'd read beneath Drew's unruffled demeanor. She'd seen it in the barn the other day. Drew wanted to be closer to his kids, but for some reason he held back.

So she'd told her story.

Now Drew and David exited the barn together. David was bouncing on his toes, excitement radiating from him. Drew said something Kaitlyn couldn't hear, and David steadied himself, visibly working to calm himself.

Soft, quick footsteps pattered behind Kaitlyn. Tillie stopped next to her and stepped onto the bottom rail of the fence. "What're they doing?"

"I don't know," Kaitlyn said.

Drew glanced over briefly, his face unreadable. "David's going to be the first to ride the colt."

The back door slammed, and Jo stepped outside. Tillie abandoned Kaitlyn and ran toward her sister, calling out, "David's gonna ride Phantom!"

The girls drifted to the corral, Tillie sticking to Jo's side. Jo didn't come near enough for Kaitlyn to converse with her. She ignored Kaitlyn completely, but at least she wasn't aggravating her sister.

Nick and Ed appeared from behind the barn, both leading horses. When they saw the crew watching the corral, they changed course and came to stand near Kaitlyn.

David and Drew stepped up to the colt. Drew held the bridle as David ran his hands along the horse's flanks and pulled on the stirrups just like his father had.

Finally, David put a foot into the stirrup and pulled himself up to stand in it. The colt stood completely steady, even after David lowered back to the ground.

"Remember the first time Drew broke a horse?" Ed wiped his hands on his pants legs. "David looks just like him."

Kaitlyn's heart was pounding hard enough for her to feel the pulse in her neck. She hadn't realized how small David would look on the horse's back. Slender like a reed.

"How old was he?" she asked Ed.

He shook his head, not understanding the question.

"Drew. The first time he rode," she clarified.

"Probably a little younger than David," Nick said.

David raised himself into the stirrup again, paused to read the horse's body language, then glanced at his pa. Drew nodded, and David swung a leg over the colt, sat straight in the saddle.

Ed's gaze flicked her way. "He didn't break anything when he got thrown."

She must've made a small gasp, because Drew turned his head briefly. He'd retreated several feet in their direction, letting David take the colt.

"You two quit telling tales. I didn't get bucked off that first time."

Nick guffawed. "Not that time. But remember when he was about fifteen and he got bucked off that black mare we had? Right into a sticker patch? He was dancin' around, waving at his—"

"Knock it off," Drew drawled. He wouldn't have seemed perturbed by his brothers' antics except for the fact that his ears were turning pink underneath his hat.

Tillie cheered for David as he had the horse take a few tentative steps forward. Jo almost cracked a smile.

"I can picture you at fifteen," she said to Drew's back. "Full of responsibility. Probably running the whole ranch."

Ed snorted, trying to hide the sound by looking down. Drew shot him a quick glare.

Nick grinned widely as he said, "Drew wasn't so responsible when he was David's age."

"He spent more hours in the barn than anywhere else," Ed said.

"Skipped going to the neighbor's for schooling a coupla times."

Drew glared at Nick again. "It was one time. And Pa's mare was foaling."

"Ma would be looking for him because he hadn't done his chores, and he'd be out riding," Ed said.

Drew's gaze cut to Kaitlyn and then back to David, who was making slow progress around the corral. Drew's gaze never left his son for long. His posture eased a fraction as Phantom followed David's commands.

Decades of affection laced the brothers' teasing. She'd seen it at work these past weeks. Ed and Nick would do anything for Drew. And vice versa.

Something twinged deep inside her. This was family.

Something she'd longed for, for longer than she cared to admit.

She wanted to be a part of it. Be the one they were teasing, have years of stories to tell.

Could that happen if all she and Drew had was a business arrangement?

She was distracted from her thoughts when the wind picked up a handful of leaves and blew them directly across Phantom's path.

The horse shied sideways, then took off.

A crowhop, then another. David slid sideways in the saddle.

"Stay with him," Ed murmured. "Turn him in."

Drew stayed silent and still, only his lips moving. He was too far away to do anything.

David regained his seat, settled deeper into the saddle. The horse bolted around the ring, his pounding hooves echoing across the corral.

"One-rein him, David. Turn him in." Nick stepped onto a higher rung.

Kaitlyn's breath caught in her chest. Her heart raced and her hands shook. If David got thrown, he could break his neck—*God, if You're listening, please help this boy.*

David slid a hand along the inside rein, grabbed hold a foot nearer the bridle.

"Attaboy, David. You've got this." Ed had settled on the highest rung of the fence, prepared to jump inside if needed. Another quarter lap, and David steadily pulled on the inside rein.

At first, nothing happened. Then slowly the horse's head lowered. His ears lifted from his head, just a little. His pace slowed.

And finally, finally, his nose came around toward his flank as he eased to a stop.

Ed slipped down a couple of rungs on the fence. "That boy's a chip off the old block, and no mistaking it."

Drew was already approaching horse and boy. Kaitlyn couldn't hear his words over Tillie's excited jabbering. She gestured for her to quiet.

Drew held the colt's bridle, drawing horse and boy toward the gate. "That was a mighty fine ride, son."

David sat straighter in the saddle, a mile-wide grin on his face.

He slipped off the horse's back, accepting congratulations from his uncles.

"We'll help take him to the barn," Nick said.

He seemed to be trying to give Drew a message with some wiggles of his eyebrows.

Kaitlyn and Drew were left standing near the corral. A couple of feet separated them, as well as a wooden fence.

She glanced over to see Tillie and Jo heading for the house, their heads together.

"You've got good instincts. With the kids." Drew's words brought her focus back to him.

She glanced toward Jo. "Not all of them."

He made a soft sound. She didn't know whether it meant he agreed or disagreed with her, but she didn't ask.

She was still standing near the railing, and when he leaned his elbows on it, her breath caught. He was almost too close.

"What was your ma like?"

His question shocked her, and a glance at his face made her think he'd surprised himself too.

The image of her mother's casket threatened to overwhelm her, as it always did when she thought of her mother. But she pushed past it. Her mother was more than the day that'd turned Kaitlyn's world inside out. She dug deeper into her memories, and a calming, simple scent rose in her mind. "She smelled like flowers." What flower? If only she knew, she'd buy the scented soap or perfume. Anything to hold on to the memories.

"What else?" Drew's deep voice softened.

"She read to me." Her eyes drifted shut as that voice echoed in her heart. "I always wanted the same book when I was little. We both had it memorized, but she still read it to me when I asked." Kaitlyn smiled. "When I was older, she teased me about it. Told me she sometimes tried to skip a page or two but that I always caught her."

"Sounds like a good ma."

"She was gentle but strong. It sounds contradictory, but she was both."

Drew's arms rested on the top rail and his head cocked to the side as he studied her. Her cheeks warmed. Was her hair a mess? She wanted to look away, to check her hair for escaped tendrils, but his gaze held her captive.

He looked away first. "I can see that in you." His voice sounded deeper, rougher than usual. He cleared his throat. "With Tillie, I mean. I can see it in you when you're with Tillie."

The girls' voices floated through the air, pulling Drew's and Kaitlyn's attention toward the house. Tillie sang a bit of a made-up song, and Jo murmured.

Kaitlyn's eyes slid closed at the sound. She'd been here over two weeks and had never heard Jo laugh. Surely she could reach her. Somehow.

She glanced at Drew. He was watching both daughters,

and his brow was creased. He worried about the kids. Had married a stranger to help his children.

And Kaitlyn wasn't lightening those worries like he'd hoped. Like she'd planned.

But she could lighten other worries.

Drew's feet shuffled. She stepped onto the bottom rung of the fence and leaned against her side of it. Her sleeves brushed his hands. She inhaled, and the air was tinted with the smell of horse and work and man. She should step back, put some distance between them. But her feet refused to move.

"Drew, do you think I could go to town sometime soon? I need to send our marriage license to my lawyer. If we can get my funds released, I can help with the costs for the cabins. You wouldn't have to sell Phantom."

Drew's eyes cooled and his jaw firmed. He stepped back and turned toward the horse. Away from her. "That's my problem, not yours. Selling horses is part of life on a ranch." He grabbed the colt's bridle and headed toward the barn.

Eight

I WILL NOT GIVE IN.

Kaitlyn wiped the already clean preparation table in the kitchen. She had finished the lunch dishes some time ago, and it wasn't time to start dinner. She peeked through the door to the dining room.

Jo sat in her chair, her upper body draped across her schoolbooks. She hadn't moved since the last time Kaitlyn had checked on her, but she wasn't asleep. No, she was stubborn.

Maybe Kaitlyn shouldn't have told her she couldn't leave the table until she finished her bookwork, but she'd tried everything else. It had been nearly a month, and Jo hadn't done more than a page or two of schoolwork. The door creaked as she pushed through. "How's the penmanship practice going?"

Jo scowled at her. "I'm never gonna need this."

"Beautiful handwriting is a worthwhile accomplishment,

though perhaps a luxury. Legible handwriting is a necessity."

Jo rolled her eyes. "Not for a rancher."

"Yes, for a rancher." Kaitlyn met Jo's gaze. There had to be some way to convince the girl to listen, but all Kaitlyn knew to do was to present her arguments. Again. "If your writing isn't clear, how will you keep your books? Write to other ranchers about purchases and sales? Leave instructions for your workers?"

"Why can't I do a nature study like David?"

Kaitlyn gritted her teeth at the whining tone but didn't allow her smile to slip. "David finished his bookwork for the day, and you haven't even started." Kaitlyn had demonstrated the individual letters of the practice page more than once, but Jo wouldn't even pick up the pen. Finally, Kaitlyn had decreed that Jo would sit there until she finished the page.

That had been three hours ago. The pen was still idle.

Discouragement made Kaitlyn want to slump. Her own teachers had managed rooms full of stubborn children. Drew only wanted her to manage three, and she was failing.

Kaitlyn glanced around the parlor. Sunlight flooded in through the now sparkling clean windows. She crossed to the bookcase and drew out a copy of *Tom Sawyer*. Should she read it aloud? She shook her head. Jo didn't deserve the treat, but more importantly, it wouldn't lead in the right direction.

She took the book to a chair by the window. Jo was watching, but Kaitlyn didn't acknowledge her gaze. Instead, she opened the book and started reading. It wasn't hard to allow a laugh or two to escape.

"What's so funny?"

"Oh, I'm reading the scene where Tom tricks his friends into doing his work."

"Read it to me?"

"Be glad to, once you finish your penmanship."

Jo muttered and sprawled back across her papers, her back to the parlor.

Kaitlyn smothered a grin. She hadn't thought it would be that easy. "You can read it yourself anytime you want once your reading improves."

"I read good enough. 'Sides, penmanship ain't reading."

"No, but they're connected. One supports the other." Kaitlyn turned the page in her book. A clink interrupted her. She looked up to see a trickle of black ink spreading across the dining room table.

"Oops." Jo's smile was sweeter than honey. "Guess you'd best clean that up. I would, but I can't get up."

Kaitlyn retrieved a rag and wiped up the spill. A bit of turpentine removed most of the stain, its sharp smell burning her nose. Then she took the paper and pen from Jo's spot at the table. Jo's smug smile faded when Kaitlyn replaced it with a slate and piece of chalk. "Less chance for accidents this way."

She sailed into the kitchen, then sank into the chair and dropped her face into her hands. She'd tried everything else. She might as well pray. God had never cared for her, but didn't He have a special love for children? Maybe He'd help for Jo's sake.

I don't know what to do, Lord. She's clinging to her anger like a mother clings to her child.

Mother. Child.

Somehow, that was the source. Except it didn't make sense. Jo's mother hadn't abandoned her. Something had happened on that trip, and no one knew what. How could she find out?

Show her your own pain.

The still, small voice echoed in her mind.

She wanted to pretend she hadn't heard it, but she'd tried everything else.

Kaitlyn made two cups of tea, liberally dosed one with honey, then carried them to the dining room. She placed the sweetened tea next to Jo, then sat next to her. "Tea sometimes makes talking easier."

Jo sat up and pushed the cup away. "I'm not allowed tea. If you was my ma, you'd know that."

"I'd like to help you, Jo. I know what it feels like to lose a mother."

Jo scoffed. "You think 'cause your ma died, I should be your friend?"

"I was younger than you when I stood beside her coffin. Even breathing hurt." Kaitlyn's chest tightened.

Jo looked down at her hands. "How did she die?"

Jo's voice had softened. Kaitlyn's hand twitched, but she restrained herself from taking Jo's. Too soon for such a move. She cleared her throat. "Her saddle girth failed. She fell badly. A stupid accident." She took a sip of tea. The warmth didn't touch the frozen lump in the pit of her stomach. "My father wanted me to learn about pressing flowers and managing a dinner party. My mother had always been my champion, insisting that everyone needed an education."

Jo rolled her eyes. "Why?"

Because you never know when your brother might force you to marry the man who holds his gambling debts. Kaitlyn placed her cup on the table. The tea sloshed but stayed inside the cup. The details were too much for an eleven-year-old. Maybe just the essence? "It's a hard world out there. No one gets through it without getting knocked down a time or two. An education gives you tools to get back up."

Jo folded her arms over her chest, a sure sign that Kaitlyn wouldn't like her next comments. "I'm gonna run a ranch. This ranch. I don't need fancy handwriting to do that."

"Doesn't your father keep notes about what works and what doesn't? What good will they do him if he can't read them later?"

"What happened after your ma died?"

Kaitlyn took a sip of tea to hide any hint of a smile she hadn't managed to suppress. Jo didn't have an answer, so she'd changed the subject. Best to go along with the change. "My mother left her assets to me in a trust. My half brother hated me for that, even though he wasn't her son. Things got hard at home. He liked to lock me into places I couldn't get out of. Never the same place, so my father couldn't find me." Not that he looked over hard. "But I was safe at school."

Jo's mouth dropped, and she looked away.

Too much truth? Maybe. Maybe not. "And that schooling meant I could answer your pa's ad. Before I saw it, I was planning to be a teacher."

Jo looked back at her. "What education did your ma have?"

"Much like my father wanted for me. Society rules. Dressing nice." Kaitlyn smiled. "My mother was so beautiful, and she had the prettiest dresses."

Jo's eyes turned wistful. "My ma had pretty dresses."

"You remember seeing them?"

"No. They're in my closet. They're not like the calico dresses she wore on the ranch. The ones Pa gave to you." Something flashed through the little girl's eyes too fast for Kaitlyn to categorize it. Then her expression settled into longing. "Maybe I could try one on?"

Kaitlyn glanced at the penmanship lesson. But this was the longest conversation she'd had with Jo since they'd met. Maybe that was a bigger step than a lesson.

Besides, one of Amanda's dresses might be made over to fit her daughter.

"That sounds like a good idea."

Jo pounded up the steps. Kaitlyn followed more slowly. Had God really told her to share her history with Jo? By the time she'd entered Jo's room, the little girl had spread a rainbow of dresses onto her bed. She came back out of her closet and added a black skirt and lace-covered shirtwaist to the collection. "They're beautiful, Jo. Which would you like to try on?"

"The one that's still in the closet. Can you get it? It's kind of heavy."

Heavy? Maybe it had a lot of beadwork.

Kaitlyn crossed to the closet and peeked inside. "I don't see anything else in there."

Jo spoke from behind her. "You have to look in the very back. I think it was her wedding dress."

Kaitlyn stepped into the closet. A whoosh of air warned her, but too late. The door slammed closed, the noise echoing through her chest.

Please, no. Not this.

She turned the handle, rattled it. No use. Locked. The spacious closet shrank around her, the walls closing in.

"Jo, this isn't funny. Open the door."

"Sorry. I got chores to do." Her footsteps faded away as she ran down the stairs.

"Jo! Josephine McGraw! Don't you leave me here!" She expelled the air in her lungs, struggled to draw in another breath.

Don't be silly. There is air here. Plenty of air.

Then why did her chest feel so tight?

"Help!" She banged on the door. No one was inside the house to hear her. She'd be here for hours.

Her pulse pounded in her ears.

Think, Kaitlyn. Think.

She dropped to her knees and ran her hands along the floor. No luck. Not that she'd expected to find a wire, since this room had only ever held clothing.

She stood up and beat her fists against the door. Pain exploded in her hands, ran up her arms, but she had to be loud. Everyone was outside. Someone would miss her eventually, but she wanted out of here now. Needed out now.

Her chest expanded, trying to find more air. She stepped

back. Only one step to the back wall. She'd never build enough momentum to pop the lock. If it could even be popped.

She tried anyway. Her shoulder crashed into the door and she bounced backward. The door stood.

"Help me!" She kicked the door, her boots offering little protection from the pain.

Some answer to prayer this had turned out to be.

They'd need to buy more seed if Kaitlyn was planning a garden this big.

Drew paced off the area his wife had marked halfway between the barn and house. The back door slammed, and Jo ran across the yard toward the barn like something was chasing her. She must have finished her schoolwork.

A thump sounded from the upstairs corner of the house. Then another.

Drew cocked his head. Was Kaitlyn moving furniture up there? He stripped his gloves from his hands and stuffed them into a back pocket. Maybe she could use a hand. When he opened the back door, the muffled thumping got louder. What was she doing up there?

"Help me!"

A chill raced through his veins and raised bumps on his skin. That was Kaitlyn's voice. Drew dashed for the stairs. "I'm coming!"

More thumps and a crash. What on earth?

He rushed into the girls' room and looked around. "Kaitlyn?"

"In here."

The choked voice came from the closet. He turned the knob, but it didn't move. How had it gotten locked?

Her voice wavered. How long had she been in there?

When the kids were young, they'd frequently locked doors that shouldn't be locked. Which casing had he used to hide a key in this room? Door, probably. He crossed the room, his heels thumping on the wooden floor.

The door to the closet rattled. "Please don't leave me!" Terror weighed her voice down.

Drew paused. "I have to find a key."

"Find one?" Her voice jumped an octave higher.

"It won't take a minute." He lowered his voice in response to her higher pitch. "Just a matter of finding the right door."

"Okay." Her voice sounded a bit steadier.

He brushed his hand across the top of the door and knocked something to the floor. It clinked and bounced toward the hallway. He snatched it up. "There. I've got it."

He turned the key in the lock, and the closet door swung open. Kaitlyn flew out, lost her footing, and stumbled. He took her arm. She was so slight that it took no effort to keep her from falling. Steadying her emotions, on the other hand? His stomach clenched. He'd never been good with emotions.

"Are you all right?"

She shook her head. A tear slipped down her ashen cheek. Her hands were red and swollen. How long had she pounded on that door? Her breath rasped in and out, and her lips quivered.

What should he do? He couldn't remember everything

from their wedding, but hadn't he promised to comfort her? Except he didn't know how.

He wiped a tear from her face. Her cheek felt like wet velvet against his calloused finger. She hiccuped, swallowing a sob. Not the right move.

Her voice had steadied when he'd used a low, soothing tone. Just like he'd use with a frightened filly.

Maybe.

He ran his hand along her back, slowly, the same as he'd touched Solomon when he first arrived.

She crumpled, buried her face in the center of his chest. Sobs shook her shoulders. His heart froze mid-beat. He'd blown it again.

Unless . . .

His ma had always claimed a woman sometimes needed a good cry. Maybe he shouldn't try to stop the tears. He pulled her closer. Wrapped his arms around her and rubbed a hand along her back. His shirt dampened.

He must be a cad for noticing how right she felt in his arms while she was so distressed. But how could he ignore her floral scent, the soft fabric of her dress under his hand, her tiny frame that still somehow filled his arms?

"I'm s-sorry."

The quiver in her voice arrowed its way into his heart.

"Shhh. It's okay. I won't melt." Though each of her tears felt like a brand. He rested his chin on the top of her head. Her warmth soaked into him. He continued rubbing his hand up and down her back.

When was the last time he'd held a woman in his arms? Amanda had turned her nose up at his honest calluses.

Kaitlyn wouldn't be able to feel them through the calico she wore, but she hadn't moved away from him when he'd touched her cheek.

She slipped one arm around his waist, then the other. He drew a deeper breath than he had been able to moments before. She wouldn't do that if he'd made things worse. He felt taller somehow. She'd turned to him as an anchor while the storm raged through her, and he'd offered her a place of security.

Eventually, her sobs quieted, but she didn't move away for some minutes after. He rubbed his cheek against the top of her head, her hair as soft as a newborn kitten. His eyes slid shut for a moment as he memorized the sensation. Then he pulled back.

"I got your shirt wet," she mumbled into his chest.

He dropped his arms from around her. "I reckon you did. You want to tell me what this was all about?"

He thought her arms dropped from his waist slowly, but that might be wishful thinking. She stepped back, glanced around the room, moved the dresses piled on Jo's bed, then took a seat there. Should he sit beside her? No, he'd draw up the chair. He put it across from her. She'd responded to his hand on her back. He reached over and took her hand. It felt so tiny in his grasp, but she didn't pull away, didn't object to the work-roughened texture.

"I don't like closed spaces."

Her tears had made that plenty clear. He'd meant to question how she'd gotten into this closet today, but if she wanted to build up to it, he'd go along.

"It all goes back to Michael. Always."

"Your brother?"

"Yes. He locked me in places many times, but it didn't usually scare me. At least not much. Not like . . ." She gestured toward the closet. "I knew Father would find me before long."

His skin crawled as tiny hairs shot to attention. How many was *many*? Ten times? A hundred? How long before her father found her? Minutes? Hours?

She remained quiet for a few moments. He ran his thumb across the back of her hand. She worked hard, but her skin felt so soft.

"Then my father died. I went to boarding school for a while, but Michael was old enough to be my guardian when I turned sixteen."

Ice flowed through his veins. Sixteen. A vulnerable age.

"My brother's friend stayed around the house a lot that summer." She shuddered. "I didn't like him. His eyes followed my every move, and his reputation was questionable. I tried to tell Michael, but he didn't care."

A growl built in Drew's chest, but he suppressed it. She might think it aimed at her instead of her worthless brother. What good was a man who didn't protect his family?

Soothing voice, he chanted to himself. "What happened next?"

"One day Brian found me alone."

She ran her hand along her wrist.

"He was so strong. I couldn't get away."

His pulse pounded in his ears. Had the man . . . He shook his head, forced his rage to a back corner of his mind. He'd release it later. Every fence post he pounded would wear the man's face. Kaitlyn needed gentle now. He tightened his grip on her hands, just enough to let her know he'd heard her.

Her unfocused gaze sharpened, flew to his face. Her cheeks flushed. "He only kissed me. That's all, I promise. You'd want to know . . . I mean, I'm your wife. You'd have the right to know—"

"Shhh." He dropped her hand and moved to sit beside her. Put his arm around her, drew her into his shoulder. She fit so well against him. "I'm glad you got away, but for your sake, not mine." He ran his hand along her arm. Touch seemed to comfort her. "How'd you do it?"

She made a sound too close to a sob for his comfort. "I locked myself in that time. But Brian didn't tell my brother where I was, or maybe Michael didn't care. I was in that closet for hours, wondering if anyone would ever find me, afraid it would be Brian who did."

Drew's eyes slid shut. Rage burned in his gut. He wasn't a violent man, but if either of those men had been here now, he'd gladly make an exception. He took a deep breath, let it out slowly. "Who found you?"

"Our cook. She started looking when I was late for breakfast the next day. Took me to the kitchen and gave me some cookies." Kaitlyn shook her head sadly. "Michael fired her that afternoon. Said he wasn't going to have me rewarded for being rude to our guests. It wasn't the first time someone paid a high price for helping me. I've always wondered if Michael didn't know or just didn't care what Brian had done."

Drew's teeth ached, and he carefully relaxed his clenched

jaw. He'd thought society women were bad. Turned out the men were even worse. "He's worthless either way."

He wiped a new tear from her cheek. She smiled at him, her lips quivering a bit at the corners—but a smile nonetheless. Warmth that had nothing to do with anger spread through him. Maybe, just maybe, he'd handled this okay.

A bump sounded from downstairs. He looked that direction, then back to Kaitlyn. "Jo did this, didn't she?"

Kaitlyn looked at her hands in her lap. "I'd rather not say."

His eyes squeezed shut. She hadn't denied it. "I'll have a word with her."

Drew left to find his daughter. From the stairs, he looked into the parlor, where Tillie had first told him a princess had come to visit. He'd looked at Kaitlyn's fancy dress and thought she'd had an easy life. How little he'd known.

She was made of strong stuff, his wife. He admired that. Living here required it.

Maybe Kaitlyn would fit in here after all.

Nine

I T WASN'T HIS DAY.

Drew glared at his horseshoe, which lay a good eight inches away from the stake. Most of his neighbors had stayed for the potluck after church. They'd moved it outside to enjoy the unseasonably warm April weather. The youngest kids were playing an energetic game of tag, and the women cleared the thrown-together tables. Before he left, he'd have to help take the sawhorse-and-board contraptions down and store them away for the next gathering.

His cousin Merritt's new husband, Jack Easton, stepped up to the line to take his turn. "You'd score higher if you'd watch the stake instead of your bride."

Drew glared at him.

Jack smiled back. "That glower doesn't work anymore. Not since last Christmas, when I saw you braiding ribbons into Tillie's hair."

Drew scrubbed a hand across his face. "Trying to, you

mean." It was a mostly good memory. Jack had relaxed with the McGraws after that. Seemed a man's scowl lost its power once its recipient saw you defeated by a hair bow.

Drew tossed his last shoe, and it didn't land any closer than the one before. He wished he could claim that Kaitlyn had nothing to do with his distraction. He certainly had other things on his mind. None of the ranchers at the after-church picnic had shown any interest in buying his bull. Jo sat off to the side of the group, sulking. Nick and Ed seemed to be enjoying organizing the boys into a baseball game, but Isaac still refused to come to town. Yep, he had enough problems to justify an off day in the horseshoe pit without looking to his bride.

And yet, he always seemed to know where she was as she flitted from one group to the next. Right now she was talking to a group of ladies across the churchyard from the horseshoe pit. Discouragement poured acid into his gut. He should be happy that she was enjoying the day, but all he could do was wonder how it compared to the lavish entertainments of her past life.

Easton threw his last shoe, and they walked to the stake to score the tosses. Sure enough, Drew hadn't scored a point.

Easton clapped him on the back. "Yep, a newlywed like yourself doesn't stand a chance against an old married man like me."

Drew shook the man's hand. "I guess that extra month of matrimony made all the difference. Not like I've seen you watching Merritt out of the corner of your eye."

Easton flushed, and Drew took the opportunity to leave the horseshoe pit while he could still claim the last word.

His neighbor, Sam Barclay, stepped up next to him, giving him a friendly nudge with his shoulder. "Haven't seen you miss that badly in a while. If that's what a wife does to your concentration, maybe I'm glad the Lord hasn't seen fit to bless me that way."

"Everyone has an off day now and then." Drew purposely didn't look toward the ladies gathered across the way. Not that he needed to. The image of Kaitlyn in her reworked green calico remained burned into his mind. That dress had never looked so good on Amanda. Kaitlyn stood tall and proud in the hand-me-down, but Amanda had always seemed ashamed to be seen in lowly calico.

His new wife continued to amaze him. Who would have thought a city girl would jump right in to help when Tillie and the dog got sprayed by a skunk? Or that she would know how to salt down beef?

Or that she'd go to all the extra work to get all three kids on horses and bring family lunch out to him on a day when he wouldn't be home until late? Kaitlyn and the kids had spent the afternoon with him, "learning real life," as Kaitlyn had put it. David and Jo had been a real help. Kaitlyn and Tillie, not so much. His lips twitched at the memory of a cow escaping Kaitlyn's attempt at herding. She'd been so outraged as she watched it run off, and even more so when Jo successfully brought it back to the herd.

No, Kaitlyn wasn't much like Amanda. But the way she flitted around this picnic talking to everyone present did seem to show that she craved more contact with people than the ranch allowed. Than his lifestyle provided. Her lifestyle now, since she'd married him.

"You having that problem, Drew?"

Drew pulled his attention from his wife. Just when had his gaze found her again? "Sorry, Sam, I missed that."

"You haven't missed much about your wife's location." Sam flashed a grin at him, then his expression turned serious. "I was wondering how your grazing's holding up. Yours should be better than most, with the river access you have."

Drew's cheeks warmed, and he turned to fully face his friend. Maybe that would focus his attention where it should be, helping to find solutions to the problems he and his neighbors were facing. "We're doing okay so far. Are a lot of folks having that problem?"

Sam nodded. "I think it contributed to the Robbins family pulling out."

Drew scrubbed a hand over his face. If he'd known, he could have offered them time on his land.

"Drew, there you are." Tom Fisher, a local carpenter, stopped next to them. "Kaitlyn said that you had an extra side of beef and you might take some shingles in exchange."

Kaitlyn? How'd she get on a first name basis with Fisher, who'd more than earned his reputation as a curmudgeon?

The man ran his hand along his grizzled cheek. "The shingles are mostly leftovers from bigger projects, so you might have to piece 'em together some, but I reckon they'd keep the rain out till you could do better."

Drew's shoulders lightened, as if a load there had been lifted. Every time he turned around, Kaitlyn found a way to help, easing the burden he carried in ways he'd never expected. "How many you willing to part with?"

"Enough to roof a cabin, I'd think, iffen it weren't too big."

"Sounds like a fair trade." Drew extended his hand, and the older man shook it, then wandered closer to the horse-shoe pit.

Drew turned back to his friend. "Maybe you could drive your herd out my way if your grazing is bad."

"Grazing isn't the worst we're facing. Have you tried to get a loan at the bank this year? They turned me down flat, and I've always paid off anything I borrowed ahead of time."

"I haven't asked for one. Only collateral I've got is the original homestead, and I don't want to put it up." He'd considered it though. Ran the numbers and had just about decided he had to do it. Now it looked like it wouldn't be an option.

Sam looked around, then lowered his voice. "You know the new bank president and Quade are thick as thieves. And Quade's out buying up land people can't prove up. Well, he ain't getting mine. No siree. I've got a year to go on my agreement, and I'm gonna keep it, loan or no loan."

Drew's lunch solidified into a lump in the pit of his stomach. He only had a month to prove up Ed's homestead. How was he going to get that lumber?

A commotion drew his attention back to the ladies. David and a few of his friends skidded to a stop in front of Kaitlyn. She cocked her head, listening to the boys, then nodded an answer. They dashed back to their abandoned baseballs and gloves.

She watched them run back to the field, her smile gentle. Then she looked his way, as if she could feel the weight of his gaze. He could no more keep himself from smiling back at her than he could hit a ringer in the horseshoe pit today, and for the same reason. His mind was on her, not the task at hand.

Just like he found himself making mental notes of things to tell her about when they had coffee in the evenings after the kids went to bed. Or looking forward to hearing her lesson plans. Or sharing a look when Tillie did something adorable.

He shook his head to clear it of memories. They had a business deal, not a marriage. That was the way it had to stay.

Even if her presence eased the burdens he carried.

One of the ladies standing near Kaitlyn, Mindy Cummins, waved briefly to her and made her way to the men. She and her husband lived on one of the ranches farthest from town and probably needed to leave early.

She paused next to Drew, her hand shading her eyes as she tried to find her husband.

Drew gestured toward the ball game. "I think he went to check on the boys, find out what sent them racing through the picnic area. Hope there wasn't trouble."

"Not a bit of it. David wanted Kaitlyn to back up his story about breaking a colt. Some of his friends thought he might be exaggerating."

"And was he?"

"Nope. Evidently, Kaitlyn told the story almost exactly the way David did. Now I'm gonna have a boy sulking around the ranch 'cause his friend got to break a horse first."

Drew's lips twitched. "I've been there. Sulky boys can be a handful."

"I'll manage him, or his father will. Just like you do with David. After the boys ran off, Kaitlyn mentioned you let David continue the ride after Phantom bucked. Said she thought that was one of the bravest things she'd ever seen, knowing how much you wanted to yank him out of harm's way."

Kaitlyn thought he was brave? He could almost feel his chest puff up at the thought, but he couldn't very well say that. "Wouldn't have done boy or horse any good for me to take over."

"You don't fool me, Drew McGraw. Nor Kaitlyn either. Letting them grow up is hard."

He nodded. It certainly was. He'd put pillows around the kids all their lives if he could.

"Kaitlyn mentioned she might have a bit of a dowry coming. I'm glad to hear it. Hope it helps you get those cabins up." She waved across the field. "Oh, there's my husband. I'd better head that way, or we'll keep missing each other."

Drew nodded, but unease lifted the hairs along his arms and on the back of his neck. Sure, they'd managed to get proof of their marriage mailed off without a hitch, but he'd rather no one knew that piece of their personal business. Or her business, anyway.

Nothing in their deal mentioned her money, so it would stay exactly that.

Hers.

Kaitlyn was starting to love this little girl.

She reached across the bed and brushed Tillie's hair from her forehead, then leaned back in her chair. Too much sun and play at the picnic had sent the little girl to bed early. Had it caused the nightmare too? Kaitlyn tucked the blanket around her. Here it was, late April, and the nights were still cold. She wiped a tear from Tillie's cheek, her chest tightening at the evidence of Tillie's fear. It had only been a nightmare, but Kaitlyn hated anything that caused her charge pain.

Jo lay in the bed beside Tillie, her eyes scrunched closed, pretending to sleep. Jo had spent most of the day pretending she didn't care that the girls at church ignored her. Kaitlyn smothered a sigh. She had stayed up late last night to finish a dress for Jo, but the girl had refused to wear it and paid the price. Was it the dress itself, or the fact that Kaitlyn had made it?

Kaitlyn shook her head. It didn't really matter. Drew had already purchased the fabric, and there was no money to spare on stubbornness.

A tear seeped out from Jo's tightly closed eyes, and Kaitlyn's heart clenched. She'd known that Jo's temper was fueled by pain, but here was direct evidence.

There had to be something she could do about it. If only she knew what.

She left the room and stretched her arms over her head, trying to relieve the ache in her shoulders. It had been a long day, and she'd dearly love to be stretching her legs and back, but that would have to wait for the privacy of her own room. She had to finish putting away the dishes first. No point in making tomorrow's breakfast harder on herself.

She entered the kitchen, then stopped. Drew stood beside the stove, studying something on the preparation table. The lamplight glinted from his dark hair, and his shoulders stretched the fabric of his dress shirt. She took another step into the room, and he looked up. "What's this?" He tapped the paper she'd left there, his head tilted uncertainly.

Her cheeks warmed, and her gaze dropped. She could hardly even look at him since he'd seen her breakdown last week. He had to think she was the most lily-livered person he'd ever met.

And now he'd found that paper. Would he think she was pushing in where she didn't belong? She only wanted to help.

Except he'd thanked her for arranging the trade for the shingles.

He tapped the paper again. Not agitated. Just reminding her of his question.

"It's a list." She moved a little closer, stepping into the pool of light from the lamp.

"I can see that. What's it for?"

His voice seemed steady, not accusing, but her cheeks got hotter. She was blushing for sure. No help for it though. "I know you need to sell the bull. Nick helped me make a list of women to talk to. Either wives that help on their ranches or townsfolk who might catch the latest gossip." She caught her lower lip between her teeth, then forced herself to release it. She hadn't done anything to be ashamed of.

Drew's eyebrows rose. "That's why you were chatting with everyone at the picnic?"

She reached for the basket holding their plates from the picnic and brushed against his arm. Her skin prickled at the touch. She ignored the reaction and pulled out a stack of plates. Thankfully, they'd been able to wash everything before they'd left the church. "Is it so surprising that I'd want to help you?"

"Yes." He ran his hand through his hair.

"Ed and Nick help you. Why wouldn't I?"

Drew grabbed the basket of dishes and the lamp and silently moved next to her. He put the light on the counter under the cabinet, then held the basket of dishes next to it, saving her multiple trips across the kitchen. How like him. He'd go miles out of his way to help those he cared about, but getting him to say more than two words? Not easy.

Unlike her own father, who'd had all the right words but never protected her from Michael.

She took more dishes from the basket, then stretched up to place them in the cabinet. "What did you think I was doing today?"

He dropped his gaze. "Nothing."

Kaitlyn smothered a smile. The man really couldn't lie. Not a bad trait in a husband. "Then why do you look like David when I caught him stealing cookies before dinner?" She placed the last of the dishes gently in their spot.

He shrugged.

Maybe if she didn't watch him? She grabbed a dishrag to wipe the counter that didn't need wiping.

"I was just thinking that you must have had a lot of friends back in St. Louis." He placed the basket back on the preparation table, avoiding her gaze. "I know it can get lonely out here. I'll just, um, get some wood for tomorrow." He stepped into the lean-to.

Kaitlyn ran the damp rag across the smooth counter. She was still missing something. Drew came back in, arms loaded with wood. Goodness, his shoulders nearly filled the doorway.

She plied her dishrag on the already clean table, much as she would have liked to look into his eyes. "Turns out I didn't have many friends in St. Louis. Not ones strong enough to ignore my brother's lies. I'd like to make stronger friendships in this community." She glanced up and took in his still-tense jaw. "There's something more to this, isn't there?"

"Amanda hated it here."

"I know." She pulled out a chair, its legs rumbling over the wooden floor. She sat down. Now if only Drew would join her. "Can you explain how Amanda comes into this?"

Drew sank into a chair across from her and eyed the table as if it held the answers to all his questions. The silence lengthened, but Kaitlyn didn't interrupt it. He seemed the type who needed to gather his thoughts before he shared them. And he'd seldom talked about his first wife.

Finally, he looked up, met her eyes. "Nothing on the ranch was good enough for Amanda. Not the food, not the clothes, not the . . . company."

Kaitlyn squeezed her hands together, forcing herself to remain silent. How could that stupid woman not have valued a man who put her needs first, gave her the best of what he had? How could she have treated a good man so badly that he questioned his own worth?

"It's lonely for a woman out here." Drew gave her a half smile. "I get that."

"And you thought I was desperate for friendships off the ranch."

He nodded. "Amanda was desperate enough to run off with a man that didn't have a penny to his name, just because he was willing to live with her in the city. Just to get away from me. The mistake she made by marrying me."

Kaitlyn folded her hands in front of her. "I'm not Amanda," she said quietly.

"I know that."

A long look passed between them, and the silence lengthened.

"Did you like it back east?" she asked finally.

She thought he'd ignore the question, but he finally said, "I understood its appeal, the convenience of shops nearby, friends nearby, but it wasn't home. I belong out here, where there's freedom to move and breathe."

"I can't see you being happy there." She paused, trying to find words for the differences she felt more than saw. "I don't miss my so-called friends who judged my family based on whether we wore the latest fashion and missed the fact that my father and brother never took care of me. You always put your children first."

"Life's hard out here though. Especially for a woman. Even my mother."

"I thought she loved it here."

"She loved my pa." His eyes went a bit unfocused, or maybe focused on the past. "She used to ride out on the range with him sometimes, and boy could she ride. Put us all to shame."

Kaitlyn's brow furrowed. "I can't imagine anyone riding better than you."

"She could."

His jaw clenched and his hands tightened into fists, his forearms corded below his turned-up sleeves.

Kaitlyn's heart turned over. She reached across the table and laid a hand on his sleeve.

His forearm relaxed under her touch. "I was back east when it happened."

She nodded and let her hand move over his sleeve, the fabric rough beneath her fingers.

"Pa got thrown from a horse and landed wrong." He shuddered. "His leg never healed right. They didn't tell me for a long time, but finally Ma sent me a telegram asking me to come back to the ranch. I didn't make it in time to say goodbye."

Kaitlyn's eyes grew moist, but she rapidly blinked back the tears. The last thing Drew needed was her crying all over him again. She tightened her grip on his forearm. At least he could know she heard him.

"When I got home, I didn't even recognize Ma. I never saw her go to the stables, much less ride across the homestead. Her smiles were gone. She didn't say much, didn't eat much…" He swallowed, his throat working against the emotion flooding him. "She just gave up. Much as I tried, I couldn't make her happy. She should have survived that cold, but it went to pneumonia, and she gave up."

Kaitlyn's heart twisted in her chest. His pain was a living thing, crowding them together. He was shouldering a burden he was never intended to carry, but he couldn't see it. "Drew, who decided that it was your job to make everyone happy?"

He stared at her. Had he really never thought of it that way? No wonder he tried to do anything to make everyone else's life easier.

He ran his hand through his hair, and his eyebrows pulled together. Finally, he collapsed against the back of his chair. "I don't know. It's just always been that way."

She tightened her grip on his arm and drew his eyes back to hers. He had to hear her. "Drew, who is supposed to make you happy?"

Ten

WOULD SHE EVER SEE THE BOTTOM of this sink?

Kaitlyn ran her fingers around the edge of the basin of soapy water, searching for any piece of silverware from lunch that she had missed in the cloudy water. Not finding anything, she picked up a few plates from the stack on the chair beside her. Some days it felt like she never got out of this kitchen and Drew never got off the range. Today he hadn't even made it back for lunch, and dinner was hours away.

She'd almost think he was avoiding her, except that when they were together, he smiled more. Shared more about his day. Listened to her share about her own.

"Hey, Marshal." Ed's surprised voice floated through the open kitchen window. Kaitlyn had already learned that May wasn't a good time for visits on a ranch. The work list was long, and spring in Wyoming was all too short. They hadn't made it to town since the picnic a week and a half ago.

Kaitlyn stacked the plates into the soap-water basin. Dishes could wait. She looked around the kitchen, then snatched the lid off the cookie jar, breathing a sigh of relief. David hadn't emptied it yet. She piled cookies onto a plate, ladled water into the teapot, and placed it on the stove. They'd have tea shortly.

Rap, rap, rap.

Her first visitor in her new home. Kaitlyn forced herself into a normal pace across the living room to the front door. Skipping would hardly give her visitor a good impression of her maturity, after all. She opened the door, and Danna stepped inside, the end of her dark braid swinging along the waistband of her pants. Kaitlyn gestured toward the parlor. "Hi, Marshal. Come on in. I've got tea warming and cookies waiting. I'm so glad to see you."

"No need to stand on formality. Coffee in the kitchen will be fine." The marshal didn't return Kaitlyn's smile. She stepped inside and examined the room, then her gaze swept Kaitlyn.

Disquiet pinged through Kaitlyn's heart. Danna was the closest law enforcement officer. Was this not a social visit? She pushed her doubts aside. The marshal had been friendly at the church picnic. Just because she was an officer didn't mean she was here on business.

Kaitlyn gestured toward the door. "The kitchen is through there."

Danna's posture would have made a finishing school graduate jealous as she passed through the dining room, but her walk was businesslike. Kaitlyn's gaze settled on the gun belt Danna wore around her hips. She bit her lip. Surely this was only a social call.

Kaitlyn followed her through the kitchen door, but she could not bring herself to hurry.

The teakettle whistled. "I'll just, um, take the teakettle off. The coffee's always hot." Kaitlyn grabbed a kitchen towel and moved the teakettle, then grabbed the coffeepot. Danna leaned against the counter.

"Do you take your coffee black?"

Danna nodded. Kaitlyn filled two coffee cups. "It's so good to see you. Thanks for stopping by."

Danna quickly scanned the kitchen, as if categorizing evidence in a case. Queasiness tried to rob Kaitlyn of her appetite. She pressed a hand to her stomach but controlled her expression. She was overreacting, surely. She'd left any danger far behind. "Have a cookie?" She nudged the plate toward the marshal.

"None for me, thanks." Danna took a sip of her coffee, then put the cup back on the counter. "Tell me, Kaitlyn, what brought you west?"

The hairs on the back of Kaitlyn's neck stood up. How could she answer that? No one around Calvin needed to know what Kaitlyn had left behind. She sipped from her cup, hiding as much of her expression as she could from the too-observant marshal. "I came here to marry Drew. You know that."

"Were you leaving trouble behind you?"

Her breath caught, but she met Danna's gaze steadily. "I

suspect nearly every woman who agrees to be a mail-order bride is leaving some kind of trouble behind her."

"Kaitlyn, I got a wire from a man claiming to be your brother."

The cookie Kaitlyn had eaten threatened to make a reappearance. She wanted to squeeze her eyes closed, wanted to go back in time to lunch and ask Drew if she and the kids could join him on the range. Anything but to be here and realize her hiding place was threatened. She swallowed hard.

Danna's gaze sharpened. Not that she had missed much before.

Kaitlyn forced her breathing to steady. "Michael Montgomery is my half brother." Why did she bother? No one had ever cared about the distinction besides her.

Her attorney must have told him where she was. She had thought that would be privileged information.

Maybe she needed a new lawyer.

"He claims you ran from a fine home," Danna said. "That you weren't in your right mind. That you might have been coerced into marriage."

Coerced into marriage. The words sent a shudder through her. The only person who'd tried to coerce her was Michael himself.

If he knew to wire the marshal in Calvin, he could find her on the McGraws' ranch. Nearly everyone in town had seen her with Drew and the children at the picnic.

Drew. The kids. The ranch. They were all in danger now.

Her first instinct was to run, and she found her gaze already out the window, whirling with wild thoughts.

If Michael could find her here, was anywhere safe?

Drew. Where are you? I need you.

Danna rested a hand on her shoulder. "I'd ask if you're in trouble, but I think the answer to that is clear."

Kaitlyn nodded. Her voice seemed frozen.

"Did Drew force you to marry him?"

"You know him better than that."

It'd be closer to the truth to say that she'd cajoled Drew into her way of thinking, but admitting that wouldn't help the situation.

Danna's tension eased. "I do, but I had to ask. How old are you?"

"I'm twenty-three."

Danna studied her. "Old enough for the wedding to be legal, then. Why would your brother think you were coerced?" She took another sip of coffee, then put the cup on the preparation table. "I can't help you if I don't know what's going on."

The words were steady, comforting, but she'd no doubt be like all the others, seeing only the smiling surface of Michael, never understanding what lurked beneath.

Except . . . everyone else had watched Michael grow up. Remembered the charming little boy he'd been, when it had suited him. And it suited him with most everyone outside of family. But Danna knew Kaitlyn first.

Hope rose within her too fast to be squelched. Maybe this time she had a chance. Michael had only just started spreading his lies.

Besides, hadn't Drew said something about Danna? The snippet of conversation floated just out of reach for a moment before it came into focus. *The marshal can be trusted,* he'd said.

Kaitlyn's eyes burned, but she refused to dash the foolish tears from them, instead blinking them away. They wouldn't serve her here. "My brother is . . . difficult. In public, he pretends to be a concerned brother, but in private he is anything but. He's struck me before. Locked me in a closet." Her pulse raced as memories of the times Michael had left bruises on her skin, spread lies about her, or locked her in a confined space flew through her mind. No one had ever listened to her.

Except Drew. Her husband had heard her story and called Michael worthless. Maybe Danna would listen too.

She forced herself to meet Danna's eyes. The marshal was still listening, anyway. "Everything my father left—it's all gone. Michael gambled it away. We were living on the allowance my mother arranged from my own inheritance." She straightened a bit. "The money that she left to me, not him, but our lawyer controls it until I turn twenty-five. Unless I marry."

Danna's eyes narrowed. "I'm guessing he didn't like the idea of you controlling it."

Kaitlyn nodded.

"And he tried to get you declared incompetent?"

Incompetent? Where had Danna come up with . . . Oh, the wire. "No, he had a better idea. Seems his friend held most of his debts. He agreed to forgive them if I, well, if I married him. I couldn't though. I just couldn't. He's a vile man. So I left."

Danna straightened from the counter. "And you figured

if you became a mail-order bride, your brother wouldn't be able to touch you."

"Yes. Especially if I lived far enough away, I didn't think he would travel there." Kaitlyn shrugged. "In person, Michael seems so reasonable, so honest. When you meet him, you'll doubt everything I said. I promise you will."

Danna's head tilted, and she gave a slight nod. "Oh. He's one of those. I've met a few in my career." She thought for a moment. "But maybe you should send him a wire. Nothing much. Just let him know you're happy here. It would help settle the gossip around town as well."

Kaitlyn sank into her chair. "Gossip? What did the telegram say?"

"Only what I told you, but I'm afraid our telegraph operator isn't as discreet as he should be."

"So now everyone is talking about Drew forcing me to marry him."

Danna nodded.

Kaitlyn's heart turned to lead inside her chest. After Drew had worked so hard to overcome the rumors about Amanda, she'd landed him in a new pile of gossip. When would she learn? Michael always got his way.

Danna took a cookie from the plate. "I need to get back to town. If you give me a message, I'll see that it's sent today."

Kaitlyn's throat burned and thoughts raced through her mind almost faster than she could register them. Confirm her location to tame the gossip? Or continue to hide and hope for the best? Maybe her brother had sent that wire to multiple law offices. She shook her head. "I need time to decide."

Danna said goodbye, and Kaitlyn returned to the kitchen. She pulled a plate from the soap-water basin, then wiped it with the dishrag. If only she could clean up her life as easily. Her stomach churned and her mind spun.

What would Michael's next step be? He'd implied she wasn't in her right mind. There had to be a reason for it. To ruin her reputation? Deprive her of friendships and support in the area? An image of the family walking into church next Sunday and all the people who had been so friendly at the picnic now turning their backs to her seared her heart. She'd lived that particular torture once before.

Except, it wouldn't be her alone that was affected this time.

What if the townspeople turned their backs on the Mc-Graws?

She dropped the plate she held, the water splashing her dress. She placed a hand on the dry sink to steady herself.

How could she bring ruin to this family? To little Tillie, who wouldn't understand why her friends ostracized her. To David, whose friends had been determined to be next to break a horse. To Jo, who was already having difficulty with girls her age.

And to Kaitlyn's husband, who was trying so hard to be everything his family needed.

Husband.

She sank into the nearest chair. Michael had mentioned marriage, somehow knew about Drew, so he knew she was here. Which meant she couldn't stay.

Drew rounded the corner of the fenced-off garden spot and approached the backyard. The marshal had just left. Kaitlyn would serve visitors refreshments, so he'd have to hustle if he wanted to find any cookies left in the jar after Danna stopped by. He grinned. He wasn't sure if Kaitlyn still thought the kids were to blame for her baked goods disappearing or if she only pretended she didn't know that Drew and his brothers also swiped them when given half a chance.

"Told ya she'd leave."

Drew paused at the sound of Jo's voice coming from the backyard. The gloating tone that could only be aimed at one of her siblings. He sighed. Not again.

"She is n-not. You're l-lying, Jo!"

Tillie, Jo's favorite target, and near tears, no less. Drew moved close enough to see the girls taking clothes down from the line and piling them in baskets. He might have to intervene, but Tillie needed to learn to stand up for herself.

"I saw her packing. Good riddance too. We don't need her." Jo stretched to reach another clothespin. Tillie wiped her eyes, her shoulders shaking.

Drew squared his shoulders. Much as he might like to ignore the squabble, Kaitlyn had taught him better. He joined his daughters and laid a hand on Tillie's shoulder. "What's going on?"

"Jo s-said—" Tillie wrapped her arms around his leg and hid her face. "Jo said—" The little girl dissolved into tears.

He smothered a sigh and looked sternly at his older daughter. "Jo said what?"

"I told her Kaitlyn's leaving." Jo's voice sounded serious now, but her expression remained smug. "Ma left. Why wouldn't Kaitlyn?"

That didn't make sense. Just last night she'd told him her plans for the kids' lessons for May. She'd even asked when she and the kids could help with the herd again.

Drew shook his head. Those weren't the actions of a woman looking to escape but of a woman planning ways to better the place she lived. "What makes you think she's leaving?"

"I heard her talking to Miss Danna. Then I saw her packing."

Tillie sobbed harder. He rubbed his hand across her back, slow and steady, just like he'd do with a frightened horse. Who knew his skill with animals could help him comfort his children? "Jo, the problem with eavesdropping is you don't get the whole story. And I know you didn't see her packing."

"I did too."

"How can you stand there and lie to my face?" Drew struggled to keep his voice level.

Jo stomped her foot. "I'm not lying. Kaitlyn's in the house packing. If Ma wouldn't stay, why'd you think Kaitlyn would? Ma was lots better than her. She loved us."

Drew wanted to stamp his own foot. "Jo, be quiet."

Jo ran from the yard, heading toward the woods.

Tillie hiccuped. "Is she really leaving, Pa? I don't want her to go."

"Kaitlyn isn't leaving, Tillie. I'm going to go inside and figure out what's going on. Are you all right?"

Two more tears tracked down Tillie's face, but she nodded.

Drew glanced at the path Jo had taken, then shook his head. He didn't have time to track her down right now. Besides, he still had no idea what Jo needed from him. Tillie was easier.

Since when do you take the easy way, McGraw?

Since talking to Jo might mean telling her what her mother had really been like. He shuddered. No child should have to know that her mother hadn't wanted any of them.

He moved through the silent kitchen, then passed the dining room table, where Kaitlyn and the kids worked on lessons. The parlor chair where she curled up, enjoying his copy of *Tom Sawyer*. He'd never have to wonder what to get for her birthday. Twain had written a lot of books.

Her birthday. When was it, anyway? He'd have to find out, make sure her day was special. And Christmas. She'd want to do something special for the kids that day, no doubt. It'd be his job to make sure she wasn't forgotten. It'd take a few years before he'd have to find another author.

He stopped in the parlor. Since when did a business deal include worrying about Christmas gifts? Probably about the same time it started including sharing stories of their days and the kids' exploits.

He set his jaw. Somehow, friendship had snuck through the fences he'd erected, but it stopped there. Not that Kaitlyn was likely to fall in love with him. No one had thought he was worth a lifetime commitment.

He knocked on the door to her room.

She opened the door a foot, just wide enough for him to see into the room behind her.

Her trunk lay half filled on her bed.

Eleven

DREW PUSHED THE DOOR OPEN FARther. Kaitlyn's clothes were scattered across the bed. His pulse pounded in his ears.

She'd really fooled him. He'd thought she was different. A muscle twitched in his jaw as he brushed past her to stand between her and the open trunk. He forced himself to pull in air, the cool May breeze feeling like cut glass as it passed into his chest.

"What do you think you're doing?"

She looked at him, her eyes blank, expressionless.

"There's a little girl out there crying because you're packing."

Kaitlyn's face paled, and she shrank in on herself, but then she squared her shoulders and walked to the other side of the bed. Good. At least she'd have to reach over the lid of the trunk from that side. He turned to face her, the bed and trunk between them.

She picked up a dress and bunched it up, then pulled it to her chest like a shield. "I need to borrow your trunk. I'll see that you get it back."

He gritted his teeth, forcing words from behind them. "What are you doing?"

She leaned over to fold the dress, hiding her expression from him. "Leaving."

"Do you even care what this will do to Tillie?"

Her shoulders twitched, but she didn't answer, didn't look up. A tear slipped down her cheek.

He paused. That didn't make sense. If she wanted to leave, why was she crying? "Why, Kaitlyn? Why are you packing?"

She shook her head, keeping her face tilted downward. Everything inside him tensed, sharpened. He needed to see her eyes. "What did the marshal say?"

Another tear slid down her cheek.

"Kaitlyn, sweetheart—"

She looked up, and his blood froze in his veins. Her tear-streaked face was white, her gaze bright with fear.

"Tell me what's wrong. Please, sweetheart. I need to know."

"I can't." She turned the trunk to face her and picked up another dress. Her hands shook as she folded it, or attempted to fold it. When she placed it in the trunk, it sprawled across the open space.

"You have to. Have you thought about what your leaving will do to Tillie?" He strode around the bed, then paused. She was afraid. He didn't want to scare her more. He took her hands and gently pulled her toward him. A shudder shook her.

She met his gaze. More tears joined the first. "You don't understand."

"Then explain it."

She took a deep breath. "It's my brother. It always is. My own personal nemesis."

He wiped a tear from her face. She stilled, but didn't pull away. "And Danna, I'd guess, since she was here. What did she say?"

"Michael sent a telegram. To her office. He knows where I am. He knows about you. And probably the kids." She bit her lip, slipped away from him, and reached down to drop a folded dress into the trunk. If only her hands would quit shaking.

He took the dress out, dropped it back on the bed. It landed in disarray. Good. That would slow down her packing. He caught her hands in his, then closed the trunk. "You're not leaving. We're facing this together. You might as well tell me. I can always ride into town and find out myself."

She sighed. "It said I wasn't in my right mind, that I couldn't have agreed to marriage. That you coerced me into marriage."

"Coerced?" Drew's brows furrowed.

"And the town knows what the wire said."

A tingle ran down his back. He needed the town's goodwill if they were going to help him prove up Ed's homestead. He shook his head. Coercion was just too far-fetched. "Knowing he said it and believing it are two different things."

She pulled her hands from his, then opened the trunk. "You don't understand my brother. He always finds a way to get what he wants."

The tingle along his spine chilled. Kaitlyn had chosen to face a three-day trip on a train to a place she didn't know to marry a man she'd never met. She didn't give into fear easy. "Give me an example."

She spun back around, and the hope in her eyes nearly did him in. Had no one ever asked so simple a question? He swept the trunk and clothing out of the way and sat on the mattress, pulling her to sit next to him.

"You know he wanted me to marry his friend."

Drew nodded.

"It was the same man I hid from when I was sixteen." She pressed a fist against her mouth, then lowered it. "Brian bought up Michael's gambling debts, promised he would forgive them the day we wed."

Drew bit back a curse. "He'd sell his sister for the price of debts he ran up himself?"

She nodded, yet another tremor passing through her. How much of her life had she spent in fear of her brother? "Has he always been this way?"

She tilted her head, considering. "He was twelve and I was six when I caught him laughing while he whipped my pony." She shuddered and her eyes filled with tears. "Blood ran down poor Buttercup's flanks." Her gaze hardened. "I tackled him and took the whip away."

"You were Tillie's age? You shouldn't have been able to do that."

She bit her lip, tears welling in her eyes. "He had heard our father just outside. When Father came in, I was holding the whip."

Drew swept her into a hug. Her chest jerked as she sobbed. He ran his hand along her spine, up and down. "Did your father believe him?"

"I d-don't think so. But he p-punished me anyway, because the schoolmaster for Michael's new school was there. He didn't want Michael to l-lose his place. That's when I figured out I was just a convenience to them. A tool to use and then cast aside."

Drew tightened his hug, careful not to squeeze too hard. "No one is disposable. Certainly not you." She felt so tiny in his arms, yet she'd faced a lifetime of trials and still found ways to see the positive. She had steel in her backbone. If only he could shield her from the memories, but hiding them hadn't helped her. He needed to know the whole of the story if he was going to keep her safe. "What happened to the inheritance?"

She pulled back from his chest and looked up at him. "He's my half brother. He has spent our father's legacy. The money that's left came to me from my mother, not his. But I only got an allowance until I turned twenty-five. Unless I married."

"I see." And he did. The whole sordid tale rooted in jealousy and greed. He tilted his head, different scenarios running through his mind. "I don't see much he can do now that we're married."

Her lips trembled. "I thought I could help here. That the money would finally do something good. Buy lumber for your homesteads. Secure David, Jo, and Tillie's future. My own as well, for that matter. But my inheritance is just as much a curse as it has always been."

He pulled her close again. He should have already had the homestead ready to prove up instead of giving her something else to worry about. "Funding the homesteads isn't your job." He ran a hand gently along her back. "Much as it would hurt my pride, I would probably have accepted money from you, if you could spare it. But it isn't worth your safety or your happiness. If letting him hang on to it keeps him in Missouri, let him have it."

She shook her head, her face rubbing against his chest, the heat of her tears soaking through the thin fabric of his shirt. "My mother left it to me, not Michael. And—I love this ranch."

His hand stilled on her back. She loved it here?

"Besides, it wouldn't be enough, not if he thinks he can have the money and his debts wiped away too. I don't know how he'll do it, but he will. Nothing ever stops him."

She pulled away from Drew and ran her hand across her wet cheeks, then crammed the unfolded dress back into the trunk. "If he comes here, I won't be the only one to suffer. He'll ruin you as well. I can't let that happen. You m-matter too much."

I matter too much?

Shock weakened his grip on her. He couldn't move, could barely breathe. She had no place to go, no money to get there, and she was willing to risk leaving to keep him safe?

His eyes squeezed closed, and he let her go. That was why she was leaving? Emotion crashed through him, shaking him.

He was the oldest brother, had always protected everyone else, and this tiny woman planned to stand between him and her brother. His throat felt thick with all the emotions he didn't have words for.

She wasn't looking at him. "I hope you don't mind me taking the dresses I've altered."

She was still planning to leave. Frightened of what her brother might do to her, but terrified of what he might do to those around her. It was way past time someone fought for her. He ran his hand across her back, the calico fabric of her dress soft under his fingers. "You're my wife. Stay, and we'll face this together."

Her face tilted up so she could meet his gaze, her hands resting on his chest. She licked her lips. "But, Drew . . ."

"No buts. You're my wife." Her face tilted just so, her lips moist and inviting, the weight of her hands against his heart—it was all too much. He lowered his head, his lips brushing hers. He tasted the salt of her tears. Tears she'd shed out of fear for him and his family. Her lips were so soft. Her hands moved, slid low on his back. She hadn't pushed him away. Her lips moved against his—gentle, innocent. Their heat felt branded against his, but he had to pull back. Kisses weren't in their bargain.

But he'd be willing to change the terms if she was.

He drew back slowly. Her eyes were dazed, and he ran a

finger along her lips. So soft. He'd never thought he could trust a woman again, never thought he'd find a woman who loved the ranch. He'd given up looking. And yet, here she was. He stepped back, and his arms felt empty. "We'll deal with Michael together. If he comes here, you won't face him alone. I'll stay right with you, protect you." He ran his knuckles along her cheek. "We'll focus on the homesteads first, since we can't do much about your brother until he gets here. If he gets here."

Kaitlyn glanced up at him, then dropped her gaze. Her cheeks flushed. "He's my half brother. And he'll come."

"Half brother. I'll remember that."

Clanging sounded through the door. He sighed. "Sounds like Jo's in the kitchen. I'd better go check on her." He moved to the door, then glanced over his shoulder. Kaitlyn hadn't moved, hadn't put anything else in the trunk. She'd been crying at the thought of leaving. Unlike Amanda, who'd cried at the thought of staying. Maybe friendship wasn't a bad addition to their deal after all.

Kaitlyn's head still throbbed, even though it had been a couple of hours since her bout of tears. Now everyone was crowded around the dinner table. Several of the brothers had glanced her way questioningly. Maybe the cold water she'd washed with hadn't erased all the puffiness.

Her stew could have used a little more seasoning, but nobody else seemed to notice. Tillie sat next to her, Ed on his niece's other side.

"My meat's too big."

Kaitlyn must've winced at the whine in Tillie's voice. Ed looked her way, but she just didn't have the energy to move. He pulled Tillie's plate in front of him and cut the meat, then handed it back to her.

Without Tillie's usual cheerful chatter, the meal felt quiet.

David scanned the table, his expression unsure. "The calves out on the range are looking good. Even the white calf is putting on weight. I think she's gonna make it."

His voice was steady, not gloating, but Jo bristled anyway. "You saw Daisy, and I got stuck with stupid laundry."

"You'll go tomorrow." David placed a hand on her shoulder, but she shrugged away from it.

Drew cleared his throat. "Jo, I've had enough of your attitude today. Apologize to your brother."

Jo's shoulders slumped. "Sorry," she muttered.

What had Jo done? Kaitlyn looked at him, tilted her head questioningly. He shook his head slightly, then tapped the pocket where his father's watch resided. Kaitlyn found the energy to smile at him. Message received. He'd tell her later. One side of his mouth quirked.

His mouth. She raised a hand to her own lips, which still tingled when she thought of the last moments in her room. He'd kissed her, held her, comforted her. And said he'd remember that Michael was her half brother, as if he knew it mattered to her.

Ed pushed back his plate and looked her way. "Why'd the marshal come out?"

"She brought me a message from town." The words

flowed as smoothly as they had when Kaitlyn had practiced them earlier.

"Must have been some message, to be worth the trip. Who sent—" Ed stopped abruptly, looking in Drew's direction. "Never mind."

Kaitlyn looked at her husband, caught the glare he'd sent to his brother.

Jo snickered. "She said Kaitlyn's in trouble."

Drew caught his daughter's eye. "Jo, that's enough."

"Well, she did. Didn't she Kaitlyn?"

Kaitlyn bit her lip. How little of the story could she get away with? She met Jo's challenging gaze. "Not in the way you think, Jo. There is trouble, but not between me and the law."

"You don't have to leave, do you?" Tillie's whining tone increased, and tears seemed imminent.

"Everyone leaves, Tillie. You're just too much of a baby to know it."

Tillie pushed her chair back, the legs scraping against the floor. She jumped down, an elbow nearly knocking over her water glass. She climbed into Kaitlyn's lap and dissolved into tears. Kaitlyn rubbed her back as she wept. Ed, Nick, and David gathered dishes and carried them into the kitchen. Happy for an excuse to avoid the drama, no doubt. Drew stood and signaled Jo to join him on the porch. Kaitlyn's hand paused on Tillie's back. She'd never seen that expression on Drew's face before. Stricken? Guilty?

He crossed the parlor and exited through the front door. Jo followed, her steps lagging.

Tillie's tears slowed, and she pulled back from Kaitlyn.

"I d-don't want you to go! You're my mama now. Mamas aren't s'posed to leave."

Tillie's dark eyes seemed so trusting. A tear spilled down her plump cheek and seared Kaitlyn's heart. She pulled Tillie closer. If Kaitlyn left, would the little girl understand how much she'd wanted to stay? Or would Jo's words continue to sow bitterness?

Michael had already shown his hand. He was coming to Wyoming. The only question that remained was what to do about it. But right now, Tillie needed her. "I know you don't, sweet pea. I don't either, but sometimes we have to do things we don't want to do."

"Now?" Tillie's voice broke on the word.

Tillie had already lost one mother. Amanda had been trying to take the girls from their father when she died, and the family hadn't been the same since. Kaitlyn couldn't stand to add to that wound. "No matter what, there's one thing you need to know. It isn't your fault. There are grown-up things going on, but they have nothing to do with you."

Tillie nodded, but doubt lingered in her eyes. Kaitlyn wiped tears off Tillie's cheeks, then stilled and laid her hand against the little girl's forehead. It was hot. Kaitlyn's stomach clenched. No wonder Tillie was emotional.

"Are you feeling okay, little one?" Kaitlyn brushed the hair from Tillie's cheek.

Tillie shook her head. "My throat hurts."

A fever and a sore throat? What if it was scarlet fever? Or diphtheria? Did they need to find a doctor?

Kaitlyn forced her breathing to calm. Tillie was whining, but she still seemed mostly normal. Drew would know what to do. "Let's go talk to your father for a minute."

David returned to the dining room, carrying a rag to wipe the table.

Kaitlyn laid her hand against Tillie's cheek. Was it warmer than just a minute ago? She signaled David to come closer. "Get some washcloths and wet them with cool water from the well. Then come to the porch." The boy nodded and closed the door.

Kaitlyn struggled to her feet with Tillie in her arms, then carried the child through the living room and opened the front door. Drew and Jo sat on the top step. Jo's head was bowed and her shoulders were slumped.

"I know I've said that." Drew's voice was serious. "But not everyone leaves. I won't leave you, not ever. Family sticks. And if Kaitlyn does leave, it isn't because of you."

Kaitlyn would have flinched if her arms weren't full of Tillie. She'd known her leaving would hurt Tillie, but David and Jo as well? Could Michael do any more harm to this family than she already had? She took in a steadying breath. Best if she didn't appear to be eavesdropping. Kaitlyn stepped onto the porch, her tread intentionally loud. "Tillie's running a fever, Drew."

Drew stood and signaled Kaitlyn to move closer. "Bring her this way."

Tillie looked at Jo, then shook her head and slipped from Kaitlyn's grasp. "I can walk. I'm not a baby, no matter what she says." She sat on the lower step, away from Jo.

Drew sat next to her and placed a hand on her forehead. "Not feeling good, punkin?"

Tillie leaned against her father and shook her head.

Kaitlyn took the seat next to Jo. Drew and Tillie turned to face them. She carefully focused on Tillie, but after the whispers at the church picnic, Jo needed to hear her story too. "I have a brother who called me names, Tillie. In fact, he did a lot worse than that. If I leave, it won't be because of you. It will be because of him."

"What'd he do?" Tillie moved into her lap, always happy for a story and a cuddle.

David stepped onto the porch and handed Kaitlyn a washrag. She smiled her thanks and ran it over Tillie's forehead and around her neck.

Jo sneered. "He probably called you ugly or something."

"You're not ugly. He's ugly for saying it." Tillie's thumb settled into her mouth. They'd have to break that habit someday, but not right now.

"That's what I wanted to tell you. If someone says something mean to you, you don't have to listen. You can choose who you listen to. I had to choose to ignore what my brother said. Instead, I listened to my mother and my teachers." She grinned. "I have to admit, they did sometimes point out a mistake I made. But their goal was to make me better, not to tear me down."

And somehow that intention had always come through. Could she pass on that gift? She tightened her grip on Tillie. "Tillie, you always want to help. That makes you a good friend."

"Me?"

Kaitlyn nodded. "You."

"Pa, I'm a good friend."

Drew nodded. He blinked a few times. "That you are, sweet pea."

Kaitlyn looked up at David, leaning against the door-jamb. "David, you have your father's way with animals. They respond to your combination of gentleness and firmness."

David blushed and looked away, but not before she saw his smile.

She turned to Jo. "Jo, your determination is going to take you far in life. Once you make up your mind, you don't let anything stop you."

Jo didn't smile, but her posture softened the tiniest bit. Kaitlyn would have to accept that.

This is your family.

The words whispered through her heart and settled into her soul. She couldn't leave them. They needed her, and she needed them. She eyed her husband. Yes, husband. If that moment in her room hadn't settled that fact, what would? "Drew, did you mean what you said earlier?"

He met her gaze, his expression determined. "Every word." His voice settled a little deeper than normal.

How to warn the kids but keep it child friendly? "My brother's name is Michael, and if he ever comes here, I want you to find your father or one of your uncles immediately. He's cruel. He was mean to our animals and said I'd done it. He'd be mean to you too."

Drew's gaze warmed, and he reached for one of her hands. "Does that mean . . ."

She smiled at him, nodded slightly. Then she turned Tillie to face her. "Ask me again, Tillie."

"Huh?" The little girl's eyes showed her confusion.

"You asked me an important question before we came out here. Ask me again."

Tillie's gaze cleared. "Are you leaving us?"

"No, Tillie. I'm staying."

Twelve

KAITLYN STEPPED ONTO THE FRONT porch and took a deep breath of honeysuckle-scented air. In the five days since Danna's visit, spring had finally arrived in Wyoming. Bees buzzed among the flowering bushes, and the sun finally brought warmth as well as light. They were going to have a great day for moving the bull.

A clatter rose behind her, and she spun to face it, then relaxed. David had piled a stack of breakfast dishes to carry into the kitchen. She should have known. Michael would be a lot quieter in his attack.

She crossed the porch to examine the honeysuckle more closely. It would need pruning next spring. Assuming Michael hadn't destroyed the ranch by then.

Tillie's illness had been over in a day, so Kaitlyn and Drew had been able to go to town not long after the marshal stopped by. They had talked to the stationmasters for both the train and the stagecoach line. Both agreed to tell the marshal if anyone asked about Kaitlyn. Finally, Danna had agreed to warn them if any news of Michael reached her. He shouldn't be able to take them by surprise.

So now they waited. Each day seemed longer than the one before, and it hadn't even been a week yet.

What would Michael do? Unease sent a chill through her, despite the warm weather. Her lists of his possible actions were likely useless. Michael didn't think like other people. Whatever move he made wouldn't be on one of those lists. She could almost guarantee it.

Last night, after the kids were in bed, Drew had taken her hand in his and asked her to come with him to the barn. Her stomach fluttered with the memory of his warm, calloused hand enclosing her own. He'd glanced at her mouth, but Nick had stepped in to ask him a question.

Had he planned to kiss her? Did she want him to?

She shook her head. Not if he chose not to love her. She'd had enough of that in her life.

Jo had refused to go with Tillie to Mrs. Boutwell's for the day. Kaitlyn sighed. Drew had thought things would go more smoothly with Jo after Kaitlyn had explained about her brother, but it hadn't been the case. Anytime she could slip away, Jo had hidden either in the barn or in her room. Chores had been finished haphazardly at best, lessons not at all.

Boots thudded on the porch behind her. Drew. The men all wore boots, but she knew his footsteps. He stopped beside her.

She turned to face him. "Any luck?"

He shook his head. "She didn't even open the door."

Kaitlyn sighed. Of course she hadn't. Jo had determined she was staying behind and refused to talk about it, hadn't even come down for breakfast. "She'll be safe here?"

Drew was silent for a moment, considering her question. Kaitlyn's heart warmed. He hadn't ignored or belittled her worries. He might not understand the threat Michael represented, but he didn't ignore it.

"She's stayed here for a morning in the past, so I think she's safe. And we need to get that bull up front where a buyer can inspect him if we're ever going to sell him." He stepped closer and reached for her hand. Their fingers easily interlaced. "Come meet your new mount. I left the horses hitched to the corral fence. Just need to tighten their girths and they'll be ready to go."

He crossed to the porch steps, tugging on her hand. She glanced over her shoulder. Should she try to talk to Jo? But what was the point? If she hadn't opened the door to her father, she wouldn't to Kaitlyn.

They passed through the yard toward the corral. The horses waited near the barn, tied to the top rail of the fence. "A new mount? Who am I meeting today?"

Drew led her to the end of the line of horses. "This is Goldie. She's sure-footed and has a bit of speed in case that bull makes a turn we aren't predicting. Just don't ask her to jump."

Kaitlyn ran her fingers over the white diamond between Goldie's eyes. The buckskin leaned into her caress. "We're going to be great friends, aren't we, girl?" The horse huffed an agreement.

The rest of the family clattered onto the porch, good-naturedly shoving each other. Their voices echoed across the yard. Kaitlyn felt happiness and warmth flow through her. They were her family, and she was spending the day with them.

Drew leaned down to tighten the mare's girth, then made final adjustments for the other mounts. He returned to her and folded his hands to make a step. "Let's get you on her before the crew gets here. Things might get a bit loud."

Kaitlyn placed her foot in his hands and pushed off to swing astride the mare, grateful for the full skirt she'd found among Amanda's things. At least something good had come from Jo locking her in that closet.

Drew checked her stirrups, then looked up at her questioningly. She moved around a bit in the saddle, checking the feel. "One notch lower, I think."

He nodded, then moved her skirt and petticoat to make the adjustments. Her legs straightened a little further. It didn't matter now, but after a full day, her knees would be happier with the lower stirrups. "That's fine." He lowered her skirt back over her boots, then patted her calf. His touch burned through both layers of fabric.

He pulled his hand back and rubbed it along his pants. He swallowed, his throat bobbing. "I'd, uh, better go check with my brothers."

She nodded, her mouth too dry to reply. Drew met the rest of the family halfway between the house and the corral.

A clatter rang from the barn. Kaitlyn looked that way, and ice poured through her veins.

Jo.

On Phantom, who was barely broken. At least he was saddled.

The roan crow-hopped under her, and Kaitlyn's heart raced. Jo clung tight, but her legs just weren't long enough to keep a firm grip. She slid a bit, then righted herself.

The horse ran toward the corral fence and sailed over. Jo lost a stirrup but stayed upright. She reached for the saddle horn, but didn't cry out.

From the corner of her eye, Kaitlyn saw Drew charge to the corral. The rest of the men followed, but they were all too far away.

Jo's horse ran flat out toward the opposite fence of the corral.

Kaitlyn's breath stuttered to a halt. Phantom was heading to Crazy Cow's pen. And taking Jo with him.

Time froze around her. Her heart lodged in her throat. She pulled hard on the reins, and her horse backed quickly. Pressure from her knee and a rein against Goldie's neck had the mare spinning . . . just in time to see Phantom sail over the second fence. This time, Jo couldn't keep her seat. She hit the ground hard.

Inside Crazy Cow's pen.

Phantom kept running, jumped another fence, and was soon out of sight.

Kaitlyn dug her heels into Goldie's sides and the horse leaped forward. Kaitlyn came down hard in the saddle, then tightened her legs around the horse and leaned forward into her gallop.

Scrabbling sounds reached her ears. Probably the men clambering over the fence, but they would still need to get mounted and get their horses turned. It would only take seconds, but it was seconds Jo might not have. Crazy Cow had already spotted the intruder to her pen.

The bovine's head came up, and she snorted, the sound chilling Kaitlyn's blood.

She leaned forward further, nearly lying on Goldie's neck, her eyes never moving from Jo's too-still form.

Get up. You have to get up.

The girl didn't obey Kaitlyn's silent pleas.

Goldie drew close to the fence. Should they jump? Kaitlyn glanced over at the mama cow. She hadn't lowered her head yet, but her hoof pawed the ground. Jumping would be faster. Assuming she managed to stay on the mare's back.

Goldie slowed, and Drew's warning drifted back through Kaitlyn's mind. This horse didn't like to jump.

Kaitlyn was off the horse before the mare stopped. She scrambled over the fence.

"Wait! Don't do it!"

Drew's anguished voice rose above the sound of Solomon's hooves. Kaitlyn stopped for a moment, but then the cow lowered her head. They didn't have time to wait.

The cow wasn't moving yet. Maybe she could draw its attention away from Jo.

The men were coming. Kaitlyn only had to survive one charge.

Only.

She swallowed hard and stepped away from Jo, then waved her arms over her head and yelled. "This way, cow. Over here, you walking hunk of beef. Gonna make steak sandwiches out of you!"

The cow looked her way, snorted. "That's right. I'm the threat. Right here."

The cow pawed the earth, then glanced back toward Jo. Kaitlyn yelled again. No words, just sound and distraction. More hoofbeats behind her. The men were closing in.

The cow ignored the noise Kaitlyn made. Her head went down and she charged.

Right at Jo.

Kaitlyn's mind froze, but her body didn't. Without conscious thought, she flung herself over Jo's still body. She covered her head with her arms, braced for the hooves to hit her back.

Please, Lord, protect us!

Nothing hit her. She peeked out between her arms. Black legs stood in front of her. Black? She looked up. Drew and Solomon had planted themselves between her and the cow. Crazy Cow slid to a stop inches away from the horse. "Get up, Kaitlyn. Back toward the fence slowly. I've got this."

"But Jo?" Her breath snagged in her throat.

"I'll get her." Ed's horse slid to a stop on her other side, and he swung down. He never took his eyes from Crazy Cow. "Get yourself over the fence. I'll take care of Jo, and that walking pile of salt beef will never get past Drew and Solomon."

Kaitlyn scrambled to her feet, her eyes on the dance between Drew and the cow. Solomon matched every move the angry bovine made with grace and precision. Jo groaned, bringing Kaitlyn back to reality.

She held herself to a slow pace as she crossed the fence.

Ed passed Jo over. Kaitlyn staggered at the young girl's

weight, but cradled her against her chest. They'd almost lost her.

Ed reached between the rails to wipe a trickle of blood from Jo's face. "Is she okay?"

Jo's eyelids fluttered, and she groaned again.

Kaitlyn laid her on the ground. "I don't know. She has a pretty big bump on her head."

"Once everyone's out of the pen, Drew can join you. He'll want to check Jo over." He swung astride Lightning and they crossed the pen, Nick following on Surrey. Both horses gracefully cleared the fence, then Drew followed on Solomon.

Kaitlyn carefully straightened the little girl's limbs. No shouts of pain. That had to be a good sign.

All three men gathered around Jo. Drew spared Kaitlyn a brief glance and ran a hand along her shoulder. "You okay?"

She nodded, and his shoulders relaxed just a bit. Then he turned to Jo, ran hands down her arms and legs. She opened her eyes and tried to sit up but sank back against the ground. Drew ran his hands along her ribcage, and she winced, but didn't cry out.

Drew released a pent-up breath. Kaitlyn felt the force of his anger. "What on earth were you thinking?"

He'd almost lost them both.

Drew leaned against the porch post and rubbed his hand across his face. In the two hours since the accident, Jo had recovered far more than he had. He'd always liked his daughter's spunky independent streak, but now it had almost gotten her killed. Nick had warned him that Jo didn't listen to anyone but him. If Drew had listened, maybe today wouldn't have happened.

Kaitlyn had put herself between Jo and Crazy Cow's hooves. The moment he'd seen her climb into that cow pen, he'd thought his heart would stop. Even now, his knees weakened and his head swam at the memory. He could be preparing them both for burial right now. He released the breath that had tangled in his chest, took another, and released it slowly before a fraction of his equilibrium returned. Another breath, maybe two, and he would be calm enough to face the storm inside the house without making it worse.

He entered the house, barely stopping himself from slamming the door behind him. Jo had to learn to listen. His heart wouldn't survive another day like today.

The door to the kitchen stood mostly open. Kaitlyn's and Jo's voices floated out from behind it. He stood still for a moment, letting those voices flow over him. He'd almost lost them, and the mere thought caused his stomach to churn. He softly closed the door, the sight of his shaking hands stopping him in his tracks. It was over, and they'd both survived.

He edged closer to the door and peeked inside. Kaitlyn had dragged a couple of chairs into the kitchen for them to sit in. She faced the doorway but didn't acknowledge his presence. She was focused on Jo, who had her back to him.

"I could have ridden him. Pa says I'm a great rider."

Even from this angle, he could tell that Jo had her arms

crossed angrily over her chest, and he could imagine her stubborn expression.

Kaitlyn squeezed the water from a washrag and dabbed it along Jo's forehead. "Hmm." The sound was kind. How could she care so deeply for a little girl who treated her so callously?

Drew could almost see Kaitlyn biting her tongue. *Be careful what you say*, she'd whispered to him as he'd carried a still-dazed Jo into the house. Now she was following her own advice.

"I could. I've ridden green-broke horses before."

"Why did this ride go so badly, do you think?"

Jo glanced down but didn't answer.

Drew stepped into the room. "I can answer that."

Jo turned swiftly, then grimaced and pressed a hand to her head. Drew pulled another chair into the kitchen and sat next to Kaitlyn so he could see every expression on Jo's face. "When you saddled Phantom, did you leave him in the big stall? Untied? Did you leave the barn?"

Jo nodded. "I, um, had to get some food. And I, well, I forgot my jacket."

"I think he rolled while he was tacked up. The saddle core splintered under his weight. When you got on, it pinched his back."

Jo crossed her arms over her chest and smirked. Her eyes cut to Kaitlyn. "See, I told you it wasn't my fault."

Determination solidified inside his chest. She had endangered herself, and Kaitlyn too. She had to be made to see that. Kaitlyn squeezed his knee, drawing his attention to her. She shook her head slightly. He bit back the angry words that swirled through his mind and nodded to her. She was probably right. Yelling at Jo wouldn't accomplish much.

Kaitlyn wiped at more dried blood on Jo's forehead. "You put yourself and several other people at risk. You need to think through what might go wrong before you act."

Drew leaned forward. "While you were out cold, Kaitlyn risked her life, lying over you so the cow would hit her first."

Jo's jaw dropped, and she glanced at Kaitlyn, then back to him. Her cheeks flushed.

Drew nodded. He had her attention now. "Your chores are doubled for the next month, and that includes inside chores. You could have both been killed."

Jo paled, and her eyes widened for a moment. Then she speared him with an angry glare. "I might have known. You wouldn't care if I broke my neck and died, but we can't endanger Kaitlyn!"

Broken neck. Bile rose in his throat. When he'd identified Amanda's body after the train wreck, her neck had been twisted at an odd angle. And he'd brought her to Wyoming. If only he'd understood his wife's desperation, her hatred of the ranch, which had put her on that train. Old grief rose inside him. If only he'd worked less, paid more attention . . .

"See, he don't even deny it." Jo's tone was angry, but her eyes were bright with unshed tears. Words. He needed words. If only he knew the right ones. Jo jumped up from her chair to leave the room.

"Stop!" Kaitlyn's shaking voice froze Jo in her tracks. "How could you say such a thing?"

Jo pointed at Drew. "Ask him! He didn't even want me. He only kept David."

His throat constricted, blocking any attempt at the words he couldn't find anyway. Didn't Jo know that Amanda had left while he was away from the house?

He glanced at Kaitlyn, seated beside him, hoping she would see his need for help.

She took his hand, her hold comforting, but she focused her attention on the child in front of her. "Your father's love for you shows in every action he takes. Ask him why he let your mother take you. I bet he has a reason."

"Pa?"

Jo's uncertain voice tore through his chest. He reached for her and drew her to his lap. "I should have told you about this a long time ago. I'm sorry I didn't."

Where to start? Images raced through his mind. Amanda unhappy. Refusing to allow the girls to leave the house and learn about the ranch—"this heathen land" as she'd called it. The girls clinging to her skirts whenever she allowed them near her.

Kaitlyn's grip tightened on his hand and brought him back to the present. Start at the beginning, with as much of the truth as an eleven-year-old could handle. "I didn't really understand just how much your ma hated it here." Was that hoarse voice his? He cleared his throat. "She didn't tell me she was leaving. I came back for lunch and she was gone." He'd run through the house trying to find her. Then the barn, where he'd found the wagon missing.

Drew wrapped his arms around Jo. "You were so young, sweetheart. Younger than Tillie is now. And Tillie was just a baby." His voice was still husky, almost choked. "I didn't go after you immediately, but it wasn't because I didn't want you."

"Then why?" Hope warred with suspicion in his little girl's eyes.

"You were so young. I thought two little girls needed their ma."

A tear ran down Jo's face. He wiped it away with the tip of his finger. Kaitlyn squeezed his other hand. Kaitlyn. Her father had punished her for Michael's misdeeds. Knowingly. No one had stood beside her since her mother had died, and the pain of that still showed today. That wasn't going to happen to Jo. Not on his watch. "Jo, you and Tillie and David mean everything to me. I love this ranch and this home my parents built, but I'd walk away from it in an instant if any one of the three of you needed me to. Nothing matters more than you three kids. Nothing."

Jo burst into tears and threw her arms around him, buried her face in his chest.

Wait a minute. Shouldn't she be happy now? He glanced at Kaitlyn. She had tears on her cheeks as well, but her radiant smile squeezed his heart. If she could look at him that way . . . He looked away.

Half an hour later, he watched through the window as Ed and Nick rode out to round up the bull and find Phantom. They'd meet up with Isaac, and the three of them should be able to get the job done, no matter how cantankerous the bull was feeling. Jo had gone upstairs to rest. Kaitlyn stopped beside him, the lavender scent of her soap comforting him.

"Thought you might like this. It's been a rough day." Her hand shook, and the coffee nearly sloshed from the mug.

He took it from her, then looked her over. Her face was pale, her eyes bright. She seemed to be moving smoothly, but there was a rip in her sleeve. It could have so easily been her body that was ripped. He pointed to her arm. "Is that from today?"

She glanced down. "I hadn't noticed. I must have done it when I climbed the fence."

He put his cup down on the prep table and took her arm in his hand. It felt cold and trembled in his grip. He rubbed it, trying to give her some of his warmth. A bit of blood had soaked through her sleeve. He rolled it up to her elbow and examined the scrape. "Why didn't you tell me you were hurt?"

"A scrape hardly counts." Her voice was low and unsteady.

"Please, let me check it." He held her gaze until she finally looked away, blushing. But she didn't pull away from him. He found her lavender soap and dipped it in the basin of water she'd been using for Jo. He rubbed it between his hands, its fragrance strong and calm. It suited her.

He ran his soapy hands over her scrape, then rinsed it. Her skin was so soft beneath his fingers. Warmth flooded him. Did she feel it too? "Any other damage?" he murmured.

She shook her head, not meeting his eyes.

She could have been killed right before his eyes. His eyes squeezed shut as the thought echoed through his mind and landed in his heart. He might never have seen her again.

Never have held her again. He pulled her into his arms. "I thought my heart would stop when you jumped into that pen." His voice sounded hoarse to his own ears.

"I knew you'd get there in time."

Warmth raced through his body, and his arms tightened around her. *I knew you'd get there in time.* She trusted him, when she'd never had experience at trusting anyone.

Even when he'd come so very close to failing.

He breathed in her lavender scent, then slowly released her. "Next time, don't trust me so much."

Except there'd better never be a next time. His heart wouldn't survive it.

Thirteen

T HEY ALL KNOW.

Kaitlyn glanced around the churchyard. Two women whispered to each other behind their hands. Their arms dropped to their sides, and they blushed before they looked away. Michael's telegram had arrived a week ago, and the McGraws seemed to be the most popular topic of conversation at church today.

Kaitlyn's cheeks heated. She'd hoped to never live this scene again, but Drew had said it would be good to attend church together and stay for the social time afterward. They'd even brought Jo, despite yesterday's accident.

Didn't he know that truth never interfered with people sharing a salacious story?

Of course he did. The stories must have flown when his wife left him.

Tillie ran up, her shoes scraping against the pebbles. "I

miss-ed you." She grabbed Kaitlyn's hand and swung it a couple of times. "Can we play one, two, three?"

Kaitlyn smiled. Tillie loved being swung between two adults when they hit three. "Maybe later, Tillie. I need someone to hold your other hand, right?"

"Okay, later. Promise?"

"I promise."

Tillie ran back to play with her friends. Kaitlyn glanced around the churchyard and found Drew standing among a group of men but watching her. One side of his mouth quirked up—his version of a comforting smile. Her chest lightened.

Gossip was still gossip, but facing it with family beside her made all the difference in the world.

Danna and Merritt stopped next to her, Danna's skirt whipping around her legs from her long strides.

Merritt tipped her head with a teasing smile. "Kaitlyn, did my cousin just smile at you? I'd almost forgotten what his smile looked like."

Kaitlyn's cheeks warmed. She'd come to know Drew's cousin, the local schoolteacher, over the past weeks. She liked Merritt. Even her teasing. "He was smiling at Tillie."

Merritt shook her head. "He checks to see where you are every few minutes. Maybe seconds."

Kaitlyn's heart skipped a beat. Could Merritt be right? She snuck a glance back at Drew. Sure enough, he was still looking her direction, and Tillie was nowhere near.

Danna cleared her throat. "That dress Tillie's wearing is adorable."

Danna and Merritt had planted themselves next to Kaitlyn and weren't moving, daring anyone to say an unkind word. "I made over one of Jo's old dresses. Tillie does love pink." And even a couple of years ago, Jo probably hadn't, since the dress showed no wear at all.

"I knew you'd made it," Danna said. "I know every ready-made item at the general store. I'm hopeless with a needle."

"But not with a badge."

Danna shrugged. "We each have our skills. It's a good thing my husband can cook, or we'd starve."

Kaitlyn scanned the area near them. No one close enough to hear. She lowered her voice. "Have you heard anything from my brother? Or found out if he contacted any other marshals?"

Danna shook her head. Apprehension churned Kaitlyn's stomach. If Michael hadn't contacted anyone else, he probably knew where she was. It had been a week. Had he arrived secretly? Hidden in a nearby town?

Danna laid a hand on Kaitlyn's shoulder. "Let me worry about him. My job is protecting my town. And my friends."

Friend.

Danna called her *friend*. Kaitlyn's stomach settled a bit. Danna wouldn't run from trouble, unlike Kaitlyn's society friends back in St. Louis.

Merritt looked toward Drew, who was still watching the three of them. Then she looked back at Kaitlyn, her lips quirking. "Yeah, you let Danna handle Michael. You need to focus on teaching my cousin a full smile now that he has the half smile down pat."

They were right, of course.

Still, Kaitlyn found herself trying to locate each of her

charges. David stood out by the wagons with some other boys. Ed had Tillie's hand.

Jo. Where was Jo?

Kaitlyn scanned the yard a couple of times before she found a cluster of girls near the back of the church. Was Jo there? "Excuse me. I'd better check this out." She made her way toward the knot of girls. They were surrounding someone. Kaitlyn picked up her pace.

"You stole it. You must have. Your family doesn't have money to waste trying to make you look pretty."

Kaitlyn winced. No doubt who that bit of meanness was aimed at. Sure enough, a break in the group revealed Jo standing in the middle, her hand clutched around the end of her braid. "It was my ma's."

"Was not. I lost it at school last week. Give it back to me. Ribbons look stupid with pants anyway." The girl tried to pull Jo's hand from her braid, but Jo clutched it tight, her other elbow landing squarely in the girl's midsection.

"Ouch." The girl stepped back from Jo and rubbed her stomach.

Kaitlyn stopped next to them. "Girls, I'm so glad to see you. I was hoping to invite some of Jo's friends out to the ranch for a visit. We could play some games."

The ringleader of the girls sniffed. "My friends live in town, not out in the country." She spun around and flounced off, the two other girls following in her wake.

Jo stared at her, anger glittering in her eyes. "Why didn't you tell them the ribbon was my ma's?"

"Because they already knew it. You didn't think she really lost a ribbon just the same color, did you?"

Jo shook her head. "If you knew they were lying, why didn't you say so?"

"In Proverbs, it says, 'A soft answer turns away wrath, but a harsh word stirs up anger.' I thought it was worth a try."

"I want to stir up anger with them. They called me a thief!"

"Well, in another verse it says to treat your enemy kindly, and in doing so you'll heap burning coals on his head." Kaitlyn paused. "Um, that means make him even madder. It isn't literal."

"I wish it was. They'd look good dancing away from coals. Next time, don't help me." Jo pulled the precious ribbon off the end of her braid and stuffed it into her pocket, then she stalked off and sat on the church steps. Kaitlyn smothered a sigh. She'd been so happy that Jo had worn the ribbon Kaitlyn had removed from one of Amanda's skirts. One step forward and two steps back seemed to characterize their relationship. But Jo needed some time to cool off, and finding a place to sit by herself was better than brawling with the other girls.

A wagon pulled out from the churchyard, the horse's harnesses jangling. Kaitlyn glanced toward the sound. It was the Cummins family. David stood near their own wagon, where he'd been keeping company with the two Cummins boys, and Drew was still with the men. David's shoulders drooped, and he kicked at the gravel. Definitely unhappy.

Kaitlyn made her way across the church grounds and stood next to him. "Missing your friends already?"

David sighed. "They're gonna be gone so long."

"Really? Where are they going?"

"Back east."

"East, hmm?" Kaitlyn tensed. "Have you ever wanted to go back east?"

"Never thought much about it."

"It'd be natural to wonder, since your mother came from there and your grandparents still live there."

David squinted at her, his cheeks flushed. "How do you know? Did you read my letter?"

She nodded. A few days ago, she'd been in his room putting up laundry. It had been open on his desk.

"That was private!" David glared at her.

Kaitlyn shoved her hands into the pockets of her skirt. Private between Drew and his father-in-law, not David. Mentioning that wouldn't help. "It's natural that you would wonder about your grandparents."

"He didn't want me, not till I grew up and I wouldn't cause him any trouble."

That's how Kaitlyn had read the letter as well, but there were other interpretations. "Maybe he meant you could come visit when you would be old enough to not be homesick."

David dropped his gaze, his toe drawing lines in the dust. "He came out here when Ma died."

David's flat tone told her a lot. The visit hadn't gone well. "Did he? What did he say?"

"He yelled at Pa. Called him a murderer for bringing his daughter out here." David looked up at her, his eyes moist. "But Ma died in a train wreck."

Kaitlyn's breath caught. So much pain and confusion in that statement. She laid a hand on David's shoulder. "He didn't mean it literally. He meant that this land is a hard place, too hard for his daughter to survive."

"But that's just stupid. Look at all of us, doing just fine. You too, and you're even a city girl."

"People say and do things when they are grieving that make no sense, not even to themselves sometimes."

David pulled away from her and ran his foot along the marks he'd left earlier in the dust, his shoulders hunched over and his arms crossed in front of himself. What had happened that day? David hadn't told her everything, that much was clear.

"Did your grandfather say anything else?"

"He said that he never wanted to see us—me and Jo and Tillie. That we'd been too much for her, no wonder she'd left."

She wished she had that man in front of her right now. She'd tell him a few things that were too much for him to hear.

Kaitlyn looked down at the boy so carefully not meeting her eyes. "That is not true. Not even a little bit. Even he knows it. That's probably why he sent that letter to your father. He's realized that he's cut himself off from three parts of his daughter that are still living, and he wants to fix the bridge he burned." She smiled at the boy. "Like I said, people say stupid things when they're grieving."

David blinked a few times, then looked away from her. "I thought it wasn't true. I'd never hurt my ma."

"If you want to visit your grandfather, you could talk to your father. I'm sure he would make arrangements."

David backed away from her, his hands clenching and

unclenching and his eyes wide. "No! I won't talk to my pa, and you can't either. You shouldn't have been reading my letter anyway. You're not getting rid of me."

She seized his hands before he could run. "I'd never try to get rid of you. I love you and your sisters, all of you. I just thought you might like to see your grandfather back east. For a short trip, not forever."

His expression calmed a bit, but his eyes were still wide. "McGraws belong in the West, just like Pa says. So don't you go bothering him about something that ain't gonna happen. And stay out of my mail!" He yanked his hands from hers and ran down the boardwalk.

How had that gone so wrong? Kaitlyn watched the boy disappear, her heart aching for all the pain this family was grappling with. She didn't know how to even start fixing the problems they faced.

Family sticks. That was what Drew had told Jo. This was Kaitlyn's family, and she was sticking.

She glanced toward the men gathered by the horseshoe pit, found Drew standing to the side. He looked so tired. So far, she'd brought more trouble than help to the ranch. She could change that, if only she could get her inheritance. She could use it to help him with supplies to build on the homesteads, to relieve some of the burdens he carried.

She sighed. Fixing finances was a lot easier than repairing broken hearts.

"The bull is worth twice that." Drew kept his voice steady with effort, his mouth so dry he was surprised he got the words out at all. He'd hoped to find someone to buy his bull in the visiting time after church, but he needed a better price than this.

Wilson wasn't a bad sort, and his ranch probably had no more to spare than the McGraws' did.

Or he knew the deadline for proving up the McGraw homesteads was only three weeks away. Three weeks, and they only had the studs up. Plus, they had used all the wood they'd chopped. They needed the money the bull would bring in—needed it to have any hope of finishing Ed's cabin.

Drew pushed the uncharitable thoughts away. Times were tight for everyone these days.

Wilson shrugged. "I'm sorry, Drew, but that's all I can spare. I could throw in some logs, but I can't cut them until ranch work slows."

Drew grimaced. Ranch work didn't slow until winter, far too late to do him any good, at least for Ed's homestead. He'd work around the clock, but swinging an axe in the dark while exhausted would be sheer stupidity. Not that he hadn't considered it. "I'll think about it. Meantime, I think Ed is looking for me."

Wilson scanned the crowd, noted Tillie pulling Ed in their direction, and shoved his hands into his pockets. "It's hard when they want your attention every second, but enjoy it as much as you can. You'll miss it when it's gone."

"That I will," Drew replied, then made his way toward Ed. His brother pointed Tillie toward the Boutwell family. Tillie took off toward her friends, and Ed ambled toward Drew, bumping into a diminutive redhead in the process.

Rebekah Edwards. Drew smothered a smile as the two glared at each other. You'd think they would have learned to ignore each other by now.

Ed signaled Drew to meet him away from the crowd. He must have heard some rumors. Drew sighed. He'd asked his brothers to listen for news about Kaitlyn or Michael but had hoped they would hear nothing.

Looked like that was asking for too much.

He joined Ed, then looked around. No one seemed to be paying attention except Rebekah. Her sharp gaze noted their movements. They'd best be careful, or she'd convince her boss to print Kaitlyn's family issues in the local paper.

Drew moved closer to Ed, then gestured toward Rebekah. "I see your schoolroom feud is still going strong."

Ed frowned. "She's a pill."

"A dangerous one if the story of Michael's telegram is circulating." Drew kept his voice low. Rebekah stood several yards away, but she had sharp ears.

"It's circulating, but as irritating as she is, she doesn't print gossip. And she doesn't control the paper anyway. She just wants to." He rubbed the back of his neck. "Besides, she's probably only wondering where Isaac is."

"Maybe." Drew glanced around, then gestured for Ed to follow him to a more isolated spot. "No one can hear us from here, so tell me what you heard about Kaitlyn."

"Nothing much about her. Just whispers that drop off if any of our family gets near. But Jack did tell me something about the Tates."

Ed's frown grew deeper, and Drew felt a cold trickle of unease. This wouldn't be good. "What about them?"

"Seems no one has seen or heard from them for more than two weeks." Ed glanced over his shoulder to see if anyone had moved closer. "Talk around town is they pulled up stakes and left."

Drew winced. The Tates had always kept to themselves, but that was a long time for no one to hear anything. Plus, they had agreed to let the McGraws use their land for grazing. Without it, he'd have to buy hay, and then where would the money for Ed's cabin come from?

He forced himself to take a deep breath. Panic wouldn't serve him well. "They can't have left. Last month, they were almost ready to prove up their land."

Ed shrugged. "I don't know. It'd be odd for them to leave when they were so close to proving up, but two weeks is a long time for no one to hear from them."

"Maybe they're sick. Or something happened to put them behind on planting. Or . . . well, it could be a hundred things."

"Either way, Jack asked if we could check on them after we get home. He said it would be a while before a deputy would be free for the trip."

Drew suppressed a sigh. One more chore in his never-ending list. Still, something might really be wrong, and he couldn't ignore that possibility. They'd have to leave soon to have time to ride over. He glanced toward their wagon. "That's strange."

"What is?"

Drew nodded toward the parking area. "David's talking with Kaitlyn. I'd expect him to be with his friends."

Ed glanced the same direction. "The Cumminses probably left already. They have even farther to go than we do."

"Hmm." Drew watched his son. The boy's shoulders were tight and his legs were planted wide. Finally, he stomped off.

Ed sighed. "That didn't look like it went well."

Drew kept his eyes on Kaitlyn. Her shoulders slumped, and she reached a hand out to the wagon as if she needed help with her balance. David had hurt her. Drew started toward her, but before he could take five steps, she pulled herself up straight and dropped her arms to her sides. Her chin lifted, and he'd bet her mouth was set in a stubborn line.

He smiled. David didn't stand a chance.

She was wearing the green dress that made her eyes glow. Sunlight caught in her blonde hair, giving it an extra sparkle. Even from here, he could see a tendril that had worked loose. His fingers itched to tuck it back behind her ear. He curled them into a fist, trying to subdue the burning.

Ed's bumped his shoulder. "See something you like, big brother?"

Drew cleared his throat and tore his gaze from Katie. His eyes scrunched closed. When had he started thinking of her as Katie?

He swallowed hard and tried to mask his expression before he faced Ed. From his younger brother's grin, he hadn't been fast enough. "What's not to like? She's great with the kids. And what she did yesterday?" Drew shook his head. Jumping in that corral and covering Jo? That took more courage than he'd seen in any woman. Most men too. "I never thought I'd see anything like what she did yesterday."

"So all you see when you look that direction is that she loves the kids. Right."

"I could do without the sarcasm."

"If you'd admit the truth, I'd omit the sarcasm."

The truth. That the burden on his shoulders felt lighter when she smiled at him? That she seemed to understand what he couldn't figure out how to say? Or that he had a hard time looking away from her anytime they were in the same room?

Ed bumped his shoulder again. "Come on, brother. You're not fooling any of us. And I'd have to say your taste in women has improved." Ed's mouth tightened at the thought of Amanda. She had hurt the kids, hurt Drew, and Ed had a hard time forgiving that.

"Ranching's a hard life for a woman. Specially a city girl like Amanda. Or Kaitlyn."

Ed laughed. "You can't seriously be comparing the two." When Drew didn't respond, Ed's smile faded. "Can't you see the difference? Kaitlyn's been brighter and more cheerful by the day since she's been here. Amanda never even tried."

Drew thought back to the day Kaitlyn had arrived. She had seemed sad, uncertain.

Ed smirked. "Seems I gave you something to think about, so let me add to it. Her smiles are warmer when they're directed at you."

"She'd have never chosen a two-bit rancher. She just got

stuck with me." Drew's gaze found Kaitlyn again without his permission.

Ed's jaw dropped, then his gaze hardened. "I'm gonna pretend I didn't hear that. If anyone else said that about you, I'd slug them. If I didn't know it originally came from Amanda, I'd . . ."

"You'd what?"

"I'd slug you myself."

"Glad to know where I stand."

"You can always depend on a brother to knock some sense into you. And enjoy the process."

"You can try, little brother. You can try."

Ed's head tilted to the side, his eyes serious. "If anyone deserves a bit of happiness, it's you. Kaitlyn isn't Amanda." Ed started toward the wagon. "Meanwhile, if we're going to check on the Tates, we'd better go."

Drew watched his brother make his way across the yard. Kaitlyn's smiles had gotten brighter over time, but that didn't necessarily mean she had feelings for him. In fact, it probably meant she felt safer the longer she was away from Michael.

Safety. He might not have the money her family had, but he could protect her. Would that be enough?

Fourteen

Y OU EXPECTING TROUBLE?" ED GUIDED his horse close to Solomon's flank. His free hand rested near the stock of his rifle.

Drew scanned the land, looking for anything out of place. Nothing. A nice spring evening with enough clouds to ensure a beautiful sunset. "No reason to."

"That wasn't an answer."

A breeze blew through. Drew forced himself to relax, then pulled his hat off to better enjoy the cool wind. The day had been hot. Finally, he faced his brother. "Just be ready for anything."

They followed the creek into a small clearing perfect for Isaac's cabin. But they had to finish Ed's first. Soon they left the trees behind and crossed onto Tate land. Strange. He should be able to see smoke from their cabin from here.

Ed eyed the empty sky. "You think Quade forced them out like he did with the Fogelsons?"

Drew reached for his canteen and took a sip. "Could be sick." He nudged Solomon into a trot. If the Tates weren't able to tend their fire, they might need Kaitlyn to send supper, and darkness was approaching.

If they were sick, that was. Not another victim of Quade.

He stopped himself from reaching for his water again. Worry, not thirst, dried his mouth.

Three cows topped a rise in front of them. Moving fast. Why weren't they with the herd in the good grazing? He looked at his brother, who appeared as confused as Drew. More cattle topped the ridge. Drew undid the strap over his rifle. From the corner of his eye, he saw Ed do the same.

They rode toward the stragglers and drove them into a bunch, then directed the cattle over the hill back the way they had come. Drew paused at the crest. What on earth? That looked like his entire herd. Four riders pushed them toward him. He pulled his rifle from its scabbard and laid it across his saddle, where it would be easier to use if he needed it. He couldn't spare his brother a glance, but Ed would follow his lead.

He stopped Solomon at the front of his herd and waited as two of the hands rode up to meet him. One had a concha hatband, and the other wore a black hat. Drew wrapped his reins around the saddle horn. Solomon responded to leg aids as well as to neck reining, and Drew might need both hands. Black Hat's eyes narrowed, and he moved one hand to his rifle.

Drew kept his hands a foot from his own gun. With it across his lap, he had enough of an advantage. No need to provoke them further. "What are you doing with our cattle?"

Conchas pulled to a stop next to his friend. "Your cattle was on our boss's land. You're lucky we didn't shoot them where they stood."

Black Hat signaled his friend to settle down. Okay, so he was in charge.

Ed pulled up beside Drew. "This land belongs to the Tates."

Black Hat shook his head. "Not anymore."

Drew's stomach roiled, but he'd deal with the implications of that statement later, when he and his brother weren't outnumbered. He pressed his left leg into Solomon's side, turning him a few degrees to the left to give him a good view of Conchas trying to sidle around to their blind side. He rested his hands on his rifle.

Black Hat scowled at Conchas. "Don't be a fool, Riley. Get back in front where everybody can see everybody. We're just returning McGraw's herd. No need to go looking for trouble." He turned back to Drew, his eyes serious, his posture tense.

The man was expecting problems. But maybe not hoping for them?

Drew lifted his hand off his weapon. Black Hat's shoulders relaxed, and he moved his hand from his rifle and raised it into the air. His other two riders stopped behind the herd.

Drew didn't drop his guard. They were still outnumbered, and none of these men looked afraid of a fight. "When did the land change hands?"

Black Hat's gaze was steady and a bit sad. "Seems Tate ran into some trouble with the land office. His improvements didn't make the cut."

Lightning sidestepped, and Ed brought him back under control. "He had a house and a lean-to. Phillips had already checked in with the Tates once. The final inspection was only a formality."

"Phillips ain't in charge no more." Conchas sneered, his hand moving back to his rifle. "His word don't count for nothin' now."

Drew intentionally relaxed his shoulders. Conchas might be a buffoon, but Black Hat didn't seem to miss much. No sense giving him any clues to work with. "So Duff isn't honoring past agreements?"

Conchas raised a scornful eyebrow. "Tate didn't have any evidence that Phillips ever came out here."

Drew forced his eyes not to squeeze shut and suppressed a wince. Ernie Duff had tried to misplace papers that showed the town owned the lot the school sat on. He'd failed that time. Evidently, the Tates hadn't been as lucky. "And their improvements didn't rate an extension?"

Conchas spat a stream of tobacco juice. "Duff don't agree with extensions. Not for anybody. This is Quade land now."

Drew's stomach clenched. Quade now held land bordering the McGraw spread. He wanted their water access. Always had.

Ed pulled his hat off and ran a hand through his hair. "Wonder just how your boss managed to force them out."

Black Hat tilted his head toward the herd. "I wouldn't

know much about that, but Boss said to tell you he won't take kindly to any further trespassing."

Take kindly? Drew shook his head. Way too many interpretations of that phrase, all of them a threat to his family and their livelihood. "Tell Quade we got his message."

The corner of Black Hat's mouth turned down. "I reckon you know the rest of the message without me saying it."

"No point in hiding it." Conchas's smile could have frozen water on a summer day. "Everyone knows Quade's gonna have his water afore long."

Drew's heart dropped to his boots. Pa had had to draw his pistol to protect the family legacy from Quade. No way was Drew going to let his family down.

And how are you gonna do that when you now need money for hay as well as lumber?

Black Hat looked over Drew's herd. "It's a lot of animals. I can spare an hour or two to get them back to your homestead."

Drew ignored the hired hand and focused on the man in charge. "We can handle it." Black Hat would probably be a help, but Quade still signed his paycheck. If the boss asked what he'd seen on McGraw land, he'd have to answer.

Black Hat nodded, then signaled his men to head back toward the Diamond Q bunkhouse.

When the four horses topped the second rise away from them, Ed ran a hand along the back of his neck. "What are we gonna do now?"

"Take the cattle home." Drew kept his voice steady, even with his heart resting somewhere around his boots.

"And after that? There's not enough grazing to get the

cattle through the summer, and we need the hay we planted for the winter."

Tell me something I don't know, little brother.

"Tomorrow's problem." Maybe they could buy some hay for the summer. Except they needed that money to prove up the first homestead. He never should have let them get this far behind on the homestead improvements. If only he'd managed things better, they wouldn't be in this fix.

The air in his lungs evaporated. He struggled to draw in more. But how was he supposed to have managed better after Amanda left him and the kids needed his time? And now, with the bottom dropping out of the cattle market… He shook his head. Jo didn't think he loved her, and he was going to lose the land. He was failing on all fronts.

He gestured for Ed to move to the side. "You take the right and I'll take the left."

With just the two of them, it took hours to push the cattle back home, and someone would still have to go back out to round up a few stragglers. Drew's body ached at the very thought.

Nick met them in the barn. "Why'd you bring the cattle up?"

Ed filled him in. Drew couldn't find the energy to care.

Nick scowled. "Quade's a snake."

"Nothing new about that." Drew swung down from Solomon and pulled his saddle off. "I'd best take another horse and head out to look for stragglers."

"Isaac can handle it. You look about done in, and he's getting antsy anyway."

Drew nodded, and Ed went to let Isaac know about the situation.

"We can still cut some logs." Nick tilted his head thoughtfully. "Make a small cabin on Ed's place. Maybe even a lean-to. Doesn't have to be fancy."

"That might not be good enough. Ernie Duff is in charge now, and he's a stickler."

Nick scoffed. "Probably in Quade's pocket."

"Wouldn't matter anyway. We've only got three weeks. Barely enough time to put up a cabin. No time left for cutting logs."

And didn't that just sum it up? Selling the bull might supply hay for the cows to survive the summer or buy supplies for cabins, but not both. There had been little interest when he'd tried to sell Phantom. He was a great horse, but the ranches around here were well stocked.

He undid the top button of his shirt. How had his collar gotten tighter in the last few hours?

He was going to have to sell some cows, maybe up to half his herd.

And how was the ranch going to come back from a loss like that?

Someone should go to Drew.

Kaitlyn carried the dishes into the kitchen. She returned to the dining room to wipe the table but detoured to look out the window. Though everyone else had eaten already, Drew remained in the barn.

Ed entered the dining room. Kaitlyn stepped into his

path. "I've kept Drew's dinner warm. Do you want to take it to him?"

Ed shook his head. "He'll come in when he's ready to eat."

Kaitlyn stared at her brother-in-law, trying to read what he wasn't saying. The concern all the men were trying to hide.

The concern they'd left Drew to face on his own.

She spun around and returned to the kitchen, where she ladled some stew into a bowl.

Ed followed her, Nick on his heels. Kaitlyn shoved the bowl at Ed, who didn't reach for it.

"He needs to eat," she said.

Neither man met her eyes.

Maybe she should go.

But what suggestions could she make about a ranching problem? The best she could do was listen, and Drew didn't like to talk.

She froze in the middle of the kitchen. Drew had listened to her about her brother, and she'd felt better afterward. He might not want to talk, but he needed to.

Kaitlyn placed Drew's bowl on a cooler corner of the stove to keep warm. With luck, she could convince him to come inside to eat. She grabbed a shawl and exited the house. Drew stood by the corral, leaning on the rail as if it were the only thing holding him up. Kaitlyn shivered, then squared her shoulders. If her husband had ever needed her, it was now.

She slipped up beside him and leaned on the rail. His brothers had given no hints about what was wrong, so she didn't know what to ask. Maybe her silence would give him room to speak. She breathed in deeply, the air scented with horse and man. The warmth from his arm next to hers reminded her of his strength, helped her relax. The sky grew darker.

He sighed. "I lied to you."

She stiffened, her breath frozen in her chest. What?

Drew faced her, his hat pulled low. "I told you I could protect you, take care of you. But the truth is, I can't. We're going to lose the homesteads." His voice cracked, and his Adam's apple bobbed. "I'm going to lose everything my family has built over the past thirty years."

Drew's shoulders caved under the weight of his grief. He'd already lost so much. How could he face this loss as well?

Kaitlyn's chest stung. She'd built walls around her heart when Drew had said he'd never love her, but bit by bit he was tearing them down. Now, in the midst of his current heartbreak, he had stopped to consider how the issues would affect her. How was she going to keep him out of her heart if he kept putting her needs first?

She moved closer to him, laid a hand on his chest. His heart thudded against it. "Tell me."

In a halting, choked voice, he told her about losing grazing land and not having enough money for both building supplies and hay for his cattle. He turned back to face the fence, his head bowed and his hat brim shadowing his face. "I'll have to sell half the herd, and prices won't be good right now."

She tried to see what had snagged his attention, but

found nothing. Was he only trying to hide wet eyes? He'd built this herd till it was the envy of every ranch around. She'd heard it discussed at the picnic, when ranchers had said they wished they could afford any stock he had to sell.

"Maybe one of your brothers would have an idea."

"It's not their job. It's mine."

"I don't understand. It's a family ranch."

He was silent for a while, then sighed. "I'm the oldest, so I'm responsible. The original land couldn't support all four of us, so my pa suggested we take other homesteads. It should have been easy, but somewhere I failed. I might even lose the original ground."

"Your brothers are grown men."

"Still my job to run the ranch. I promised."

"Promised?"

"When Pa left me this land, he made me promise there'd always be a place for my brothers here. And Ma, well, on her deathbed, she asked me to keep the family together. But even before that . . ." His hands tightened on the fence, his knuckles white.

A trickle of cold brushed Kaitlyn's skin. She held her breath. It was the *before* that held the key, she just knew it. "Go on."

"My pa told me I always had to watch out for my brothers." His shoulders drooped and his chin lowered. "That I was the oldest and they'd look up to me."

"Sounds like there's a story there."

"I was doing chores, grumbling about them. I should have paid more attention. I knew better." He cleared his throat. "Anyway, Isaac was just a little guy, younger than Tillie, and he had followed me out. First I knew of it, Isaac wandered into a horse's stall. The horse got spooked. I couldn't get Isaac out, and the horse broke my brother's leg. That's the night Pa reminded me that my brothers would follow my example, and I had to remember that."

Drew turned to face her, his expression agonized. "I didn't protect Isaac, and now I can't protect you."

Kaitlyn swallowed hard, trying to hide the feelings she felt for that long-ago Drew. The current one needed her strength. But the ranch. How could they lose it? All they needed was money, and she had plenty. She just had to get it.

"I should've followed up with the judge before now, but we could go to St. Louis and talk to him. Surely if he sees us together, he'll understand I am with you willingly."

Drew shook his head, his shoulders sagging and his arms hanging limp at his sides. "I can't take the time to go to St. Louis. Not if I'm going to get those buildings up. Besides, if I'm standing beside you, it might convince him I'm threatening you."

Kaitlyn looked across the corral. She could travel by herself. She'd done it before. Except this time she was going toward Michael, not away from him. No one had ever believed her over him. Why would the judge believe her now?

She pulled her shawl more tightly around herself, trying to shut out the chill that consumed her. Michael. Her own personal tormentor. Would she never escape him?

She glanced back to Drew. His shoulders were slumped and his arms draped over the corral rail. He was willing to stand with her. Shouldn't she be willing to stand with him?

She squared her shoulders. She was going. But going alone would likely fail. Who could go with her?

She mentally reviewed the people she'd met. "Merritt."

Drew glanced her way. "Merritt?"

"She'd go with me to St. Louis, don't you think? She went with you. And the judge may need someone to speak about our relationship. Someone who's seen it."

Drew straightened but then leaned against the fence again. "You said he's dangerous. I won't put you in danger."

"I have to go. Can you spare one of your brothers to go with me?"

He slowly shook his head. "It will take all of us to get the cabin up." He paused, his head tilted. "But maybe . . ." His brow furrowed, then he nodded. "Take the marshal. She's well-known as a stickler for the law. Plus, she's a great shot."

A great shot. Kaitlyn's heart rate sped up. She bit her lip. She didn't want to go anywhere where she needed a good shot to escort her.

Lord, I only want what is mine. Why is this so hard?

The love of money is the root of all kinds of evil.

Kaitlyn swallowed the sour taste in her mouth. Michael did love money, and he would commit any evil to get hers. If she went to St. Louis, she'd be in his domain. He'd convinced the entire city that she'd run after a married man. No one would speak for her, while he'd have legions on his side.

Drew stared into the darkness. "You don't have to do this."

Once again, he was putting her first. She knew what she had to do. She lifted her head and calmly met his gaze. "Yes, I do."

Losing the ranch would destroy him. And he had already torn down enough of her walls that watching the destruction would break her heart. Maybe putting some distance between them would be a good thing. He didn't want love in this relationship, and she was dangerously close to breaking that rule.

Fifteen

HOW DID I EVER LIVE LIKE THIS?

Kaitlyn tried and failed to take a deep breath. In only two months, she'd gotten used to the looser fashions in the West. Her tweed traveling suit with its required corset was strangling her.

Danna coughed, and Merritt wiped watering eyes. Coal smoke from a thousand cookstoves tickled Kaitlyn's throat. In the four days they'd spent attempting to get an audience with the judge, she hadn't drawn an easy breath. Neither had her traveling companions.

They passed another crossroad. Businesses jostled each other for their tiny slice of street front. On the other side of the street, grand mansions had large yards. Well, large by city standards. They were nothing close to the wide open ranges in Wyoming.

Thankfully, they only had half a block to go. The sooner this task was finished, the better.

"Those are some fine houses," Merritt said.

And they make fine prisons. Kaitlyn squeezed her eyes closed. Not every family in St. Louis was like hers. She needed to remember that.

They entered the courthouse, and Kaitlyn's heels echoed against the mosaic floor. The dome above their heads glowed with warm terra-cotta between ivory ribs. This building dedicated to upholding the law felt like a cathedral. Surely she would finally get justice here.

Danna laid a hand on her shoulder. "Do you have your appearance request?"

Kaitlyn took a deep breath, then brought out the letter from Judge Peterson. "Room 211. Upstairs, I guess." In a matter of moments, they stood before the door to the judge's office.

Danna reached to open it, but Merritt rested a hand on her shoulder. "Just a minute, Danna." She turned to Kaitlyn. "Remember, we're here for you, no matter what. That's what family does."

Family sticks. Drew's words echoed in Kaitlyn's memory. Drew. The kids. The brothers. The ranch.

Lord, I only want what's supposed to be mine so I can help the only real family I've ever known. Please help us.

Kaitlyn smiled at Merritt and Danna. "Thank you. I appreciate you both." Then she opened the door.

The judge sat behind his desk, and Michael stood beside him. His suit was cut to perfection, but he didn't have the shoulders to fill it out. Not like Drew.

Her stomach roiled. Drew wasn't here.

She wanted to run all the way back to Wyoming, where

a rough cowboy had been the first man to ever make her feel safe.

She squared her shoulders. Drew needed her here.

The judge stood, his black robe flowing to his feet. His expression was serious. "Please, come in. Sit down."

There were only two chairs in front of the judge's desk.

Danna stepped beside her. "We're still here, right behind you," she said softly. Kaitlyn was aware of her friends' every move as Danna and Merritt found spots on the bench behind the chairs.

Kaitlyn slipped her hand into her pocket, running her finger over the paper hidden there. Tillie had drawn a picture of the five of them as a family. Kaitlyn stiffened her backbone. She'd come a long way to speak the truth. Michael wouldn't stop her. She sat in the chair on the left.

Michael sat next to her. His cologne turned her stomach. She focused on the judge. His hair was the color of iron, and his posture was just as unyielding. He gestured to Michael. "Your brother has been telling me some of his concerns."

From the corner of her eye, she saw Michael look her way and smile. "I've been so worried about you, sister."

She ignored her brother and focused on Judge Peterson. "Your Honor, I'm here to claim my inheritance. I've married, which meets the requirements—"

Michael shook his head. "Your Honor, the marriage is under investigation."

The judge stared at them both, frowning. "I'm going to tell you both how it works in my chambers. You will each have your turn, and you will not interrupt each other. Is that clear?"

"Of course, Your Honor." Michael's expression couldn't have been more sincere, except for the subtle tightening around his eyes.

Kaitlyn nodded. A chill raised the hairs on her arms, and she resisted the urge to rub them. Michael would notice. The judge might, as well.

"Very well." The judge removed his spectacles and leaned back. "Since the young lady's argument is straightforward, I want to hear from you, Mr. Montgomery. Why is her marriage under investigation?"

Michael rose to his feet. "I'm her brother and her guardian. I didn't give my permission for her marriage."

"How old is your sister?"

"Twenty-three, Your Honor."

"Old enough to marry without a guardian's permission."

"Under normal circumstances. I'm afraid the circumstances are not normal. You see, Kaitlyn hasn't been the same since our father died. She stopped seeing her friends. Fired the entire staff in a fit of hysterics. I thought she was doing better when she started spending time with me again instead of staying alone in her room. I'm afraid I let my guard down. Then I found out she was . . ." Michael's gaze dropped. "Well, Your Honor, I'd rather not say the words, not about my own sister."

Kaitlyn's cheeks warmed, but she refused to drop her eyes. She'd done nothing wrong.

The judge studied each of them for a moment before focusing on Michael. "Young man, this is a courtroom. Facts must be presented, not implied."

Michael's lips narrowed. "Yes, Your Honor. I learned my sister was having an affair with a married man. I kept her home, but she snuck out of the house and ran away. She left a diary filled with rambling entries showing she clearly wasn't in her right mind." Michael held up a book. "I brought it to show you."

Kaitlyn's heart banged in her chest. That diary was fabricated. It didn't belong to her—Michael must've written it. Or hired someone to do it. She watched the judge's face. Would he believe her brother's lies?

"I looked for her everywhere," Michael continued. "I take my duty to my sister seriously, but I feared she was dead."

Michael withdrew a bundle of papers from his jacket pocket. "I didn't know she'd married until her lawyer contacted mine. And then I learned the name of the groom." He put the papers on the judge's desk, along with the leather book. "Your Honor, this Drew McGraw was so desperate for a wife that he let my sister substitute for his mail-order bride, and she agreed to it. That's clearly not a sane decision."

The judge took the letters. "Where did you get these?"

"From the woman who had the good sense to refuse to marry a stranger. I only wish my sister had done the same."

The judge nodded, pulled out the first letter, and skimmed it.

Michael's gaze cut to Kaitlyn. He returned to his chair, his eyes narrowing slightly.

The chill spread from her limbs and invaded her heart. He was sure he had won.

Finally, the judge looked up. "I'm not going to take the time to read all of these at this moment, but I may need to before I make a decision. Meanwhile, I've heard your arguments." He turned to Kaitlyn. "What do you have to say about this?"

She rose, her knees wobbling under her. "Your Honor, the stories about my..." She swallowed hard. Even her ears were burning now. "... activities are just that, stories. They aren't true. The facts in this case come down to money." Her voice trembled. She swallowed a couple of times, trying to steady it. "My brother has managed my inheritance since my father passed away. He used the money in ways that only benefitted himself. It is true that I let the staff go. He mismanaged the funds so badly that there was no choice."

Michael scoffed. "Your Honor, financial matters are beyond the ken of the feminine mind."

The judge eyed Michael, his expression stern. "You have had your turn. It is hers now."

Kaitlyn's heart rose from her boots. The judge wasn't allowing Michael's interruption.

Her voice strengthened. "I managed our household as best I could, but he continued to squander the money we had left." She met the judge's gaze squarely. "I was completely in my right mind when I went to the train station on my own and when I met Drew McGraw. No one forced me into marriage." She touched the picture in her pocket. She couldn't wait to get back home and hug that little artist.

Home. The ranch was home. Or was it Drew that made it home?

"Your Honor, the two months I've spent in Wyoming have been the happiest in my life."

Danna stood and cleared her throat.

The judge looked at her. "Do you have something to add?" She stepped forward and placed the copy of Kaitlyn's marriage license on the judge's desk. "Your Honor, the character of Mr. McGraw is not the question today, though I can speak to it, if you wish me to."

"And you are?"

"The marshal of Calvin, Wyoming. I've known Mr. McGraw for years. He's not rich, but he is an honorable man. He'd never steal from anyone, much less his sister like Mr. Montgomery here did. But the only question today is if Mrs. McGraw's marriage is legal. When this issue came to my attention, I found the county's copy of the marriage license and questioned the preacher who performed the ceremony. He told me very clearly that Kaitlyn was present of her own free will."

Michael moved closer to the judge's desk. "Your Honor, no woman in her right mind would make the decisions my sister made. She left a good home to marry a stranger."

"Your Honor, not only has my brother taken my inheritance for his own use, he has also prevented me from following paths to support myself. When I had an offer to teach school, he found the letter and the train ticket and burned them. All because he was determined that I should marry his friend, Brian Matthews. I could not agree to his ultimatum, and I was forced to sneak out of my own home."

The judge templed his fingers in front of his lips and stared at Kaitlyn for a long moment. She didn't drop her gaze. She'd only told the truth.

After what felt like an eternity, the judge dropped his hands. His lips were compressed to a thin line. "Would this be the same Brian Matthews that I am familiar with?"

"If you mean the man that runs most of the illegal gambling and other . . . activities in St. Louis, then yes."

The judge examined the license in front of him, then measured Kaitlyn and Danna with a glance. He inspected Michael, and his lips twisted slightly. He looked back to Kaitlyn. "I've heard enough. I'm ordering that your inheritance be released to you."

Michael jumped to his feet. "You can't do that."

The judge's eyes narrowed. "You will not tell me what I can and can't do in my own courtroom. You may leave now. Your sister has some papers to sign."

Kaitlyn's eyes slid closed for a moment, and her heart leapt against its tethers. She had won. She hadn't thought it possible, but she had won. She smiled at the judge. "Thank you, Your Honor."

"I wish you well in your marriage."

Michael glared at Kaitlyn, then stormed out.

Merritt pulled her into a hug. "You did it, Kaitlyn. You did it."

Kaitlyn watched her brother leave. Hopefully, she'd never see him again and she could focus on Drew and the kids. Her real family.

After signing multiple legal papers, Kaitlyn finally left the courthouse with her friends. Their next stop was the bank. The sooner they worked out the paperwork for the money transfer, the better. The crowd pressed in close, and Merritt stumbled into the street.

Clopping hooves and a shout rang out, and Danna rushed to reach her.

From out of the crowd, someone pressed close to Kaitlyn. A hand circled her upper arm, squeezing tight enough to leave bruises.

Michael.

"This isn't over." His voice vibrated with threat, but then he was gone, disappeared into the crowd.

Merritt and Danna rejoined her as she scanned the crowd.

Merritt brushed her skirt with her hands. "Someone shoved me into the street."

Shock tore the breath from her lungs. Michael had pushed Merritt, just to create a distraction. He hadn't cared if Merritt got hurt. Or even killed. Spots danced before her eyes, and she forced her chest to expand, to pull in the polluted air.

Danna looked at Kaitlyn carefully. "Are you okay?"

Kaitlyn rubbed her chest. "I will be, as soon as I'm home."

"Looks like you're behind, McGraw." Quade drew his chestnut thoroughbred to a halt at the empty foundation of what would be Ed's cabin. "Wonder what's slowing you down."

Drew's pulse pounded in his ears. Quade knew very well what was slowing them down. He'd sent his hands to scatter their herd, and now he was here to gloat. Drew stopped by the water barrel and got a drink. He wanted to pour it over Quade's head, except with the sun as hot as it was, the man would probably enjoy it.

Quade leaned forward in his saddle and made a show of examining the work the McGraws hadn't completed. If the man were on the ground, he'd be swaggering.

"I'd still like to buy your spread," Quade said. "Of course, I'd have to decrease my offer, seeing as how you're so close to missing your deadline. I'd guess half my previous offer would be about right. It'd be better than nothing."

Drew's hands fisted at his sides. "This is my land, and you aren't welcome here."

"Fair enough, but I'll be back in a couple of days. With Ernie Duff. You won't be able to run me off this land then. And I'll get it for even less."

Drew watched Quade ride off until the man passed the main homestead half a mile away. Then he turned to watch his brother.

Ed walked the foundation of his soon-to-be home, checking for loose boards. He knelt to check the level at each corner.

The land was cleared and leveled over a much larger area. The area originally planned for his brother's house. Before they had accepted they would have to take Wilson's offer for the bull. Before they'd lost the grazing rights to their neighbor's land.

Now all they could afford was a twelve-by-fourteen shack.

And where was the hay going to come from?

Drew shook his head. He'd hoped Kaitlyn would be able to settle her inheritance quickly, but something was delaying her. He'd told her not to send a telegram so they didn't tip their hand to Quade, but he regretted it now. She'd left over two weeks ago, and he didn't have much time left. He'd have to go through his herd and make some hard decisions. Selling half his cattle would buy enough hay to keep the other half alive.

Hopefully.

Ed stopped next to him. "We're ready to go. Best get at it if we're to get things done by the deadline. Probably have to work straight through if we're to even have a chance."

The deadline. Three days to raise a shed. Not that hard if they had all the material on hand. Which they didn't. Haskin's lumberyard had raised its prices. They'd had to settle for green lumber, and only half enough to do the job.

Drew rubbed a hand across the back of his neck. Why was he even out here? His time would be better spent separating his herd. This was impossible.

With God, all things are possible.

Well, unless God planned to multiply the boards like He had the bread and fishes so long ago, they were done for. But they were McGraws. They didn't know when to quit. "Think I'd better check on Quade first. I want to make sure he didn't find his way back onto our land. Still, you should have your own roof in a couple of days."

Ed shrugged. "The bunkhouse ain't so bad. Sure miss Kaitlyn's cooking though."

Kaitlyn. Drew had missed more than her cooking. He'd missed the times they shared a joke with a simple look. The times she'd brought him a cup of coffee when he was working in the barn. The smell of lavender she carried with her. The small joys she'd brought with her had snuck up on him, and now he wondered how he'd ever lived without them.

Drew ran his hammer through his belt loop and followed the trail to the main house. Quade's horse stood near the entrance to the road.

Drew's chest seized up. Several men on horseback accompanied a wagon. Dust obscured the people's identities. Who could be headed this way? If Quade had moved aside for them, it couldn't be good.

A door slammed. Tillie ran across the yard. "Kaitlyn! It's Kaitlyn!"

Drew strained his eyes against the dust and caught sight of a patch of green calico and a bit of blonde hair. His knees weakened and his heart floated free. She'd come back.

Quade's eyes narrowed as the wagon passed him and entered the path to their house.

The driver stopped at the corral. Tillie climbed into the wagon and clung to Kaitlyn like a little monkey. Not that Kaitlyn seemed to mind. She wore his favorite green dress, her blonde hair a bit ragged from travel and Tillie's greeting, but he'd never seen a more beautiful sight. She slid Tillie to the ground and gathered her skirt to climb down herself. Drew hurried to help her. She'd been in the wagon a long time, so her legs might be weak. And if it gave him an excuse to touch her, well, he was her husband after all. He put one hand on either side of her waist and lifted her down. How could someone who didn't weigh much more than one of his calves transform an entire ranch? Nothing had felt right while she was gone.

One of the riders chuckled, and Drew released Kaitlyn's waist. His hands tingled from the too-brief contact. "You're late," he murmured.

Kaitlyn's cheeks reddened, and she looked down. "We couldn't get in to see the judge for a few days. And the banker took a few days more."

"I missed you," Drew murmured.

"Your wife said you had work for us, McGraw."

With difficulty, Drew tore his gaze from Kaitlyn's face. It wasn't that he hadn't seen the riders. They just hadn't mattered. Not once he'd seen Kaitlyn. He forced himself to step back from her. "What's all this?" He gestured to the men surrounding them.

Her smile rivaled the sunrise. "We did it. The judge released my funds. Most of it was transferred to the bank at Calvin, but I brought enough with me to buy lumber for Ed's house. Good seasoned lumber, just like he wanted. I had a bit left over, so I brought along some hands to work."

The driver pulled a lever on the wagon and the brake screeched.

Kaitlyn spun, one hand to her chest.

Drew stepped closer. She was jumpy. Like she'd been the first few days after she'd gotten here. What else had happened in St. Louis? He drew her against him and pointed toward Ed back at his building site. "Go ahead and take the supplies over there. We'll be along shortly."

Ed gestured for the workers to come toward him. The

men on horseback moved that way, and the wagon followed.

Drew glanced at Tillie. "Go get your brother and sister. We're all going to the building site."

"But Pa. Kaitlyn just gotted back."

"Which is why Jo and David need to be told she is here. Go on, now."

Tillie trudged across the yard, looking back to Kaitlyn as often as she watched where she was going.

Once she was inside, Drew turned Kaitlyn to face him. "What happened? Tell me the rest of it before the kids get back."

"Like I said, the judge couldn't see us immediately, but once he did, he was fair. He didn't accept Michael's word—"

"Michael was there?" Drew's hands fisted, wanting to pummel her worthless half brother. "I knew I should have gone with you. Did he touch you, hurt you?"

"He took my arm a couple of times."

And left bruises, he'd guess, by the look on her face. "Are you okay, Katie?"

Her face crumpled at the endearment, and she flung herself into his chest. "I was so scared! But I remembered you and the kids, how much this mattered. I told the truth, and the judge listened. I couldn't wait to get home."

Home.

A door slammed and feet pounded across the porch. The kids would be here soon. Kaitlyn pulled back and pushed a few tendrils behind her ears.

Drew took her hand in his, her return filling the empty

places Amanda's desertion had left in his heart. "That's my girl. Good job."

"What'd Kaitlyn do good?" Tillie stopped beside him, breathless from her run.

Kaitlyn pulled Tillie up against her. "It's boring grown-up stuff. Not like the boxes in the wagon. Think we should follow it to find out what's in there?"

Tillie squirmed down. "Presents? I'll find mine." She took off after the wagon.

David and Jo hesitated. Kaitlyn smiled at them. "Go on. I didn't forget you. Just watch Tillie around the horses."

David and Jo followed Tillie. Kaitlyn looked at Drew, her expression serious. "Drew, Michael found me after the hearing. He told me he wasn't finished. I'm still worried he'll come here. He'll try something."

The judge had accepted her marriage and released her inheritance. The money was in Kaitlyn's bank account. Michael couldn't do anything now. Could he?

He shook his head. Today's problem was raising a cabin. He took Kaitlyn's hand and guided her toward the building site. Too bad the walk couldn't be longer. He could get used to her small hand in his.

A few minutes later, they reached the site. Ed stood near the back of the wagon, talking to the workers and gesturing toward the foundation. Drew moved toward him, and Kaitlyn followed.

Brady touched Ed's arm. "I can stand guard tonight, if you want."

Ed looked puzzled. "Stand guard?"

"It's no secret Quade wants this land. They never proved

how the Fogelsons' cabin burned down, and he bought the Tates' homestead right out from under them."

Ed looked Drew's way as he stopped beside him. "Thanks for the offer. We may take you up on it."

Drew glanced around the worksite, mentally cataloging the work remaining. They were so close, but they didn't have approval yet. First, they had to get the cabin up, then they had to keep it up. Yeah, they might need a watch at night. What if Quade sent men over to burn down Ed's new house?

Tillie ran toward him, waving the doll she'd no doubt found in the back of the wagon. Drew caught her and rescued the doll. "Careful, sweet pea. You don't want to break her."

Kaitlyn winced. "I should have left the gifts at the house."

Drew placed the doll back in its padded box. "If it survived the trip all the way from St. Louis, it should be fine here for a few more hours." He turned to Tillie. "You need to leave her there."

Tillie nodded. "Yes, Pa."

Jo and David showed him the new bridles Kaitlyn had brought for their horses. Kaitlyn retrieved another box. "This one's for you."

He took the box Kaitlyn held out to him and opened it to find a black hat. The label inside proclaimed it a Stetson. He swallowed hard. How had she known he'd been wanting one of those hats? They were rugged and waterproof yet stylish. He removed his beat-up work hat and put on the one she'd brought him. It fit perfectly. How had she known his size? He placed it back in its box. "That'll be my Sunday hat."

She laughed, and he soaked in the sound. She didn't laugh enough. He planned to fix that.

"I knew you'd say that." She nudged him with her shoulder. "Look in the other box."

What had she done? She didn't have to bring all these things. Didn't she know she was enough? He gently opened the other box to find the same hat in a light gray.

Kaitlyn laid a hand on his arm. "The dark will stand up to work on a ranch. The gray's for going to town. It will match your eyes." She flushed and cleared her throat. "Plus, there are leather gloves for you and your brothers."

"Kaitlyn, you shouldn't have done this. It's too much."

"Nothing's too much for my . . . family."

He caught the hesitation and looked closer. Her eyes didn't hold reluctance but hope. Her words lodged themselves into his heart. *Her family*. Her eyes sparkled as she watched the children's joy. She probably thought they were only excited about the gifts she'd brought, but that wasn't true. Even Jo had been out of sorts while Kaitlyn had been gone. More so than normal, that was.

He slid the dark hat on, and she reached to adjust the brim. "It looks good on you."

Their gazes caught and tangled before his fell to her lips. They looked so soft. He jerked his eyes back to hers. "You'll spoil us all."

Her cheeks reddened. "This family deserves a little spoiling. Especially you, Drew."

Her eyes were the color of rain-drenched moss. His finger reached out to touch her soft lips. If only they were alone.

"Kaitlyn?" Tillie's voice echoed across the worksite.

Kaitlyn bit her lip and slowly turned away.

Her family, she'd said.

He wanted that. Wanted them to be a true family with love as the foundation.

But they'd made a deal to keep love out of their marriage. A deal he now regretted.

Maybe it wasn't too late to change the terms.

Sixteen

I HAVEN'T SEEN YOU THIS RELAXED IN months, maybe ever." Barclay took his hat off and ran his hand through his hair. "You finished that cabin?"

The churchyard was full as the congregation visited after service. Drew stood off to the side as Kaitlyn talked to a few of the women. Her blue dress made her hair brighter, and her smile made his heart lighter. The gossip still left its mark, but it was fading. Nick and Ed had gone to check on the horses. The kids were behind the church with their friends.

Drew shook his head to answer his friend's question. The cabin wasn't done, but Kaitlyn was back. Somehow, he couldn't help smiling.

The train whistle blew its first warning. It must be getting close to one o'clock if it was preparing to pull out.

They'd need to leave soon. He wanted to finish the cabin today so he could turn his attention to more important things, namely spending time with Kaitlyn. But she had insisted they go to church. She was right, of course. They had so much to be grateful for.

Ed's cabin only needed a few more rows of shingles and some windowpanes to make it watertight. They could work on that after church, even finish on Monday morning before Duff arrived if they had to.

All because of Kaitlyn.

The men she'd brought had made all the difference in the project, just as her coffee and encouragement made a long night of work almost pleasant. Then there'd been breakfast. He'd stayed to help her clear the table. She'd had no more sleep than anyone else, after all.

And she'd offered to buy hay for his cattle.

He'd argued, and she'd asked if he really wanted to let *their* cattle starve.

He'd promised to pay her back, and she'd poked her finger into his chest. With flashing eyes, she'd asked if the ranch was her home.

How he'd wanted to say yes, but *home* implied love, and he sure didn't want to bring that up in the middle of an argument. He didn't claim to understand women, but even he knew better than that.

He'd resisted the urge to kiss her as well. He wouldn't kiss her again until they knew where they stood. Until he knew if he could tear down the last of the fences around his heart or if he had to rebuild them higher than before.

Lord, I could sure use some help in the silver-tongue department.

Barclay laid a hand on his arm. "Who's that?"

Drew followed his gaze. A blond man pushed through the small group of women and stopped too close to Kaitlyn, his body crowding her. Kaitlyn stepped back, and the man followed her. Her face paled. Her lips formed the word *Michael.*

Drew's vision tunneled and sounds around him faded. He was too far away. He whistled. Solomon wasn't here to answer, but his brothers would recognize the notes and be right behind him. The crowd quieted and searched for the source of the noise.

Why didn't they help Kaitlyn?

She backed up another step, but the church building blocked any further retreat.

He sprinted across the churchyard.

Every eye followed his path.

Ed and Nick rounded the corner of the building, but too many people stood between him and his brothers.

Kaitlyn pulled against the grip her brother had on her, but he didn't release her. Drew's heart raced. No more. He'd promised Michael would never lay a hand on her again.

Michael clutched her arm. "It's all right, Kaitlyn. I'm here to help you." His voice was pitched to carry. He wanted everyone to hear.

Judging by the people's expressions, it was working.

Several cowboys elbowed their way into the crowd. Maybe they'd help.

"Your letter said that McGraw forced this marriage." Michael shook a piece of paper.

Kaitlyn violently shook her head.

Drew was close enough. Finally. "Get your hands off her." He grabbed Michael's shoulder and spun him around.

Kaitlyn stumbled free.

Michael stepped toward her, a look of concern on his face. He was a good actor.

No. That man was never going to touch his wife again. Drew swung at Michael's jaw, but the other man moved. Drew's punch landed on Michael's shoulder, but it was still enough to make Michael stagger. Good. How many bruises had he left on Kaitlyn over the years?

A cowhand joined Michael but shoved Drew.

Hadn't he seen Kaitlyn struggling to get away? "I have to get to my wife."

The man shoved Drew back a few steps. "Hey, mister. This guy's just defending his sister."

The cowhand blocked his path, sidestepped to stay in front of him.

Fury poured through Drew, turning the edges of his vision red with rage. His fist crunched into the cowhand's cheek. Kaitlyn. He had to find her.

Two men grabbed his arms from behind and turned him back to face the cowhand, who landed a fist into his gut. Drew wheezed. Nick and Ed pulled his captors away only to have more men join the fight.

Too many men.

Men blocked him from his brothers. Two men shoved Nick to the ground. Drew ran toward him only to be caught from behind.

Where was Kaitlyn?

A flash of blue. There. In the crowd. Barclay and Fisher were close by.

"What's going on here?" Drew turned toward the voice. A deputy. He'd have sounded more authoritative if his voice hadn't gone shrill. A fist hit Drew's kidney. He faced the man who'd thrown it.

Ed grabbed Drew's arm, his knuckles reddened. "The law will help, Drew. Danna will get this sorted. You can stop now."

Drew exhaled, then nodded to his younger brother, who had a scrape across his cheek. Danna knew the situation. She'd protect Katie.

Quade stepped onto the boardwalk to stand beside the deputy.

Drew shook his head. What was Quade doing here?

Quade stepped forward. "Deputy. I walked out of church to find these men roughing up my hands."

"That's not how it happened." Ed stepped up beside Drew. His shirt had come untucked, and it looked like he'd soon have a black eye. Drew's own wounds stung harder in sympathy.

Drew straightened, ignoring the ache in his kidney. "Where's Danna?" he demanded. His split lip stung as he formed the words. Had Danna warned her men about Michael? If she hadn't, would anyone listen?

The first cowhand got into his face. "He punched me first."

"I was trying to get to my wife. That man was threatening her."

"That man is her brother." The cowhand put on his hat.

It had conchas.

This was Quade's man.

Quade, in his perfect three-piece suit, laid a hand on the deputy's shoulder.

The very young deputy.

This was a setup.

Drew pivoted. Where was Kaitlyn? He couldn't see her in the crowd.

He bumped into Conchas, who grabbed him. Drew struggled free, but more cowboys restrained him.

"Kaitlyn!"

"Marshal won't look kindly on a public disturbance," the young deputy said. "You're all coming over to the jail until we can sort this out."

Quade caught Drew's eye and smiled. "Fine by me. I'm sure my men were only acting in the interests of that young woman."

Drew turned to the crowd. "But you saw him. That man took my wife with him. I have to find her!"

The deputy came forward and took his arm. "You need to come with me." He turned to the men around them. "You too."

Drew's gut ached from more than a punch. He scanned the crowd. Michael and Kaitlyn had disappeared. His heart froze in his chest. "Barclay! Find Kaitlyn! Help my wife!" The deputy grabbed him. He pulled free. "Barclay!" More arms restrained him.

Had his friend heard him?

"Barclay!"

"No!"

Kaitlyn pulled against Michael's viselike grip. Pain exploded through her upper arm. This couldn't be happening.

Shouts broke out to her right, and Michael looked that direction. Kaitlyn yanked her arm from his grasp and ran, shoving through the stunned crowd.

The kids. Where were the kids?

She spotted David and Tillie at the edge of a swarm of men. She barreled toward them while scanning the area for Jo. She located Drew in the midst of the melee and then Jo trying to wade into the fray. Kaitlyn's heart leapt to her throat, nearly choking her. Jo wouldn't think twice about joining the ruckus, and she was short enough most of the men wouldn't see her. One misplaced punch would knock her down—or worse.

Kaitlyn shoved through the people between her and Jo and caught the little girl's shoulder. Jo spun around from the force of Kaitlyn's grip, but she didn't dare loosen her hold.

She slid her hand down the girl's arm and grabbed her hand. "You stay with me."

Jo stomped Kaitlyn's foot. "Let me go."

Pain flared, but Kaitlyn didn't release Jo's hand. "No. You will stay with me." Kaitlyn's jaw tightened enough to make her neck ache. She didn't know where Michael was. She had to get the children.

Jo tried to fold her arms over her chest, but Kaitlyn dragged her to where David and Tillie stood. She took Tillie's hand. "David, take Jo's other hand. We have to stay together."

"But Pa needs us," David said.

"Remember when your father protected Jo from Crazy Cow?"

David nodded.

"If you go over there, he'll want to protect you, and he needs to focus on the men around him." And on Michael. No telling what he would do next.

David's shoulders slumped, but he nodded.

Kaitlyn looked back to the brawl. It seemed to have calmed some. She moved to get a better view.

The deputy was restraining Drew.

Ice squeezed around her heart. If the brothers were in jail, who would protect the children from Michael?

Drew's voice rose above the fray. "Barclay! Take care of Kaitlyn!"

If only she knew where Barclay was.

She spun around, her gaze sorting through the people gathered in front of the church. No one was coming in her direction. The few who looked her way wore grim expressions, then looked away.

She scanned the people around her. She couldn't let Michael get near the kids. There had been desperation in his eyes. No matter what he did to her, she couldn't let him touch the children.

Please, God, I'll do anything. Just protect this family.

"David, where's the wagon?"

"By the general store. Remember? Pa didn't want to park at the churchyard so we could get out quicker."

She stopped, took a deep breath. Then another. That was right. Drew had said they could leave quicker that way, if the ladies didn't want to talk to Kaitlyn too long. Then he'd winked at her, taking any sting out of the words.

He'd winked. Just this morning. An hour ago? Two?

Was it always going to be this way? Building a life only to have her brother crash it down?

One more deep breath. She didn't matter. Only Drew and the children did. If she could leave the kids at the wagon, they would be safe. Michael wouldn't recognize the children, only her.

"That's right, David. I remember now." She changed directions and took them toward the general store.

She took Jo's hand, and the little girl was frightened enough to let her.

A shadow moved, stepped out from the space between two storefronts. Hands shoved her to the side. She stumbled, dropped down to one knee before regaining her balance. Tillie's hand slipped from her grip.

Kaitlyn surged to her feet. Too late. He'd found them. She slowly turned to face her brother.

Michael pulled Tillie toward himself with one hand and waved a gun in the other.

Kaitlyn's eyes locked on the weapon. Her heart pounded and her skin grew clammy. He'd never practiced shooting, didn't even know to control where it pointed. She launched herself into Michael, jarring Tillie loose from his grip. "Run!" she screamed. "Find Merritt and Jack."

The children scattered. Michael wrapped her into a bear hug. She struggled, but he shoved his gun into his pocket and grabbed her chin, forcing her to look at him.

She screamed as he spun her around and pulled her back against his chest. He slammed his hand over her mouth.

"No more of that, sister dear. Not unless you want me to find those children again. It wasn't hard to hire men for a brawl. Rounding up a few squirming brats shouldn't cost much either."

Kaitlyn froze.

"That's more like it." His hot breath on her neck made her shudder. "Maybe I should round up one of the children anyway. Just to keep you in line."

Kaitlyn's breath seized. In an instant, she was back in that storage closet in St. Louis. Except this time, Tillie was beside her. The image seemed so real she wanted to scream and pound the walls. Her breath came in quick pants, but she managed to remain silent.

Michael shook her. Once. Twice. Her neck popped from the force. She jammed her teeth together to trap a cry of pain.

"Now, my dearest sister, you are coming back to St. Louis with me to get this ridiculous marriage annulled. We have an appointment with a judge who understands the limitations of the female mind."

Ice burned a trail to her heart. He'd paid off a judge. There was no way out.

Seventeen

W HERE'S KAITLYN? IS SHE SAFE?

Drew glanced around the overfull jail. Two hours in the stone room with iron bars had caused a chill to settle into his soul. Judging by the smell, Quade's men had spent a few hours in the saloon this morning. At least the lockup had two cells, so he and his brothers didn't have to share with the Diamond Q cowhands. Too bad he could still see them through the bars that separated the cells.

Conchas snickered. "McGraw ain't much of a man iffen he had to beat a woman to get her to marry him."

Drew glared at Conchas, but the cowhand just smirked.

Nick rested a red-knuckled hand on Drew's arm. "Ignore him."

Drew rose to pace the area at the front of his cell. Had Barclay heard his shouted request? Had he understood the threat Michael posed? Or was Kaitlyn even now in her brother's hands?

Six steps. Turn. Six steps. Turn.

Nick stood in his path. "She's okay, Drew. Come, sit down."

Ed scooted to the end of the cot so there'd be room for all three of them. Nick moved that way, limping from a kick he'd received in the brawl. Blood oozed from a cut on Ed's forehead.

Some job Drew had done protecting his brothers. His mother would be ashamed of him.

He sat in the space his brothers made for him. His ribs ached, as did his lower back. That punch in his kidney had packed a wallop.

"Course he couldn't protect his pretty little wife either. Worthless, he is."

"Shut up, Riley. Riling him up will only keep us here longer, and I want a drink."

Drew rose from the cot and moved to the front of his cell.

Six steps. Turn.

Barclay had Kaitlyn. Of course he did. And Kaitlyn had the kids. She wouldn't leave them.

Six steps. Turn.

Nick leaned toward Ed. "Odd that Quade's men left the saloon just as Michael appeared."

Ed nodded. "Never known those boys to leave a watering hole early."

Drew grimaced. He'd been thinking the same thing but

had hoped he was just being paranoid. Not likely, if his brothers thought so too.

Six steps. Turn.

Ed rested his head against the stone wall behind him. "Hope that deputy gets here soon."

Drew grunted his agreement. It had been long enough already. Would the deputy bring Kaitlyn with him? His heart was torn. He longed to see her, but he didn't want her to see him here.

Six steps. Turn.

The door opened, and Deputy Wallace entered, his smooth face looking like it didn't need a razor more than once a week. If that. How had Quade arranged for Danna and Jack to be called out of town? Drew shook his head. He'd probably never know.

Quade followed Wallace through the door, a smirk matching the gleam of satisfaction in his eyes as he glanced around.

Drew squared his shoulders and straightened to his full height. What was Quade doing here? And why hadn't Wallace brought Kaitlyn?

"Where's my wife?"

"On the train to St. Louis." Quade's smirk grew more intense.

Couldn't Wallace hear the man's perverse glee?

Drew inhaled and released the breath slowly.

Nick stepped beside him. "My brother wouldn't trust a word you said, Quade."

True, he shouldn't. And yet that glee had a source.

Quade adopted a more serious expression and stepped into the deputy's line of sight. "You tell him, Wallace."

"She caught the train."

Drew's knees weakened. He grabbed the bars in front of him. The deputy backed up a step, and his hand dropped to his gun. "Don't go getting riled up. It was her choice."

"Was someone with her? A blond man?"

"Yes."

Rough areas of the bar bit into his palms. "You've got to let me out of here. Her brother's a no-good rotten scoundrel—"

Wallace dropped his hand to his pistol. "Calm down, McGraw. I questioned both of them. Thoroughly. She made it quite clear she was going of her own volition."

Drew's blood ran cold. She'd gone willingly? He shook his head. He'd seen the terror on her face when Michael cornered her.

"Sounds like your city peacock didn't take to country ways." Conchas chuckled. "Guess you weren't man enough to win *or* keep her, either one."

"Shut up," Ed muttered.

Nick shook his head. "She wouldn't have agreed, not unless he'd threatened her. Was he holding a gun on her?"

The deputy glared at Nick. "You think I didn't think of that?"

"I think you're holding us in here while the real crook gets away." A muscle ticked in Nick's jaw. "She'd never go with him. Never."

The deputy's glare intensified. "I questioned them separately. She sent a message to McGraw. Wanted me to tell you that the marriage was a mistake and she wished she'd never done it."

Drew sagged against the bars, his knees refusing to hold him. The words hit him like Crazy Cow's hooves, knocked the breath out of him. If the kid had questioned them separately, Michael couldn't have threatened her into leaving.

Mistake.

The word bounced around inside his head, stinging like nettles every place it landed.

"I need to see about getting my boys out of here." Quade's voice rubbed salt into every nettle sting. "They were only trying to help that young lady, after all."

Ed joined Nick and Drew at the wall of bars. Too close. He couldn't breathe. Drew stepped back and sat on the cot, needing the small separation from his hovering brothers.

"When is Danna getting back?"

Ed's question sounded as if it came from a thousand miles away. Drew shook his head, trying to drown out that word. *Mistake.* It echoed in his mind. He'd trusted another city woman and brought his brothers to this jail cell.

Wallace turned to Ed. "I don't know." The deputy's tone was sharp. He faced Quade. "I have witnesses that say McGraw threw the first punch, that he and his brothers instigated the brawl."

Drew's eyes slid closed. Of course they had. Because Michael had been threatening Kaitlyn, and they would always protect their own.

Or one they thought of as their own.

Images flashed through his mind. He hadn't had a clear view of her. Had she really been struggling?

Wallace's voice tugged him back to the present. "But your men outnumbered them. They chose to continue throwing punches when restraining the McGraws would have been sufficient."

Quade nodded. "I understand. If you have to keep them all here until Danna gets back, I can live with that."

"Boss!" Conchas moved forward in his own cell. "You didn't say nuttin'—"

"Shut it, Riley. You made your bed." Quade tossed a gloating look toward the McGraws, then faced Wallace. "There's no urgent work on my spread. No major deadline. Be a shame if there was over at the McGraw place."

Ed shook the cell bars. "You low-down skunk."

Quade slipped out the front door.

The nettle stings in Drew's chest became raw burns. Ed was going to lose his homestead. They wouldn't be out of this cell in time to meet the deadline.

And Quade had been a part of it all.

Nick sat beside him and laid a hand on Drew's shoulder. "Isaac is still there. He can finish it. There's not much left."

Drew shook his head. "You think Isaac will leave us here while he works on the cabin? When we don't come home, he'll come looking for us."

Nick shook his hand back and forth. Drew nodded. He thought it was about a fifty-fifty chance as well.

Conchas moved toward the bars separating the two cells and grinned. "Be a right shame for a half-built house to catch fire," he muttered.

Ed launched himself toward the cowhand, who snickered as he stepped back out of reach.

"Get back from those bars, McGraw," the deputy roared.

Nick turned to Drew, his face pale. "If Kaitlyn's gone, where are the kids?"

How did I end up here?

Kaitlyn shifted in her seat next to Michael. This train was taking her to prison. No one was going to save her, not even herself. Not at the price of the children.

The young boy in the seat across the aisle from them was restless after a couple of hours on the train. He stepped into the aisle and bumped into Michael. Her brother shoved him back a step.

The boy ran to his mother, who held him close while she glared at Michael.

Kaitlyn had held Tillie like that. The night Kaitlyn had packed her trunk, Tillie had cried, not wanting Kaitlyn to leave. Would she remember Kaitlyn telling her that no matter what, it wasn't her fault? She hoped so.

Her brother knew no limits, and neither did Quade. Michael had thanked the rancher for locating his wayward sister. The men had shaken hands before Quade had sneered at her. His words still echoed in her ears and bounced around her chest.

You'd best do what your brother says, he'd said. *Be a shame for something to happen to the McGraw kids.*

How had she been so mistaken in her first impression of the man? She hadn't wanted to believe Drew and his brothers were right, but she'd been wrong. So very wrong.

The pain of Michael's grip was nothing compared to the

pain in her heart. She'd lied to the deputy at the train station. What's more, she'd been cruel. Used the one word guaranteed to push Drew away.

Mistake. The word his ex-wife had used.

But how could she have done otherwise? Michael wouldn't hesitate to hurt a child if it meant getting what he wanted. Quade probably wouldn't either. So she'd done the only thing she could think of to guarantee Drew wouldn't follow her. He had to stay and protect the children.

And she had to protect him.

Lord, who's going to protect me?

Kaitlyn shifted on the hard train bench. Michael intentionally took up more room so he could box her in. She ignored him to look out the window at the countryside streaming by. Smoke made the image waver. Or was that tears?

The steady rocking of the train car felt comforting while seated, but she knew from her trip west that it trapped her nearly as much as her brother's large body. If she should stand to escape, her balance would be precarious at best.

Of course, Michael's would be as well. She glanced around the car. There were only a few other passengers. Could she get to them before Michael drew his gun? Most of the men this far west were armed. Would any of them help her?

A man sat three rows behind her. She tried to catch his eye, but his expression hardened and he looked away.

Everyone looked away.

Kaitlyn turned back to the window. Open land rushed by, mocking her prison.

She blinked rapidly. She dared not show weakness. "Tickets?"

She suppressed a start at the voice so close to her shoulder. Maybe Michael hadn't felt the slight movement. He had to know she was on edge, but no need to give him more of an upper hand.

He reached into his jacket and pulled out two slips of paper, making sure she could see the gun tucked into his pants.

As if she needed reminding.

The conductor left. Michael leaned close. "Good girl," he murmured, his breath humid against her cheek.

She swallowed hard and tried to move closer to the wall, but there was no space, no way to get away from him. Even the few inches she gained, he erased by moving closer.

Kaitlyn leaned against the window next to her. She was right back where she'd started. When would she learn? Nothing stopped her brother. Not distance, not laws, not even marriage vows. She'd gambled, and she'd lost.

Except this time she'd lost more than herself. She'd lost her family.

She let herself drift into memories of the ranch. Of David after riding Phantom. Jo refusing to do penmanship. Tillie asking if Kaitlyn's shoes were made of glass.

And Drew. Always Drew.

"Thought she could get the best of me."

She didn't allow Michael's mutters to pull her from her dreams. At least she'd known happiness for a little while. She could guarantee she never would again. Her brother would see to that.

Eighteen

DREW BURIED HIS HEAD IN HIS HANDS, the stingy mattress on the jail cell cot feeling like it was stuffed with rocks. The echo of Quade's boots had barely faded.

Everything had gone wrong. Ed's homestead. Without it, they couldn't support the herd.

Kaitlyn.

She'd left.

Mistake.

Air wheezed into his chest. He wanted to curl into a ball on the cot, but that would require moving. He didn't have the energy. Or the willpower. Or something.

Except he couldn't give up. The kids needed him. He forced himself to his feet and closer to the cell bars. "Wallace, where are my children?"

The deputy's face whitened. "You don't know?"

Fury surged through Drew. "You arrested their father and

uncles, escorted their stepmother to the train, and didn't even stop to think about where they were?" He gripped the bars, his knuckles white. He wanted to shake them, kick them, reach through them and shake the deputy who hadn't given a thought to his kids. None of that would get them help faster. "You need to let me out." The words were gritted out between clenched teeth. "I have to find them."

Ed joined him, close enough to the bars for his belt buckle to clink against them. "Didn't you hear the threat to our homestead? What if the children are there when they burn the house?"

Uncertainty flashed across the young deputy's face before his expression hardened into determination. "I can't let you out, but as soon as my backup gets here, we'll round up men to find the children. Besides, the only thing that might have been a threat came from Riley, and he's in the next cell."

"Yeah, McGraw. What threat am I, behind bars like this?" Riley snickered. "Not like *I* can tell my friends to burn anything."

Drew didn't move. Oh, he heard the emphasis Duncan placed on the word *I*. But why respond to a taunting implication when he already recognized the danger? Quade would send his men to Ed's place soon. Drew couldn't stop it.

Please, God, let it be soon, before my kids get there. Don't let Isaac try to stop it. Not by himself. Just help him protect the kids.

Where were his children? Not on the train, or Wallace would have told him. Surely.

No, they were in town. Somewhere. A neighbor would keep them safe. Physically, anyway. They had to be frightened. Barclay, Merritt, Pastor Carson—someone would protect them.

But it was his job, and he wasn't doing it. One more failure.

Someone sat beside him. "I don't understand it." Nick's voice sounded the same as when he hadn't been able to solve a math problem back in school. The wooden bed frame creaked as he leaned back against the wall. "Why would she go with him?"

Because the ranch wasn't enough.

And neither was he.

The door from the street creaked open, and footsteps rushed across the floor. Light footsteps. Children's footsteps?

He looked up. Merritt was closing the door halfway, letting some air into the stale jail. Tillie rushed to the cell bars, tears streaking her face.

Drew sagged against the cell bars. They were safe. He blinked a few times.

Tillie placed her hands on the bars, but didn't quite manage to meet his eyes. Drew summoned his own smile and held his hand through the bars for her to take. "It's gonna be okay, princess."

"But Pa, Kaitlyn's the princess, and she's gone."

"We'll be okay without her." And they would. Eventually.

Jo moved closer. He looked at his middle daughter and his heart missed a beat. Or several. Jo's eyes were red. She'd been crying. Jo never cried. And he was stuck in here where he couldn't help.

"We're not the ones in danger, Pa." Jo's voice wavered. More tears streamed down her face, and her shoulders hitched with a partially swallowed sob.

Someone in danger? David? Drew quickly looked around. No, there was his son, standing next to Merritt. David wouldn't meet Drew's eyes, and he shifted his weight restlessly from one foot to the other, but he was safe. Drew signaled Merritt to move closer.

"Pa, you gotta listen!" Jo shouted the words, if a sob-drenched voice could be said to shout.

"Tell me, Jo." He ran his hand along her head, and the tears she'd been fighting won. Tillie's knees folded and she sank to the floor, but Jo still stood. She'd be better able to explain. "Deep breaths, Jo, in and out."

Conchas chuckled. "Look, he even has to tell them how to breathe."

Wallace glared at the cowhand. "That's enough out of you. Silence, or I'll make sure you stay a few days longer." Then he stopped next to Jo and put a hand under her elbow. "You can lean on me, iffen you need to."

Fire returned to Jo's eyes. "Ain't you the one who put my Pa in there? I reckon you done helped enough!" Tears still ran down her cheeks, but her voice was steadier.

Wallace stepped back from her, his expression set and his legs planted wide. "You can stay a few more minutes, then you gotta go. This ain't no hotel."

Drew laid a hand on Jo's shoulder. "Tell me what happened, Jo."

"Kaitlyn s-saved us, P-Pa."

What?

Jo's neck worked as she swallowed another sob. "A b-bad man had a g-gun. He grabbed Tillie. Kaitlyn plowed into him, t-told us to run. B-but she didn't get away."

"What if he shoots her?" Tillie wailed.

A gun. Anger ran like fire through his veins. Someone had pointed a gun at Kaitlyn. His Kaitlyn. His wife. Drew glared at Wallace. "You said there wasn't a gun."

The deputy's brow furrowed. "There wasn't. And I took her several yards from her brother. Plenty far enough for her to feel safe. Be safe."

Drew shook his head, his mind racing. Wallace was right. Except . . . He sorted and discarded possibilities until . . . "Were the kids nearby when you found them?"

Wallace shook his head.

"So he had plenty of time to threaten the children before you got there."

Jo stepped closer to him, her breath shuddering in and out. "Why'd she do that, Pa? Go with him so we'd be safe."

Because she cared more about their safety than her own. But Jo needed to come to that conclusion on her own.

"Why do you think?" he asked his middle daughter.

One more tear ran down Jo's cheek. "'Cause she loves us."

Drew nodded, the certainty flowing soul-deep. Kaitlyn loved those kids. Enough to sacrifice herself for them. He thought back over her message to him. *Mistake.* She loved him enough to use the one word sure to push him away, to make sure he focused on the kids.

Maybe even to protect him.

His shoulders shook. She loved him enough to put herself into the hands of a madman, just so he would be safe. How could he have doubted her?

David moved next to his sisters. "What're we gonna do, Pa? I couldn't save her. I tried, but I couldn't . . ."

"David, you did good. You're growing into a man that folks can depend on. But you're not a man yet, and no one expects you to be. As for what we're going to do? Wallace here is going to let us out of this cell, and we're going to rescue my wife."

"Who says I'm letting you out?" Wallace puffed his chest out and raised his chin.

"I do." Danna slid through the half-open door. Her voice had Wallace whirling to face her. "Or at least, I probably will, once I have a few answers."

She turned to the McGraws. "I heard the children. Seems like you have a few problems. Kaitlyn's brother came to town?"

"Yes, and he has her."

She tapped her fingers on her thigh. "And why are you a guest of my fine establishment?"

Riley leaped to his feet. "Why don't you ask us that?"

The rest of Quade's men added their thoughts to the commotion. Then Ed and Nick joined in.

Danna demanded silence and then signaled Drew to continue. He quickly filled her in about the scuffle caused by both groups supposedly thinking they were protecting Kaitlyn. He promised to return in time to face any charges brought if she would release him to find his wife.

In a matter of moments, the McGraws were out of their cell. Wallace returned the guns he'd taken from them.

Drew turned to his cousin. "Merritt, can you keep the kids?"

Merritt agreed.

Danna led the way out of the jail. "The train pulled out quite a while ago. I'm going to send telegrams to the sheriff's offices along the railway. No way you can catch up."

How long had Kaitlyn already spent with Michael? Two hours? More? She'd have new bruises, no doubt. But Michael couldn't shoot her. Not in front of a train full of witnesses. "She'll get off the train somehow. I've got to be there when she does." He swallowed hard. Away from the train, it'd be easier for her brother to get her by herself. He had to find her before that happened. He never should have doubted her.

Ed stepped up next to Drew, Nick close behind. "*We've* got to be there, Drew. Not you. *We.*"

We. What a beautiful word. The bands around Drew's chest relaxed a fraction to allow a slightly deeper breath. He wasn't in this alone.

Maybe he never had been.

It was hopeless.

A porter passed by their seat, but Kaitlyn didn't try to catch his eye. What was the point? He wouldn't believe her. No one ever had.

No one except Drew.

Yeah, and look how that'd ended. Kaitlyn closed her

mind to the still, small voice she had begun to think she could trust. Look where trust had gotten her.

Michael nudged her shoulder.

She didn't look away from the sun-drenched prairie outside the window. It was easier to pretend she was free if she couldn't see him. Imagining herself far away had saved her sanity when he'd locked her in the storage room back home.

A clatter drew her attention to the seat across the aisle. The boy had dropped his toy soldier. He picked it up and hugged it to himself, just like Tillie had hugged her doll. Jo and David had loved the bridles she'd brought, and Drew had loved his hats.

He'd worn the dark Stetson while he'd worked on Ed's cabin, at least until the sun had gone down. When she'd asked him to stop and eat, he'd said this was going to be a new chapter in the McGraw family legacy. He couldn't give up. McGraws didn't quit.

McGraw. Drew had given her a new name.

She was a McGraw. Drew never gave up. She couldn't either.

But she'd have to wait for her opportunity.

The car swayed, and Kaitlyn brushed against Michael. Hard to ignore him when he sat so close. Her stomach complained, since she'd missed lunch. Michael hadn't brought any food with them. Dinner was a long time away. She settled in to wait. It wasn't the first time she'd gone without. Probably wouldn't be the last.

Her brother shifted again, then eased his pistol into his coat pocket and poked her with the barrel. "If you weren't so valuable, I'd take care of you right here." He snickered. "At least you've caused me the last trouble you ever will. Brian is just the man to teach a woman how to behave. I'm looking forward to watching."

Kaitlyn glared at him. "What will you do when you go into debt all over again with no sister to sell off?"

He poked her with the gun barrel harder. "Shut up."

She turned her back to him.

The porter came through again. "Next stop, Blackthorn. Blackthorn, ten minutes."

She didn't take her eyes from the window but felt someone's gaze on her. A man's reflection flashed across the window. She glanced over her shoulder. The man who had been a few seats behind them had moved across the aisle to be behind the mother and little boy. He'd looked puzzled in the brief moment a trick of the changing light allowed his image to be seen. Inwardly, she shrugged. She'd never understood her brother either.

The constant bumping emphasized another need. She was going to have to find a toilet.

And wasn't Michael going to love that. Still, he could hardly keep her chained to his side for the entire three-day trip. Could that be her chance?

She nudged his arm. "I need the lavatory."

"Hold it."

"It's a three-day trip, Michael. I'm going to need the water closet before we get back to St. Louis." So would he, for that matter, but she'd hardly gain points by pointing it out.

She met his narrowed gaze easily. She'd had a lot of practice. Finally, he stood and gestured for her to precede him toward the back of the car.

Her pulse raced, and her mouth dried. She walked slowly, trying to see everything without moving her head. Eventually, Michael would get less vigilant with her restroom breaks. She'd need to be ready.

Or could this be her chance? The train's sway would make his balance uncertain. Could she take advantage of that?

The man who'd been watching cleared his throat as they walked by, but she ignored him. Even if he wanted to help, he'd only get a bullet for his trouble. With all the potential witnesses in front of them and facing forward, Michael could spin any story he wanted. He probably wouldn't even be arrested.

They reached the back of the car, and Michael opened a door. Kaitlyn glanced inside, then tried to step back. This was a small office, probably for the mail clerk. Hands centered on her back and gave a hard shove. Pain flared through her knees as she hit the floor. Michael slammed the door behind her.

No windows. The darkness swallowed her. Her breath came in pants. She stifled the sob that wanted to escape. The walls closed in around her, and her stomach lurched. There was no way out. There never had been. She'd been lying to herself, and in the process had torn down a good man and his family.

The air grew heavy, suffocating.

Breathe, Kaitlyn. It felt like inhaling syrup. *Breathe in. Breathe out.* She started the chant that had gotten her through years of confined spaces, but her lungs refused to respond.

She was going to die here. Tears ran down her cheeks.

The train whistle split the air, and the clickety-clack of the wheels slowed.

Kaitlyn curled into a ball, pulling her knees to her chest. No one would help her. She didn't matter. She never had.

You matter to me, daughter.

Kaitlyn stilled. Images of Drew flooded her mind. *Family sticks*, he'd told Jo. That was what a father was supposed to do.

God would do more. So much more.

Maybe God hadn't forgotten her when He'd left her with Michael. He'd eventually led her to Drew. Kaitlyn gathered every scrap of faith she could find in her soul.

What do I do?

Trust. And don't quit.

The train slowed more. They were approaching a town. Maybe someone could hear her. "Help me. Someone help me." She pounded on the wall, kicked it, anything to make noise. Someone had to hear her. "Please, someone help me."

A voice responded. One from inside the car. "Mister, I don't think she wants to be in there."

The other passenger. God had put him there. She pounded again. "Please help me."

Michael spoke, but she couldn't understand his words. Not over the pounding of her own heart. "Help me. Please help me."

The sounds of a scuffle echoed through Kaitlyn's prison. She pushed against the door.

It moved.

Her brother was out there. He might catch her again. He might hurt her more. Might even kill her.

She left the storeroom. She might die, but Michael didn't control her anymore.

She mattered.

She swept the train car in a glance. Her brother had backed the stranger toward the front of the car. The stranger caught her eye, then gave the slightest nod toward the exit. The rocking of the car was so slight that they must be entering a station. She could survive a jump at this speed.

She slipped through the exit onto the end platform. The wind plastered her skirt to her legs. The train was moving slowly but hadn't stopped. The station was so close, with the town beyond it. She shook her head. That would be the first place Michael would look.

She turned the other direction and launched herself off the platform.

Nineteen

PLEASE LET HER BE HERE.

Drew pulled back Solomon's reins as he passed the first shops of Blackthorn. "Easy, boy. We're here now." Solomon slowed to a walk. His breath shuddered. The horse had given his all on this trip. His brothers reined their mounts in as well. All the horses needed to be walked, rubbed down, watered, and rested. He had time for none of it.

Kaitlyn needed him.

His brothers moved closer. "How are Lightning and Surrey?"

Ed rubbed Lightning's neck. "He's got more to give, considering the circumstances."

Solomon sidestepped. *Circumstances.* What a simple word to cover Kaitlyn in the hands of a madman. She had to be terrified. Better than anyone, she knew what her brother was capable of. Had she managed to get off the train? Had

Michael followed her? Where would she hide in a town she didn't know? Find help in a town shut down for the night?

Nick urged his horse up next to Solomon. "Surrey is tired, but he can go a bit farther. We need to search the town."

An uneasy peace settled into Drew. If Michael wanted Kaitlyn's inheritance, he couldn't kill her before she signed it over to him. He'd have to find a judge to witness the transaction. That gave Drew time to find her. This town, or the next, or the one after that—it didn't matter. He'd find her.

Just stay alive, sweetheart. I'm coming.

The town was dark, empty. As would be expected at eight o'clock at night. The train should have pulled out two hours ago. Had it been dark when she arrived? Getting there, probably. Where would she go?

Nick laid a hand on his shoulder. "She's at the sheriff's office. She'd feel safe there."

Ed frowned. "After Wallace locked us up for protecting her? Not likely. She'll seek people. The hotel. Or maybe the church." He stopped a man passing by. "Your church hold evening services?"

The man shook his head.

There went that idea. But Kaitlyn wouldn't seek crowds. Too many people had let her down. The parsonage? Maybe. Or would she hide? "There's too much ground to cover."

Ed pulled his hat off and ran a hand through his hair. "Danna's bringing help, but it'll take a while for her to round up enough men."

A polite way of saying that no one in town wanted to

side against Quade. Help would be an hour behind them at least. Maybe more. They couldn't wait that long. "Nick, check the sheriff's office. Ed, the hotel. I'll try the parsonage. But keep your eyes open. If her brother followed her, she may simply hide. We'll meet at the hotel."

Nick and Ed split off in different directions. Drew followed a side street that ran behind Main Street. The backs of businesses lay on his left and small houses on his right. Only a little light from the saloon and hotel reached this far. His eyes slowly adjusted to the gloom.

Something rustled, then scurried in the garbage behind what must be a restaurant, judging by the aromas. A back door opened. He swiveled in the saddle only to swallow Kaitlyn's name before it could escape. A shopkeeper waved a hand before adding wood from broken-down crates onto a pile.

Drew turned to the houses on the other side of the street. Windows glowed from hurricane lanterns, but no sounds escaped. The wind picked up, rubbing tree limbs against the building next to him.

A twig snapped. Drew spun to gaze into the alley between the two stores beside him. There. A shadow moved.

There was someone back there.

A shoe sole scuffed against a rock. The shadow slipped closer to a huddle of blue leaning against the wall.

Blue. Kaitlyn's dress was blue.

Every muscle stiffened, then he flung himself from Solomon, not even taking time to ground tie him. That was Kaitlyn. He knew it was. He ran down the alleyway.

The shadow slunk closer to Kaitlyn. Michael. It had to

be. It grabbed Kaitlyn's arm and yanked her to her feet. "Did you really think you could escape me?"

Drew hit Michael at a dead run. The other man stumbled away from Kaitlyn. His Kaitlyn. How he wanted to check with her, see how she was, but he didn't dare take his eyes off the man in front of him. Drew's hand dropped to his holster, but he didn't draw his gun. Michael had held a gun on Kaitlyn in Calvin. Drawing his own would only escalate this, and he didn't want Kaitlyn anywhere near a gun fight.

Michael shoved him. He took a step back and heard Kaitlyn stumble, then hit the ground. "Drew! He has a gun!" Her voice shook. Was she okay? He caught a movement from the corner of his eye too late to dodge Michael's punch to his gut. His breath wheezed out, and pain flared.

Michael pulled a gun from his jacket pocket.

The blood froze in Drew's veins, but his body didn't wait for instructions. He threw his shoulder into the smaller man's stomach and wrapped both hands around the gun. He should have drawn while he'd had the chance.

Sounds came from behind him. The scuffle of boots gaining a foothold. Kaitlyn was standing. "Down, Katie. Get down!"

"Michael, stop! It's over." Kaitlyn's voice echoed through the alley.

Footsteps pounded away down Main Street's boardwalk. Going to get the sheriff? He could only hope. Nick might still be there too. The more reinforcements, the better.

Michael tried to pull his gun free. "It's not over until I say it is. You've ruined everything." He brought his other hand up toward Drew's face. Drew dodged his attempt to gouge his eye but didn't manage to avoid the fingernails on his cheek.

Michael slipped his gun hand free and fired. The shot went wide.

Drew charged Michael and wrapped him in a bear hug. "Run, Kaitlyn! Find Ed and Nick!"

"She ain't going nowhere." Michael lifted the gun and brought the butt down onto Drew's head.

Stars exploded behind his eyes. No! He couldn't pass out. He tightened his grip. He couldn't let go.

God, help me!

His fist crashed into Michael's gut, then his face. Somehow, he didn't feel the impact. He punched again. And again.

This beast had hurt Kaitlyn. *Crash.*

Bruised her. *Crash.*

Frightened her. *Crash.*

Now his knuckles stung, but he ignored them.

Michael dropped the gun. Drew grabbed it and aimed it at Michael. "This ends. Now."

Michael froze. A door opened, letting light into the alley. Drew met Michael's gaze. A predator's gaze, but worse. Evil lurked in those eyes.

Kaitlyn stepped up beside Drew. Her lavender scent untied the knots in his gut. She was safe. Alive. He spared her a quick glance. The bruise on her cheek sent fury racing through him. His finger moved to the trigger. "Maybe I'll just shoot him."

Kaitlyn laid a cool hand on his arm. "Drew, no. Think about the kids."

He pulled in a shuddering breath. Another. She was right. He wasn't a murderer. And he wasn't going to let Michael turn him into one. "Your sister is more merciful than I am." He drew in another steadying breath. "It's time to let this go. Kaitlyn is my wife. All we want is a peaceful life."

"What about what I want?" Michael shouted. "Kaitlyn is set to marry my friend."

"It's too late for that. She's already married to me."

Nick entered the alley and stopped in the splash of light from the open shop door. "Drew? Kaitlyn? Are you okay? We heard a shot."

Drew glanced toward his brother. Michael lunged forward, knocking the gun aside. He raced toward the back of the alley, heading toward Solomon, Nick and Ed on his heels.

It seemed to happen in slow motion. Michael put his foot in the stirrup. When he stepped up, attempting to get into the saddle, Solomon danced sideways. The movement jostled Michael, who tried to hang on to the saddle. Solomon kicked his hind feet in the air, sending Michael flying.

There was an audible thud when he landed.

Ed got to him first, knelt to check for a pulse. Then he stood and stopped Nick from checking, shaking his head.

Drew swallowed hard, then turned Kaitlyn into his chest. If his brothers had left Michael, the man no longer had to worry about facing a jury of his peers. Instead, he stood before the ultimate judge.

Kaitlyn shuddered in his arms.

A deputy rode up beside Solomon, dismounted, and examined Michael's body. Then he led his horse through the alley and stopped next to Nick and Ed. Their words didn't reach Drew, and he didn't care. His world was in his arms.

Kaitlyn's arms tightened around his waist. "Is he . . ."

He rubbed his cheek across the top of her head, her hair catching in his stubble. "He's gone. He won't bother you ever again."

She sobbed. "I d-didn't w-want it t-to end this way."

"I know, sweetheart. I know."

Her tears wet his shirt. He rubbed her back soothingly, the warmth of her in his arms reminding him she was alive. "It's over. At least now it's over."

It was over.

He'd lost Ed's homestead, but Katie was safe. That was all the victory he needed.

Kaitlyn couldn't stop shaking.

She buried her face in her husband's chest, the tears seemingly unstoppable. Drew's arms surrounded her, enveloped her. Warmth flooded her heart. He had come for her.

Drew's arms tightened around her. Strong from hard work providing for his family. Protecting his loved ones. She leaned against him, and he let her, didn't move away.

His hand ran down her spine, then up to her nape. His fingers dug into her hair. "Shh, now. It's over. Everything's over."

A shuddering breath escaped her. Michael was dead. She had lived her entire life in fear of him, and now he was gone.

It didn't feel as wonderful as she would have guessed. She had never wanted him dead.

She forced another deep breath, and sobs quieted, though the tears still flowed.

Thank You, God, for sending Drew.

There was no place she'd rather be than in her husband's arms. "I pushed you away, but you still came," she murmured.

He guided her toward the main street and tilted her head so the light fell on her cheek. He ran his finger across the mark that Michael had left. "I should have got here sooner."

She leaned back to look into his eyes. Warm, gray eyes. Loving eyes? She leaned toward him, her heart warming. Could it be?

His hand tightened on her waist in a brief caress. "I knew you'd find a way off that train. My clever, clever girl."

His praise filled a deep pit inside her soul. A pit dug by all the times she'd been told not to discuss anything more important than the latest fashion. That men didn't want women who thought for themselves. Maybe she'd had to travel a thousand miles to find a man with the confidence to let her be herself, but it had been worth the trip.

She ran a finger along the red marks her brother had left on Drew's cheek. "How'd you know?"

"I knew you." He smiled. "Didn't know for sure you'd manage it this soon, but that didn't matter. If you weren't here, I'd have checked the next town, and the next, all the way to St. Louis if I had to."

She grinned impishly. "Think Solomon could carry you that far?"

"I know he would. He wanted you back near as much as I did. Did you think I didn't notice the treats you slipped him?"

Kaitlyn's cheeks warmed. "I needed someone to help me hide my mistakes in the kitchen." She froze as her comment echoed in her mind. *Mistake.* She pulled away from him slightly. He hadn't heard what she'd said back in Calvin. He wouldn't be here if he had.

The deputy moved toward them. "The sheriff will want to take statements from both of you in his office."

Drew pulled Kaitlyn close. "We'll be there shortly. As soon as my wife catches her breath."

My wife. Would he still call her that if he knew?

The deputy swept her with a glance. Somehow, she knew he hadn't missed her tears or the bruise on her cheek, even in the low light from the surrounding buildings. "Quicker is better though. Less time to dread it that way."

Drew nodded.

Less time to dread it. There was wisdom in that statement. She gathered the shreds of her courage that remained after escaping her brother and faced her husband. "I have to tell you something." Her cheeks burned, and her gaze dropped to the ground.

"Okay."

"I, um, said some things to the deputy back in Calvin. Things I, well, things I didn't mean."

He tugged her back into his embrace. "Shh, Kaitlyn. I know."

She shook her head. He couldn't know. She had to tell him. "I was trying to—"

He stepped back just enough that he could lift her chin with his finger. His gaze met hers steadily. "Protect me and the kids. Kaitlyn, I know."

His emphasis on the last two words arrowed into her heart. His eyes remained warm and loving. He did know, and there was no anger anywhere in his expression. More tears found their way down her cheeks, but her smile stretched wide. She melted against him, finding her home in his embrace. He knew, and he'd come after her anyway.

"If I'm completely honest, I have to say I believed it at first. I had to calm down before I could realize that I knew you better than that. Knew you would do whatever it took to keep the kids safe. To keep the ranch safe. Even say the one thing guaranteed to make me turn away from you toward them."

The ranch. Her smile fell, and she stepped back from him. Chills traveled over her skin. *Oh, Lord, the ranch.* "If you and Ed and Nick came after me . . ."

He nodded, his eyes serious. "We won't be able to finish the cabin. Quade won. But Kaitlyn, I have you. I won too."

"I'm so sorry, Drew." Her voice trembled and her throat grew tight.

"I'm not. When we walked out of that jail, the choice was the homestead or you. I didn't have to think about that, not even for a split second. There is always more land. There is only one you."

He pulled her closer again, and his warmth seeped into the cold places in her heart. He rubbed his cheek against her hair. "I love you, Kaitlyn. I told myself to wait until the cabin was finished, till I could give you my full attention and convince you how I felt. But the truth is, I was scared. Scared of opening my heart again."

She pulled back a bit and saw a flicker of uncertainty in his expression. She laid a hand against his cheek, fingering the marks he'd gotten fighting for her. "I was scared too. Scared I wouldn't be enough for you. For the kids."

"How could you not be enough? You're everything, Kaitlyn. My everything."

He rubbed a tear away with his thumb, his calloused hand rough against her cheek. She turned her face into the caress as warmth flooded her soul. Protection. Acceptance. Love. Understanding. It was all there in his gaze, his touch. "Oh, Drew, I love you so much!"

He kissed her forehead. Her cheek. The tip of her nose. She rose on tiptoe as he lowered his head to hers, his lips firm against hers. She felt commitment in that kiss. Homecoming.

He raised his head enough to whisper, "I want this to be a real marriage. A marriage with love at its center."

A smile spread across her face, and her eyes brightened with joy. "I want that too. So much."

Later, much later, she snuggled next to him in a hotel bed, her cheek resting on his chest, her mind drifting over the eventful day.

She'd never thought she'd feel grateful for brothers, but Nick and Ed were nothing like Michael. She might not know Isaac as well, but she knew enough to know he wasn't either. When Ed had hugged her to welcome her to the family, he'd whispered, "I've never seen my brother so happy. The cabin doesn't matter. Don't you give it another thought."

Except how was she supposed to do that? It was supposed to be his home, and he was her family now. There had to be a way. Maybe they could try to prove up a different piece of land. She bit her lip. Or . . .

"Drew, what happens to the land if we can't prove it up?"

Drew blinked awake from the pillow next to hers. "Hmm—what?" His voice was still rough from sleep.

She sat up, tugging the blankets around her shoulders. "It goes up for sale, right?"

Drew nodded.

Her grip tightened on the blankets. "The bank will be open, and my money is there. What if we buy the land before anyone else can?"

Drew looked thoughtful for a moment, then he smiled. "The land office is in Calvin."

"Then I guess we'd best get moving, Mr. McGraw."

Twenty

"KAITLYN!"

Kaitlyn looked up to see Tillie scampering down Merritt's steps, the midmorning sun glinting from her dark braids. Yesterday, she'd wondered if she would ever see this child again. She pulled her hand from Drew's and stepped in front of him just in time to catch Tillie. Warmth flooded her at the embrace of this little girl who had accepted her from the first. The little girl she loved as her very own. She ran her fingers through Tillie's hair.

"Don't have to be a card sharp to read that welcome," Jack murmured behind her.

Drew chuckled.

Tillie looked up, her smile stretching nearly from ear to ear. "The bad guy didn't getted you." The smile dimmed a bit. "I thought he hurted you."

Boots clattered on Merritt's porch steps. David rushed toward them, followed by Nick and Ed. Merritt made her way to stand beside her husband. Jo trailed the group more slowly and hung off to the side.

Nick grinned at Kaitlyn. "Well, did you get it done?"

Kaitlyn nodded. "Thanks for coming here with Ed to let the children know we were safe, and for sending Jack. Having a deputy there kept everyone on their best behavior."

David edged a bit closer. Kaitlyn shifted Tillie to a one-armed hug and opened her other arm to the boy. Her son. He rushed to her and threw his arms around her. He seemed to have grown in the last two months. Another year and he'd be taller than she was.

The boy's brow wrinkled. "I was so worried."

"I bet you took good care of your sisters."

He nodded.

"Good job. I'm proud of you."

He smiled shyly and pulled her back into a bear hug, surreptitiously rubbing a tear from his cheek. She whispered "I'll never tell" into his ear. He grinned and backed away.

Drew took Kaitlyn's hand and pulled her to stand next to him, his calloused palm a perfect fit against her softer one. "What's more, there'll be no more talk of her leaving. I love her, and she's more than proved she's tough enough for our West."

Tillie squealed, then looked up at Kaitlyn. "You're staying, Kaitlyn? You'll be my ma for real? Can I call you Ma?"

Kaitlyn smiled at the little girl. "If you want to. I love your pa, and I'm staying."

Ed stepped closer to them. "'Bout time you two got things figured out. We've all known you loved each other for ages."

Nick slapped Drew's shoulder. "Yeah. It's not like you did that great a job hiding it."

Drew shoved against Ed's shoulder, but he put very little effort into it, and his smile made it all the way to his eyes. Like it had ever since they'd declared their love for each other. Like she hoped it would for the rest of their lives.

Kaitlyn glanced to the side of the yard, where Jo still stood off by herself. That would never do. It was high time Jo knew her place in this family and in Kaitlyn's heart. Kaitlyn left Tillie and crossed the yard to where Jo stood. "I'm not going to try to take the place of your mother."

Jo nodded, not meeting her eyes.

Kaitlyn's arms ached to hug this child, but she would let Jo move at her own pace. "Were you hurt yesterday? I know you must've been scared."

Jo's lip quivered and her eyes were bright with tears she still fought.

Slowly, Kaitlyn held out her arms. Jo's face crumpled, and she flung her thin arms around Kaitlyn's waist, and what remained of Kaitlyn's heart melted. She rubbed a hand over Jo's head and down to her shoulder.

After only a moment, Jo stepped back, but Kaitlyn knew that moment would be engraved on her heart for the rest of her life.

Jo wiped her eyes. "You went with him to save us."

Remembered fear knocked at her mind, but Kaitlyn refused to open the door. Michael was gone. God had protected them all. "I did. I was so worried about you."

Jo inhaled, then released the air in a shudder. "You're really staying."

"Yes. I love your father. And I love you."

Jo scrubbed a hand across her cheek. Kaitlyn reached across and gently wiped one tear the little girl had missed. Jo turned into the caress. "I wasn't crying."

"Of course not."

Jo smiled at her. Not the malicious smile Kaitlyn had seen so often when she'd burned biscuits or fallen in the calves' stall. No, this smile held only joy and hope.

Kaitlyn felt Drew's gaze on her and glanced over her shoulder to meet his eyes. His loving eyes. He looked at her, then Jo, then back at her. His smile grew broader. Kaitlyn took Jo's hand and guided her to join the rest of the family.

Drew turned back to Merritt. "It was Kaitlyn's brilliant idea. Since we didn't prove up the homestead, it was available for purchase. Jack rousted Ernie Duff from his bed before the sun was up. Kaitlyn brought the banker and bought the land free and clear."

"Ed's land is yours now?" Jo's brow furrowed.

Kaitlyn tugged her closer. "Ed's homestead is ours. It's McGraw land, and the McGraw herd will run there, just like it did before. There is no mine and yours, only ours."

"That's just as it should be." Merritt winked.

Drew moved closer to Kaitlyn and took her hand. Would she ever get tired of holding his hand?

Ed bumped Drew's shoulder. "Did Quade show up?"

Drew nodded, his satisfied grin stretching almost as wide as Tillie's had.

Kaitlyn smiled too. It had been so satisfying to see Quade show up, ready to buy the land, only to see them leaving the land office after purchasing it. When they'd asked Mr.

Duff the price, he'd frowned and stalled but ultimately had no choice but to sell it to them.

Quade had been furious, but they had bought the land fair and square. They still had time to prove up Nick's and Isaac's homesteads, and her inheritance could buy the supplies they'd need to do it. The house in St. Louis would probably be sold to cover Michael's debts, but his death and the finalized deed to Ed's land removed the threat to the children.

"It's all because of Kaitlyn." Drew brought her hand to his lips. Her cheeks warmed, and he smiled at her, then lowered their hands. "We were all focused on getting the land through homesteading. It took a brilliant outsider to see an opportunity in the disaster of missing the deadline."

Murmurs of "great job" and "genius" and "wish I'd seen it" made her heart light. Not that she was really brilliant. Learning to observe carefully had been her protection from Michael.

Protection from Michael.

Lord, You did that. You gave me the skill and taught me to hone it. And now it has saved the first place I've ever really called home.

She felt Him smiling down at her as she realized His gift. What Michael had done was not good, but God had brought good from it, just as He promised.

He'd restored to her what she'd never had. A family and a place of her own.

Later that night, Drew leaned back into the sofa. Nick

and Ed had settled into the chairs across from it. Drew stretched out his legs and let his head fall back. Home. He was in his own home, Nick and Ed nearby. All the men had left their boots at the door to protect Kaitlyn's spotless floors.

Isaac had stopped in earlier to congratulate him but said he'd ride out to keep an eye on the herd. Someone had tried to take a few head while he'd been here alone, but he'd stopped them.

Drew wasn't fooled. His next younger brother was still feeling stifled inside four walls. Whatever wounds he carried hadn't healed.

But for now, Drew's herd had land to graze, his house was no longer at risk, his family was safe, and his wife had ingredients to put food on the table.

His wife. Katie.

Her voice floated down the stairs to the men in the parlor as she tucked covers around his little girls.

Ed nudged Nick and grinned, his eyes sparking mischief. "Reckon we'll be moving Kaitlyn's stuff back downstairs. Think that closet is big enough for her things as well as Drew's?"

Nick frowned at Ed. "Kaitlyn isn't Amanda. She's not gonna need a lot of extra space for doodads."

Drew smiled. Kaitlyn wasn't Amanda, that was for sure, but she might just need a little more space than he and his brothers did. That was okay. He'd gladly frame in another closet if she wanted. This was her home too, after all.

Ed nudged Drew's outstretched foot with his own. "You

should hide that silly grin. Someone might think you're in love with your wife."

Kaitlyn's footsteps paused on the stairs. Was she waiting to hear his answer? That was okay. He'd say it as often as she needed to hear it. He might still prefer actions, but the words weren't that hard. "They'd be right. I am in love with my wife. Then they'd be jealous that I have such an extraordinary woman to be in love with."

Kaitlyn entered the room, then settled in next to him on the sofa. "The kids are all in bed."

He threw an arm over her shoulders and pulled her in close. Blonde tendrils escaped and tickled his chin. The scent of lavender soothed him. Maybe he'd plant her a lavender patch. Who knew? They might even be able to sell the excess. But if it only made his bride smile, he'd be sufficiently recompensed.

A wolf howled in the distance. Drew cocked his head. "That sounded close. We'll have to put out some traps."

Nick rolled his shoulders, then leaned in closer to Drew. "They aren't the only threat. Quade won't give up so easy."

"Not much he can do," Ed replied. "We bought the homestead free and clear, and we have plenty of time and supplies for the others."

Drew scowled. "He fights dirty. He paid his cowhands to distract us so Michael could get Kaitlyn to the train." He rubbed his hand along Kaitlyn's arm. "A man's pretty low-down if he takes the fight to the women and children."

Nick and Ed nodded, their expressions serious.

Drew sighed. "We need Isaac."

Ed scoffed. "He ain't been much use lately."

That was true. When he'd joined the U.S. Marshals, Isaac had been so self-assured he'd bordered on cocky. He'd come home withdrawn and quiet.

Drew had promised his ma that he'd take care of his brothers, but he hadn't promised he'd do it alone. "Isaac's suffering. What do you think we can do to help?"

Nick caught his eye. "You need to talk to him, find out what happened. He'll listen to you, Drew. Ed and I are just pesky little brothers."

Drew nodded slowly. Maybe he needed to make it a point to spend some time with Isaac. They'd always been close as kids.

Ed put down his coffee cup. "He's too stubborn to listen to anyone."

"He's not the only stubborn one." Nick glared at Ed. "I saw you arguing with Rebekah outside the store. When are you gonna let that grudge go?"

Ed glared right back. "About the time she does."

Drew smothered a smile. That old schoolroom feud was funny to everyone but Ed. Kaitlyn moved closer, and Drew took her hand with his free hand, entwined their fingers. She laid her head against his shoulder.

Nick stood up. "It's been a long day. I hear my bunk calling me."

Ed chuckled. "Subtle, Nick. Real subtle." But he picked up the empty cup he'd left by his feet and stood. Then he caught Drew's gaze. "Whatever changed Isaac has to be big, and it's eating him up inside. If he'll talk to anyone, it'll be you." He left through the back door, Nick right behind him.

Kaitlyn snuggled closer, and he tightened his hold on her. His wife. What had he ever done to deserve this moment with her in his arms?

"Jo wants to try riding the colt again," she murmured.

He chuckled. "Of course she does. But she's gonna have to grow some, get a little stronger. Meantime, maybe you can teach her that things inside the house are just as important."

"The ranch is in her blood. But I think she liked the fabric we picked for her dress." She grinned up at him. "It wasn't pink, after all."

He leaned down to kiss her, her soft lips still tasting of coffee and pie. Slowly, he drew back. "I'm so glad you found that letter. When you arrived, I couldn't believe God would send me another city girl. If I could have seen this moment, I would have rushed you to the pastor that very night."

"Think how I feel. He gave me you and an entire family."

"But Katie, before you got here, we were just a bunch of people related by blood. You made us a family."

He lowered his head, felt her soft lips again, and knew she was the best blessing he could ever hope for.

Bonus Epilogue

Are you are member of our new releases newsletter? You can receive a special gift, available only to newsletters subscribers. This Bonus Epilogue to *A Steadfast Heart* will not be released on any retailer platform—it's only available to newsletter subscribers.

Find out what happens next with Drew and Kaitlyn. Scan this QR code to subscribe and get your free gift. Unsubscribe at any time.

Thank you again for reading *A Steadfast Heart*. We hope you enjoyed the story. If you did, would you be willing to do us a favor and leave a review? It doesn't have to be long—just a few words to help other readers know what they're getting. (But no spoilers! We don't want to wreck the fun!) Thank you again for reading!

We'd love to hear from you—not only about this story, but about any characters or stories you'd like to read in the future. Contact us at www.sunrisepublishing.com/contact.

Read on for more from the

Wind River
MAIL-ORDER BRIDES
SERIES

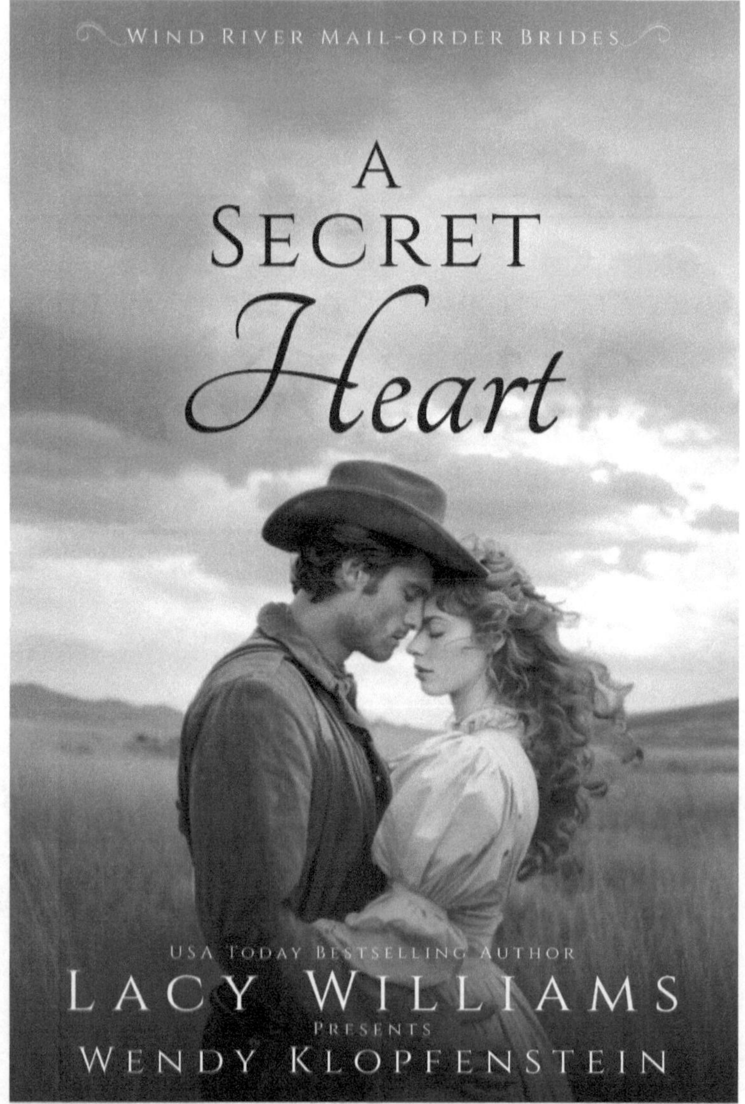
Wind River Mail-Order Brides
A
Secret
Heart
USA Today Bestselling Author
Lacy Williams
Presents
Wendy Klopfenstein

The last thing middle brother Ed McGraw wants is to be tangled up in a scheme to find a mail-order bride for his black-sheep brother. But that's right where Ed finds himself... writing love letters and not signing his own name.

Intrigued by the woman who writes back.

Rebekah Edwards keeps her dreams to herself and finds contentment working for the local newspaper running matrimonial advertisements. Until the day a new ad appears—one written by the very rancher Rebekah has pined for her entire life.

But just as she strikes up a correspondence, Rebekah finds herself drawn inexplicably to Ed McGraw—the wrong McGraw brother for her. What will happen when she finds out the author's true identity?

This sweet historical romance is perfect for fans of the following tropes:

*mistaken identity
*love letters
*matchmaking gone wrong

One

June, 1893

H E'D MADE A MISTAKE.

Ed McGraw took two steps backward and pressed his foot on one of the new wood planks of the small porch of his Wyoming cabin.

Squeak.

There it was again.

Somehow, he must've missed catching a warped board. Now the spot squeaked when he stepped on it. That wouldn't do. Not for a would-be carpenter like him.

He paused just outside the door, glancing over his shoulder. The view of the radiant sunrise glinting across the Laramie Mountains made a man want to share it with someone, but Ed had zero prospects. And finding a wife was the last thing he had time for.

He needed to hurry if he was going to finish detailing the wooden cradle waiting for him inside his cabin-turned-workshop. Morning chores were finished, but his older brother Drew would have a list of work that needed doin' today the length of Ed's arm when Ed joined the family down at the main house for breakfast. Drew had kept the four McGraw brothers together after they'd lost both parents within two years, taking on the mantle of family patriarch, but there was always too much work to be done on the McGraw homestead.

Hoofbeats sounded. Too late to finish his project now.

"Uncle Ed!"

Ed lifted his head to acknowledge his fourteen-year-old nephew, riding past Ed's cabin on a pony.

With the awkward frame of a boy growing too tall too fast, David was the spitting image of Drew at that age.

David took a slight detour and reined in yards away from Ed's porch. "Pa wants me to check the water level in the little pond in the east pasture. And see if Uncle Isaac is up there."

If David was already riding out, that meant Ed had missed breakfast. His stomach growled a protest. He needed another hour or two's work on the wooden cradle before it'd be ready for delivery. Didn't seem like he was getting that hour today.

"Be careful," Ed warned his nephew. "Isaac's been tracking wolves around the high pasture."

Too much like his pa at that age, David lit up instead of appearing worried. "I'll look for tracks!"

And he was gone.

Ed cracked open the door long enough for a glance at

the unstained wooden cradle sitting along the wall before he closed the door with a soft snick.

A sigh slipped from Ed's lips. Would his family ever understand? He loved the feeling of a piece—chair, bed frame, shelf, anything—coming to life in his hands. He wasn't so fanciful as to think wood spoke to him, but when he sketched out a new item to build with pencil and paper, he felt as if some hidden part of him came to life. One at a time, his arms slipped through the suspenders hanging at his side as he started toward the worn path between his cabin and the main house. His fingers riffled through his hair, sending a fine layer of sawdust tumbling through the orange-tipped rays of sunlight.

The main house had been built by Ed's pa. After Isaac had joined the family, Pa had built onto the house, adding a second story and another bedroom downstairs. Ed had grown up running and riding all over this land, along with his older brothers Drew and Isaac and their youngest brother Nick. The McGraw spread was their legacy, a hard-fought family heritage.

Only, he wasn't sure he wanted it any longer.

The kitchen window was open, and once he got close enough, girlish voices floated from inside. Drew's daughters, at eleven and six, couldn't have been more different. Jo was a tried-and-true tomboy, wearing trousers more often than anything else. Tillie, never without a ribbon in her hair, loved playing family with her dolls.

Ed would do anything for them, but when he opened the door and stepped inside, his first urge was to turn back around.

"Don't pull!" Tillie whined. She sat in one of the straight-backed chairs, her face all screwed up.

Standing behind her younger sister, Jo scowled at the top of her head. "It's a braid. They're gonna hurt some."

Drew's wife Kaitlyn swiveled from gathering the dishes at the table, where Drew and Nick were still seated, to admonish her stepdaughters. "Stop arguing. The quicker you finish, the quicker you can head outside to the barn." That was directed at Jo. And the pointed words hit home. Jo focused on Tillie's braid, her tongue peeping out of the corner of her mouth.

Kaitlyn had only married into the family a few months ago, but she was whip-smart, and the children had taken to her. Now she glanced up and caught sight of Ed. He watched a minuscule grimace flit over her expression.

"I'm sorry. I forgot you were coming. I don't know how much breakfast is left."

Before he could say anything, she was already moving to the kitchen, bringing the dirty dishes with her. Ed scanned the table as Nick nodded to him. A strip of bacon remained. It'd go great with the last biscuit. No longer warm to the touch, but it was something. If he'd ignore the projects he kept hidden at his house, he might secure himself a big hot breakfast.

"Need a plate?" Kaitlyn returned from the kitchen. Evidence of her fancy upbringing slipped out again as she handed him a china plate and enough silverware for a four-course meal. She expected a level of societal propriety the brothers hadn't been used to abiding by before she'd shown up from St. Louis. She also brought more smiles to Drew's face than Ed had seen in a long time, so he guessed he could forgive her.

"I'm fine." No need for her to wash another plate for a piece of bacon stuffed in a biscuit. A cold biscuit. He tore off a bite as he pulled out a chair with his free hand to sit at the table, despite the wrinkle in Kaitlyn's brow.

His brothers eyed him while Drew kept talking. "Isaac needs to be here. He can't sulk alone forever."

Isaac had been with the U.S. Marshals for years before he'd come home a year ago, subdued and quiet—not the brother Ed had grown up with. And now they were having a discussion of how to draw his older brother in from the old cabin at the far end of the McGraw property. Why hadn't anyone bothered to wait for him to have this conversation?

"He'll come around." Nick leaned back in his chair, seemingly unaffected by their brother's absence. Always a peacemaker, he also possessed an uncanny understanding of Isaac.

"I'm not so sure." Kaitlyn put in her two bits from behind them. "The last time he came down for supplies, he seemed...lonely. As if he carried a burden and had no one to share it with."

Lonely? How did Kaitlyn figure that? More like Isaac went around as if he had lemon stuck in his teeth. Had ever since he'd hung up his hat as a marshal, coming home only to spend his time repairing the old cabin or moving the cattle from pasture to pasture. It would've been nice to have him show up for the planting, but that would've meant socializing with other people. Like his brothers. Like Ed.

With only a year between them, Isaac being the older,

they'd been close as boys until Isaac had started beating Ed at everything. And now Isaac had shut them all out. If he was lonely, it was his own doing.

Ed took another bite of biscuit. One with bacon in it this time. His eyes darted between Nick and Drew.

"Isaac will show his face when he wants to. When he's ready." Nick barely raised his voice.

"What if he had a wife?" Kaitlyn leaned in to grip the back of Drew's chair. "Someone to care for him, to come home to."

A gleam danced in Drew's eye. "Who do you suggest? Widow Mayberry?"

Ed chuckled before shoving another bite in. Even Nick grinned. Heart-breaking, tough-guy Isaac married to Widow Mayberry. She had to be twenty years older, and she talked nonstop. At least hard-nosed Drew's recent marriage to Kaitlyn had drawn out a bit of a sense of humor in him.

"Not funny." Kaitlyn pretended to bristle, then another spark lit her face. "What about Rebekah Edwards? She isn't married. Didn't you say she was sweet on Isaac?"

The biscuit lodged in Ed's throat. He choked back a cough. Not Rebekah. A quick wit and all those fiery red curls wrapped up in an annoying, although what some called "pretty," package. Ed would take anyone but Rebekah for a sister-in-law. It was bad enough he had to put up with her as a neighbor. The nagging crumbs in his throat threatened to break him into a full-blown coughing fit. He went for Nick's coffee. One swig and he set the cup down.

Nick gave him a sideways scowl.

"Rebekah's too busy working at the paper." Another

sip of coffee gave Ed time to pull his thoughts together. "Speaking of the newspaper, they're doing a special section for those mail-order bride ads now. You know, like the one you ran."

"An ad?" Drew raised a brow in question. While he had run an ad, it'd been a rough road and a twist of fate that'd landed Kaitlyn here as his mail-order bride. "Sounds good."

Drew sounded as if Ed had suggested a perfect idea when he'd only meant to divert the conversation.

"You'd post a matrimonial ad for Isaac?" Ed followed up. After all they'd been through with Drew's ad, he wanted to try this again? "Our Isaac?"

His brother obviously wasn't thinking straight. There had to be a better way to find Isaac a wife, if he even wanted one.

Nick shifted in his chair. "He doesn't need us poking our noses where they don't belong. Give him time to come around." Nick had always been close to Isaac. It wasn't a wonder that he was protective now.

"And if he doesn't come around? If he hides out the rest of his life up in that sorry excuse for a cabin? Or worse?" Drew fixed his eyes on Nick as he jabbed his finger at the table. "I can't even get him to tell me why he came back."

"Wouldn't be too bad to have his help around here either." Ed dusted the crumbs from his hands. All eyes fixed on him as if he were interrupting. "Might do him good to be around family more. That's all."

"A wife will do the trick." A dreaminess filled Kaitlyn's words. "Someone to love the rough edges away."

"He'll never go for it." Wise words from Nick. Surely

no one imagined Isaac would agree to their plan. It might even drive him further away. But Drew wasn't used to being questioned.

"We don't have to tell him." Ed finished the last of Nick's coffee. He rose to refill the cup from the pot Kaitlyn had placed at the other end of the table. Steam rose from the liquid. Even if breakfast hadn't warmed his belly, the coffee had.

"Good point." Drew ran a hand along his chin. "We don't tell him at first. We run an ad, evaluate the replies, then pick a woman or two that might fit him. We turn it over to Isaac from there."

Nick shook his head. "I don't know."

"He'll go for it when a pretty lady shows up," Kaitlyn said. She shared another glance with Drew. Obviously, the honeymoon phase hadn't passed yet.

Ed cleared his throat. Now was as good a time as any to tell them he'd be at his place working for a couple of hours. If he finished the cradle, he might have time to get it to town today.

"That's decided, then." Drew rose from the table before Ed got a word out. "Nick, are you ready to go see about that mare? Ed, I promised one of us would take the Boutwells to town. I need you to take care of that. Put in that ad while you're there."

What had led his brother to think he'd be available? Drew lived and breathed this homestead, thinking he needed to command them all like an army regiment. What if Ed refused? What if he dared to want more?

"I've got things to do here." Helping the Boutwells wasn't

so bad, but more than likely, he'd end up with Rebekah wanting to join them. She hadn't changed one bit from their school days, back when there'd been a little school on the edge of Heath Quade's property that all the neighbors had attended. Before Quade's wife had passed and he'd sent his younger girls off to boarding school, closing the local schoolhouse down. But that'd been after all the McGraws and Rebekah had graduated. Time with Rebekah still rubbed him wrong, like a sand burr stuck inside his boot.

Drew halted for the briefest second, then waved off Ed's faint complaint.

Ed swallowed back another protest. Wouldn't do him any good. The cradle would have to wait. He glanced at Nick. "You want to write the ad? You're the one with all the book smarts."

Nick rose to follow Drew without a look back. "I'll leave the ad to you two."

"Do the ad next trip. Time's a-wasting to get the neighbors to their train." Drew waved it off. Which meant Ed would get saddled with writing the ad too.

The sooner he got this over with, the better.

"I can always count on you, Ed." Drew's words settled heavy in Ed's chest as Ed stepped past his brothers on the way to the door.

One more thing added to the endless list of jobs everyone counted on him to do. All he wanted was a chance to prove his woodworking could be a means to bring in money. A reason for him to have the time to work on it. But how would he do that if he never caught a break to even finish this one project?

It simply has to be Isaac McGraw.

Rebekah Edwards stood at the kitchen window and strained her eyes to make out the identity of the driver approaching the farmhouse. Her heart beat out a fluttering rhythm. If Isaac drove to town, she'd add each minute of the long ride to her collective memories of every move he had ever made in her presence.

But the man's hat was down, and the morning sun coming through the kitchen windowpane blurred the figure on the wagon seat. He sat broad-shouldered, muscles flexing as he halted in front of the house.

If only his head would tilt to reveal Issac, his eyes the deep green of the pine trees and his dimpled smile so endearing. She hadn't seen him in town recently, but she was still holding out hope.

"Are you listening, Rebekah? I don't want to leave you here alone. Not with all the rumors about Quade's men." Aunt Opal's words pulled Rebekah's stare from the window. The men's voices were muffled through the wall.

Despite her excitement at the possibility of seeing Isaac, nothing in Rebekah relished being separated from her aunt and uncle. She'd lived with them on this farm since coming west over fifteen years ago at the tender age of eleven. While she stayed by herself in the loft over the newspaper office in Calvin during part of each week due to the distance, she'd never stayed on the farm alone. Rumors of Quade and his men harassing local farmers until they agreed to sell their land didn't help matters any.

"I can't leave the paper. It wouldn't make it a month without me." Rebekah leaned against the kitchen counter, cluttered with the meat and cheese her aunt was preparing for sandwiches, as she folded the checkered cloth around the loaf of freshly baked bread. Her statement held no bravado, only the bitter truth.

She'd worked at her beloved paper since the summer after she'd graduated from school, and it was struggling. If it didn't turn around soon, there'd be nothing for Mr. Sullivan to leave her. If she lost her paper, she'd lose her dream of independence.

Aunt Opal's brows knit together, further deepening the lines of worry as she layered the sandwiches together, working on the little counter space that remained. "I don't understand how you staying is going to make it better."

The yeasty scent of the bread tempted Rebekah as she shoved the loaf into the basket. How would she stretch it out for as many days as possible, this hug in a loaf? It would be all she had of her aunt's cooking for a long while. She stepped closer to Opal, looping her arm around the petite woman's shoulders. This woman who'd been closer to her than her own mother all these years.

"We've added a special section to take on more matrimonial ads. They're my specialty. Mr. Sullivan left them totally in my hands. I even convinced a larger paper to run them for broader circulation." She leaned in to give her aunt a squeeze in an effort to silence her arguments. Rebekah didn't need to add her aunt's concerns to her own worries about looking after the garden, the canning, and the endless list of chores inside the house as well as performing her duties at the newspaper. At least their closest neighbors, the McGraws, had agreed to help with the livestock.

Opal's weary smile faded. "Mind you, I don't want you talking to Quade while we're gone."

Rebekah suspected the fire in her aunt's voice hid a mountain of worries. For their homestead. For Uncle Vess. For Rebekah. Not to mention the trip east. It echoed Rebekah's own worries of staying here alone. The ones she'd been pushing aside for the sake of her dreams.

Opal cast another glance her way. The creases between her brows deepened as if she'd been reading Rebekah's thoughts. "And if he ever shows up here, you go get the McGraw brothers."

Heath Quade had been by more than once to make an offer on their place. The first one had made Rebekah whistle, which had garnered a scolding from Aunt Opal for being unladylike. The second one had come with a veiled threat. Rebekah hadn't heard it herself, but she had no reason to doubt Uncle Vess's word.

"I doubt Quade will come here while you're gone. I likely won't even see him unless he does something worthy of a news article." Not that Rebekah would mind going to get one particular McGraw, even if she could handle Mr. Quade on her own.

"You and that paper." Aunt Opal's weathered hands settled the sandwiches for her and Uncle Vess's train trip in another basket. "Make sure you weed the vegetable garden.

Watch out for that hen that tries to slip out of the coop." She glanced up from shuffling the sandwiches. "And lock the door at night."

All of Aunt Opal's talk meant more than the words she spoke. It meant she would miss Rebekah and worry about her. That she loved her. In a funny sort of way, the words wrapped themselves around Rebekah tighter than any hug ever could. She stepped closer to enclose the woman in her arms.

"What's all this?" Aunt Opal's words wobbled with emotion.

Rebekah leaned closer to her ear. "A little something to remind you of me while you're gone."

Aunt Opal gave Rebekah's arm a squeeze before backing away to swipe at a tear with the back of her other hand. "We'll be back, you know. Before you have time to even miss us."

"I doubt that." *I miss you already.*

Opal sniffed, then straightened. "Doesn't your uncle know it's high time for us to be leaving? I wish he wouldn't overwork himself walking all around giving out instructions. As if the McGraws don't know their way around a farm."

"Stop your worrying, Opal." Dear Uncle Vess leaned his lanky form into the doorway, blocking the view outside as another cough racked his body. "Everything is loaded but us. And whatever delicious-smelling bread you have there."

Rebekah's brow furrowed at his cough as she picked up the loaf and placed it in her makeshift bag. She had everything she'd need to remain in town for a day or two.

Her regular trips to help oversee things at the newspaper office were usually a source of joy to her. If only her aunt and uncle weren't catching a train. The only source of joy today, putting butterflies in her stomach, was the hope of Isaac driving them.

She'd thought she'd grown out of the feelings she'd held for him back when she'd attended the one-room schoolhouse with Isaac and his brothers. Until the day she'd caught a glimpse of him returning to town after serving as a marshal. He'd still exuded all the manliness of a genuine hero, striding from the train station to meet his brother Ed. No one else lived up to the legendary Isaac McGraw. Not back in school. Not now.

Rebekah smoothed her dark woolen skirt with one hand as she grasped her bag in the other, then followed her aunt out into the sunlight. She angled her free hand under her hat to shield her eyes as the McGraw near the wagon turned to greet them.

"Morning, Mrs. Boutwell."

Not Isaac.

A lock of mahogany hair escaped beneath the edge of Ed McGraw's hat as he greeted Aunt Opal with a nod. Awkward seconds passed before he offered a faint "Miss Edwards."

Rebekah stiffened. *Him. Hmph.* Had no one else noticed the drop in his voice when he'd finally said her name? Did they ever notice his slights? Two weeks ago, he'd been by to change out a wagon wheel for Uncle Vess. She must have stood by the wagon for half an hour before Ed had acknowledged her only to refuse the lemonade Aunt Opal had insisted she take out to him. Infuriating man.

"I'll load that for you." He motioned to her satchel.

"I can do it." She attempted to pull her satchel back from his reach, but not before his fingers brushed hers as they tightened around the handle, leaving her bristling.

Ed tightened his jaw. He didn't glance her way as she let go. She knew that tic of his. He was none too happy to see her either.

"How is Isaac?" The words left her mouth unplanned.

Her aunt and uncle gave her a curious look.

"Haven't seen him in a few days." Ed flicked a glance her way as he pursed his lips. He placed her satchel under the seat with the other bags, then walked to the back of the wagon. He held out a hand to Aunt Opal. "I put in some hay to make the ride more comfortable."

"You are too kind to an old woman's aching bones." Aunt Opal stepped toward him and slipped her hand in his.

Ignored again. Rebekah rolled her eyes to avoid the distraction of his muscled arms hoisting her aunt into the wagon. The very arms she had so easily envisioned belonging to Isaac earlier.

Vess handed the basket of food to his wife once she was settled, then turned to face Ed. "You will look after Rebekah, won't you?"

"I'm a grown woman, Uncle Vess. I can look after myself." Rebekah's words fell on deaf ears as her uncle kept his eyes trained on Ed. Neither of them acknowledged her.

"My brothers and I will look after the place," Ed hedged.

She barely held in a snort. Uncle Vess might as well forget getting a promise out of Ed to look after her. Which suited her just fine.

Vess lingered by the side of the wagon, his hand running across the top board. "Promise me you'll be sure she gets to town and back safely. You're a man of your word, and I trust you."

"I'll check with Drew to see if he can spare me." Ed half mumbled the words, the way he'd always mumbled when the teacher had asked about missing homework back in school. He didn't want to drive her any more than she wanted him to.

"Rebekah is precious to me." Vess coughed again.

She swallowed hard, fighting the pull of concern over his illness that she'd been trying so hard to tamp down, at least until they got to the train. One quick turn of her head, and Ed's stormy glance her way stilled the rising swell of tears, filling her with resolve.

"Don't be silly, Uncle Vess. I'm perfectly capable of saddling up a horse and riding to town." Surely her assurance would ease his mind and end this.

Rebekah shot a pleading look at her uncle, but his focus held on Ed. A man-to-man sort of stare-down, as if Ed owed him this and he was calling in his favors. Ed broke the stare.

"You McGraws have been good neighbors to us. But

it's not Drew's promise I'm after. I'd like your word, Ed McGraw."

Rebekah shifted her gaze from the men to the horses in an effort to control her rising frustration. Uncle Vess wouldn't settle for anything but Ed's promise.

A sigh from Ed filled the air. "No need to worry about a thing, sir. You have my word."

Tired of waiting for Ed to offer her a hand up, Rebekah scrambled into the back of the wagon herself. Her shin clanged against the edge of the wagon, and pain shot up her leg, deepening her annoyance. She caught the twitch of Ed's jaw before he nodded to a small container nestled in the hay. "Almost forgot. Kaitlyn sent a jar of jam for you."

Rebekah hugged the gift from her friend close, smiling as she placed the jar in her satchel and settled herself beside her aunt atop the hay. The wagon jostled, and she looked behind her to the front of the wagon. Her gaze connected with Ed's as he hoisted himself onto the seat. She felt her smile fading to match his expression, and she could almost read his mind.

It's going to be a long summer.

And for once in her life, she agreed with him.

Acknowledgments

So many people contribute to making a book come to life. I'd like to thank my agent, Tamela Hancock Murray, whose support was essential at many different stages in the process. My editors, Sara Shull, Katie Donovan, and Charity Henico, made the book better than I thought it could be. Lacy Williams was the lead author, lead coach, and lead cheerleader in this project. Susan May Warren and everyone at Sunrise Publishing offered me the chance to learn with the best.

My parents and my daughter supported me from a distance. My husband was in the trenches with me every step of the way.

And finally, I want to thank God for giving me the gift and the training to use it.

Also by Lacy Williams

Christmas Bells and Wedding Vows (anthology)

Wagon Train Matches
A Trail So Lonesome
Trail of Secrets
A Trail Untamed
Wild Heart's Haven
A Rugged Beauty

Wind River Hearts series
Marrying Miss Marshal
Counterfeit Cowboy
Cowboy Pride
The Homesteader's Sweetheart
Courted by a Cowboy
Roping the Wrangler
Return of the Cowboy Doctor
The Wrangler's Inconvenient Wife
A Cowboy for Christmas
Her Convenient Cowboy
Her Cowboy Deputy
Catching the Cowgirl
The Cowboy's Honor
Winning the Schoolmarm
The Wrangler's Ready-Made Family
Christmas Homecoming
Heart of Gold

USA Today bestselling author **Lacy Williams** is devoted to bringing her readers heartwarming love stories about cowboys and the women that tame them. She is the author of over fifty-five books, including the acclaimed Wind River Hearts and Sutter's Hollow series. Her books have been nominated for the RT Book Reviews' Seal of Excellence as well as finaled in RT's Reviewers' Choice Awards. She has been a puppy parent almost her whole life and often writes with one of her dogs snuggled in her lap. She is a mom of four and spends her non-writing time buried under piles of laundry and dishes.

Learn more at lacywilliams.net.

Martha Hutchens is a history nerd who loves nothing more than finding a new place and time to explore. She won the 2019 Golden Heart for Romance with Religious and Spiritual Elements. In 2018, she was a finalist in ACFW's Genesis contest, in 2013 one of her manuscripts was in the top 50 of Harlequin's So You Think You Can Write. Two of her manuscripts were finalists in the 2020 Maggie contest. She is an active member of Faith, Hope, and Love Christian Writers and ACFW. A former analytical chemist and retired homeschool mom, Martha is frequently found working on her latest knitting project when she isn't writing.

Learn more at marthahutchens.com.

Wind River
MAIL-ORDER BRIDES

USA Today Bestselling Author Lacy Williams

Martha Hutchens, Wendy Klopfenstein, Wendy Galinetti, Traci Summeril

In the wild and untamed landscape of old west Wyoming, the McGraw brothers navigate the challenges of ranch life, unexpected love, and the transformative power of second chances. As each mail-order bride enters their lives, these steadfast men discover that love can bloom in the most unlikely places. Love comes softly in Wind River...

We solve the problem of what we read next.

Available on Amazon

BLOOD OF KINGS: LEGENDS

Award-winning author
JILL WILLIAMSON

with Andrew Swearingen, Kelly Fernlake, & Niki Florica

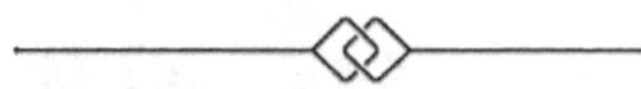

Return to the world of Er'Rets in an epic fantasy series brimming with richly woven tales of loyalty, love, and sacrifice…

We solve the problem of what we read next.   Available on Amazon

YOU MAY ALSO LIKE...

When a blizzard strikes Deep Haven and Megan is overrun with catastrophes, it takes a former Ranger to step in and help. But the more he comes to her rescue, the sooner she'll move out... Come home to Deep Haven in this magical tale about the one who got away... and came back.

Still the One by Susan May Warren and Rachel D. Russell

Grace Howell leaves her life as a ballerina and returns to Heritage, Michigan, to heal. Teaching dance is just a temporary gig, until she finds herself unexpectedly charmed by small-town life and her growing attachment to Seth Warner, a man from her past with a troubled history of his own.

You're the Reason by Tari Faris

Dani Sullivan is determined to revive Jonathon Island's fading charm and reunite her fractured family. Her plan? Reopen the Grand Sullivan Hotel. But without the funds to restore the hotel, Dani's forced to accept help from Liam Stone—a big-city hotel developer whose sleek, modern vision is everything she's trying to avoid.

Meet Me at the Grand by Lindsay Harrel

We solve the problem of what we read next.   Available on Amazon

sunrise
PUBLISHING

WHERE EVERY STORY IS A FRIEND, AND EVERY CHAPTER IS A NEW JOURNEY...

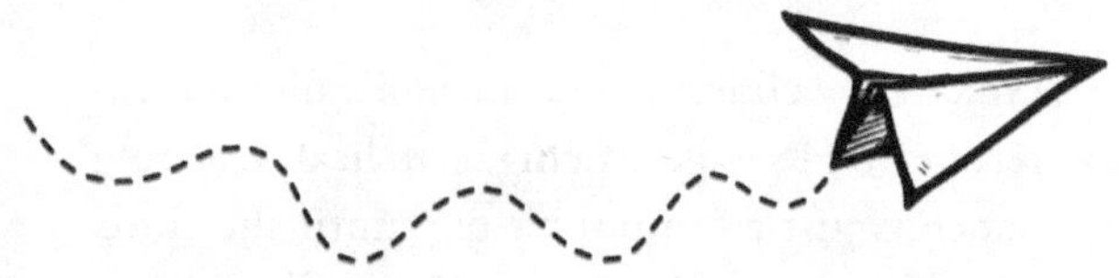

Subscribe to our newsletter for a free book, the latest news, weekly giveaways, exclusive author interviews, and more!

@sunrisemediagroup

@sunrisepublish

@sunrisepublishing

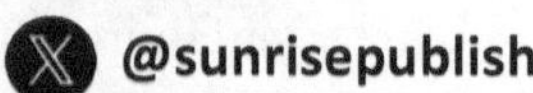
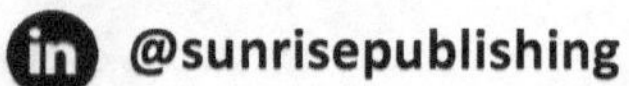

Shop paperbacks, ebooks, audiobooks, and more at
SUNRISEPUBLISHING.MYSHOPIFY.COM

www.ingramcontent.com/pod-product-compliance
Lightning Source LLC
Chambersburg PA
CBHW021027310726
48969CB00006B/1576